EVERYDAY PEOPLE

Visit us at www.boldstrokesbooks.com

EVERYDAY PEOPLE

by

Louis Barr

2020

EVERYDAY PEOPLE

ISBN 13: 978-1-63555-698-8

This Trade Paperback Original Is Published By
Bold Strokes Books, Inc.
P.O. Box 249
Valley Falls, NY 12185

First Edition: May 2020

CREDITS

EDITORS: JERRY L. WHEELER AND STACIA SEAMAN
PRODUCTION DESIGN: STACIA SEAMAN
COVER DESIGN BY JEANINE HENNING

Author's Note

I exercised due diligence while researching this novel. I, however, took literary and dramatic liberties in many scenes involving technology, police procedures, common laws, et alia; thus, nothing in this novel should be considered real, accurate, or factual.

For my silver fox. Long shall we run.

Sic volvere Parcas.
Virgil, *Aeneid*

PROLOGUE

Retro Grunge Rage

Shane Danning, Jugs & Mugs Saloon, Hollywood, Wednesday, April 25

From the corner of my eye, I glimpsed a young couple sitting down at a nearby table. I swiveled my barstool for a better look.

Cloaked in retro grunge rage, Doc Marten boredom, and Debbie Harry torment, the pair were unconventional to say the least. But it was a goddammed good-looking unconventional. I smiled at them.

Retro Grunge One smirked.

Retro Grunge Two frowned as if someone nearby farted.

A closer look told me both were about one shot shy of shitfaced. The last thing I needed was one or both of them puking in my bed. Dismissing them with a headshake, I finished my beer, tipped the bartender, and headed out. Then I committed the unthinkable for a native Angeleno: I began walking home.

I stopped at an intersection not far from my house. The city lights along the block ahead were out. Squinting into the shadows, I didn't see anything unusual. I stepped off the curb.

A van rolled past me as I crossed the street. The driver parked at the far end of the block and doused the headlights.

I heard the van's engine idling as I neared its rear bumper. Something primal stirred the fine hairs on the back of my neck. I stopped dead in my tracks.

A tall man slid from behind the wheel and blocked my path. It had come down to fight or flight.

The big sonofabitch moved fast in the dark. I saw the red dots on my chest a split second before I dropped to the sidewalk, convulsing from the Taser's electrical pulses.

CHAPTER ONE

The First Rule

Steele & Whitman Investigations, Sunset Strip, Monday, April 30

I stood as she stepped into my office.

On the big screen, Diana Danning had always looked stunning. But seeing her in person for the first time in years almost made me forget to breathe.

Following our handshake, I told her to have a seat. She sat in one of the leather armchairs angled in front of my desk.

I sat, woke my tablet, and said, "Ms. Danning, my business partner tells me that you'd like us to search for your son."

She said in her breathy voice, "Yes, please find Shane." She paused, spoke: "And it's Diana, please. I've worked with your family too many years for us to use titles." She flashed her billion-watt smile. "So, Mr. Steele, do you go by Clinton or Clint?"

I returned her smile. "Everyone calls me Clint."

I knew Diana Danning was in her mid-forties, yet she looked about a dozen years younger. But more important, she still radiated that indefinable presence that the cameras captured and the public adored.

Diana learned early in her film career to roll with the punches. Her versatility, talent, and professionalism set new standards for leading ladies, netting her almost thirty years of starring roles, worldwide fame, multimillion-dollar product endorsements, seven Best Actress Oscar nominations (she won five), six ex-husbands, four Golden Globes, two Emmys, and probably a partridge in a palm tree at her "Birds Neighborhood" estate.

And over the past thirty years, Diana had tried to keep her only child, Shane, out of the spotlights and far, far away from the media.

But Shane's Hollywood good looks, crooked smile, and continual antics made him the darling of tabloid reporters and photographers. They stalked him relentlessly.

At the age of eleven, Shane took a joyride along Rodeo Drive in Diana's Mercedes, sideswiping two police cruisers during a low-speed attempt to pull him over. A tabloid reporter captured it all on film.

At sixteen, he mooned a paparazzo in a London park. Shane's adolescent ass made the covers of tabloids across the United Kingdom and a few in the United States.

At eighteen, Shane again became a media darling when electrical system failures forced him to crash land his twin-engine plane, leaving a path of destruction across the manicured lawns of three Bel Air estates. The starboard wing clipped a tree; the airframe burst into flames. Shane escaped through the cockpit's emergency exit, dazed and bruised but uninjured.

An international buzz ensued during his sophomore year at MIT after a classmate shot candid locker room pics of Shane and sold the full-frontal nude photos to a glossy women's magazine. It took a team of lawyers, a preliminary injunction, and stacks of cash to retrieve the photos.

After the MIT incident, Shane stayed out of the headlines for several years until five nights ago, when he vanished after leaving the Jugs & Mugs Saloon—a Hollywood dive popular with grad students, bohos, and young professionals. Once again, his name and face appeared in broadcast and print media around the world and all across the web.

I saw Diana looking at the city nightscapes I'd photographed, framed, and hung on one wall. She studied each of the five poster-sized prints as though she might spot her son in one of them. Tears began to line her flawless face.

A woman in tears breaks my private investigator's cold black heart. I slid a box of Kleenex to the edge of my desk. She plucked two tissues and dabbed her signature violet eyes.

I leaned back in my chair. "What do you think happened to Shane?"

Diana shook her head. "I don't know. There's been no activity on his credit cards or bank accounts. He's neither called me, nor his airline employer, nor any of his pilot colleagues. No one has made a ransom demand."

I couldn't say what happened to Shane either. He may have been kidnapped, but the ransom demand typically comes within twenty-four hours of the abduction. More likely, he met someone and went off on an extended "date."

"Did Shane mention having problems with something or someone?"

"The police asked me that. The answer is no."

I tried another slant. "Has anything out of the ordinary happened to you over the past few weeks?"

She looked at me as if my IQ had suddenly dropped below fifty.

"Humor me."

She sighed. "Darling, you know out-of-the-ordinary things happen all the time when you're living the Hollywood dream."

"Uh-huh. When did you last see or speak to Shane?"

"He dropped by my dressing room on the morning of April twenty-fifth, about fifteen hours before he vanished."

I asked her what she and Shane had talked about.

She gathered her thoughts, then said, "He thanked me again for the Porsche I gave him last month for his thirtieth birthday. He said he had a packed flight to Vegas that afternoon, would return to LAX that evening, and might stop for a beer before going home." She paused, then added, "Oh, he talked about missing his ex."

I looked up from my notetaking. "Who's the ex?"

"Kristina Morgotti."

I held my poker face. "Do you mean Kristina Morgotti as in *Hollywood Nights* Kristina Morgotti?"

"Yes."

I'd neither heard nor read anything about Shane Danning's involvement with Tinsel Town's Queen of Snark. I sometimes glanced at a *Hollywood Nights* gossip column or web post, but only when my Aunt Vona called on a rant about Morgotti's latest batch of wild-assed suppositions and fabrications.

I shifted in my chair. "Did your son and Morgotti part amicably?"

"They did according to Shane." She shrugged. "But who knows. I'm certain the cops questioned Morgotti at length."

With a water board, car battery, and electrodes, I thought. Most celebrities avoided Morgotti like a case of genital warts—until they needed their latest projects promoted.

During the initial interview, I apply the First Rule of Investigating: Assume most of what your client tells you is bullshit. After listening for voice modulations, watching eye movements and other body language, I'd neither seen, nor heard, nor sensed a trace of dishonesty.

Then again, she'd made millions and millions and millions and millions of dollars as a world class actress.

What the fuck was I thinking? Her son, her only child, was missing. She was worried sick; same as I'd be if my son disappeared.

"What do the cops say about Shane's disappearance?"

"They think Shane left on his own volition."

"Diana, the LAPD investigates around three hundred missing person reports every month. These cases are given investigative priority, placing a due diligence duty on the Missing Persons Unit." I paused briefly, allowing Diana to reflect on those facts, then concluded, "Everyone with the MPU knows his or her job and does it well."

"You don't want to look into what happened to my son."

She'd called that one right. The last thing I needed at this time was a high profile case.

But Diana and my family had professional ties. I couldn't tell her to get the hell out of my office and find another private detective.

"What I'm saying is if the LAPD didn't find evidence of foul play, you might want to wait for Shane to contact you before retaining my services." I didn't smile while I said, "I may come easy, but I don't come cheap."

She raised her voice. "*I do not give a shit about the cost or what the fucking cops think!*"

She pulled in a long breath and slowly let it out. "I'm sorry. I only want you to find Shane and bring him home."

And forget whatever it is Shane wants to do, I thought, but said, "Who's the lead investigator?"

She said in a voice that neither brightened nor bristled, "Harlan Flynn."

Given Diana's Hollywood royalty status, it came as no surprise that one of the Police Administration Building's elite investigators took the case from the Hollywood station. "I know Captain Flynn well."

She smiled. "I told Flynn I planned to hire you. He said you're one of the best private eyes in Southern California when it comes to finding missing people."

With Captain Flynn's glowing endorsement, I knew what that sneaky bastard had up his sleeve. As a private investigator, I could take actions that would cost Flynn his gold shield, gun, and gonads. And he doubtless wanted to keep his gonads, having grown attached to them.

My dark blues directly met Diana's beautiful violet eyes. "I'll search for Shane. May I take a look inside your son's house?"

She opened her bag and set a key on my desk. I added Shane's address to my tablet notes.

I saw it had gotten late in the day. "I'll talk with Captain Flynn first thing tomorrow morning."

The breathy voice returned. "You'll call me the moment you learn something."

"You can count on it." I pulled out a business card and printed my cell and home landline numbers on the back. "Please call, day or night, when Shane or anyone else involved in his disappearance contacts you."

"I shall."

She tucked my card into one of her bag's array of secret hidey holes, flapped pouches with snaps, zippered pockets, and probably a goddammed trap door. I wondered how the hell women ever found anything in those purses. It had to be a gal thing.

She stood.

I stood and walked her to my office door.

She turned, studied my face, and said, "You look so much like your father."

I'd often heard I looked like Liam Steele, my movie director father. But I had a more muscular build and stood six inches taller than Dad. My West Point football teammates nicknamed me Moose. But that's locker room banter.

Diana thanked me.

Then she stood on the tips of her toes and kissed me.

CHAPTER TWO

Big Papa Phallus

Clint, Steele & Whitman Investigations, Monday, April 30

I watched Diana gracefully walk down the hall in heels that would've brought me a face-to-floor meeting with my first step. It had to be another gal thing.

I wouldn't mind standing at Diana's door with a dozen roses—make that two dozen—and a dinner reservation at one of L.A.'s tony restaurants du jour.

I love and revere women. Their smiles, intelligence, feminine mystique, curves, voices, grace, inner strength, and eyes always capture my attention.

But I also appreciate the male form and men's sexuality.

I'm not gay. I'm not straight either. I'm bi. And I'm not claiming to be bisexual to downplay my attraction to men. I was happily married to a woman, and throughout those years, I remained bisexual, but a monogamous husband. Sierra, my late wife, was and would always be the female love of my life.

Anyone taking the time to JFGI (Just Fucking Google It) will learn there's a long list of sexuality options beyond LGBTQA, and new choices seem to come out of Seattle monthly.

The never-debunked *Kinsey Reports* ("Sexual Behavior in the Human Male," 1948; and "Sexual Behavior in the Human Female," 1953) found that only ten percent of the population is purely heterosexual, only ten percent of the population is purely homosexual, and the other eighty percent of us might, at some point or points in our lives, try or consider trying other sexuality options. (Kinsey defined sexuality as either physical contact, or strictly psychological, such as sexual attraction, desire, and/or fantasy.) Simply put, queer is more predominant than most people care to recognize.

Hope Whitman, my business partner, office manager, explosives expert, and knower of all things great and small, charged into my office, shoving the door shut with one of her sensible heels. Then she barreled toward me like the Tasmanian Devil.

"'Sup?"

Hope scowled. "Some might find that red gloss on your lips quite fetching. You ask me, ya look like you rushed leaving clown school today."

She snapped a tissue from the box on my desk and thrust it at me—the tissue, not my desk. "Are your privates smeared red too?"

I wiped away the remnants of Diana's kiss. "Did you want to discuss something with me other than my lip gloss and the color of my boy parts?"

Hope let out a long breath. "A stranger came in shortly after I sent Diana Danning to your office. He wants to speak with you. I got his ass parked in reception."

Hope and I met with prospective clients by appointment only. We then cherry-picked the cases we wanted to take. I met Hope's eyes. "Did this stranger give you a name?"

"Says he's Scott Davidson."

My mind raced, trying to place him, but I drew a blank. "What does Davidson want?"

Hope unloosed one of her prissy New Englander's sniffs. "I asked him. He told me it's a personal matter, and I should mind my own goddammed business."

Steele & Whitman's files were sometimes subpoenaed. And it wasn't unusual for either Hope or me to get slapped with a summons to testify in court about a closed case. "Does Davidson look like a process server?"

"Maybe, but he reminds me of a dime-store cowboy. My gut tells me he's up to no good."

Seventy-year-old Hope Whitman had pulled the plug from the LAPD after riding in patrol cars for twenty years, followed by five years on the bomb squad and her last five as the police chief's administrative assistant.

She kept a wheel gun in her desk. Threaten her, and she could go all Ma Barker (JFGI) on your ass. Scott Davidson should consider himself lucky he hadn't gotten gut shot.

Hope has lived with Stella, her wife, for over thirty years. Besides keeping Hope from shit-fitting herself into a stroke, Stella works as my son's nanny and home teacher. I'd figured anyone who could bring Hope down from a rant could manage my rambunctious six-year-old son.

"Please tell Davidson I'll speak with him. And be polite. He could be the salt of the earth."

"Yeah, or a process server, or the Zodiac Killer." She started for the door, turned, and added, "Watch him."

I trusted Hope's cop instincts. Opening my desk's top right drawer, I pulled out my weapon of choice, a compact forty caliber Glock. I racked a round and moved the gun to the desk's center drawer, leaving it open several inches.

I shot my cuffs, cinched my tie, and said, "Clinton Steele, you are duly served."

About a minute later, Scott Davidson knocked on my open office door. With one look, I knew he didn't wear the stripes of a Captain Douchebag process server.

Davidson was easy on the eyes in a laid back, Lee Majors (JFGI) "boy-howdy" cowboy, big papa phallus sort of way. I stood and invited him in, while closing the desk drawer and stowing my Glock for some future shooting incident.

I shook Davidson's callused hand and noticed his farmer's tan. He pulled out one of the client chairs and sat military straight, keeping his spit-shined black cowboy boots flat on the floor.

I sat and leaned back in my chair. "What can I do for you?"

Davidson cut to the chase. "I'm looking for a full-time job."

"You've worked either as a private investigator, or in security, or in law enforcement," I stated.

"I worked as a Kern County deputy sheriff for twenty-five years," Davidson said.

"You're retired?"

"Yes, I'd had enough of department politics, budget cuts, and complaints about the maltreatment meted out to lawbreaking assholes." He quickly added, "Sorry."

I smiled. Seriously, meted? That's a verb you use to prove you're a college grad. I turned to my PC and clicked. The printer slid an employment application into the tray. Handing Davidson the form and a pen, I pointed at the writing table outside my office.

I opened and scanned the latest edition of the LAPD's *Police Beat*

E-zine, occasionally glancing at Davidson. He looked like a rough and tumble kind of guy, someone not to be fucked with in any way, shape, or form.

I closed the E-zine, turned, and looked at the framed desk photo of Sierra, my late wife. She stood hooded and gowned, scrolled sheepskin in hand, having earned her doctorate in economics. She softly smiled as I stood behind the camera, framing the shot.

The luckiest moment of my life came when I first saw Sierra in a mom-and-pop coffee shop. I couldn't drum up the chutzpah to cross the room and try to start a conversation with this drop-dead beautiful woman. She was focused on her laptop, her fingers flying over the keys. She looked busier than a one-legged Rockette. She might tell me to take a flying fuck at the moon if I interrupted her work. I walked out of the shop, espresso in hand.

I'd thought the Ma-and-Pa shop served the most unremarkable coffee in all of Los Angeles. Still, I'd stopped by the following morning, hoping to see the pretty woman with the dark auburn hair. I spotted her again, keyboarding her laptop. She looked up—and straight through me. I felt like a stalker or a perv taking a coffee break. I left with my head down and my tail between my legs.

On my third day of unexceptional coffee, she looked directly at me and smiled. I grinned as if I'd just made a successful prison break. Our smiles held. Espresso in hand, I walked straight to her table and asked if I could join her.

She closed her laptop. "Please sit down. I've been waiting the past three days for you to talk to me."

Fuck my life.

After a few weeks of lunch and dinner dates, holding hands at the movies, talking as we took long walks, necking, and finally sleeping together, we both knew our lonely days and nights had become things of the past.

When we were dating, I told her about the one bisexual relationship I'd had with my West Point barracks mate. But she knew when we spoke our wedding vows I would be a faithful husband. We were happily married for about five years before Ian, our then four-year-old son, and I lost her in an auto accident. I died inside.

Now I missed my wife, loved my son, enjoyed my job, owned my house, remained in perfect health, and received a great income from Aunt Vona's and my closely held corporation, Steele Productions. At thirty-three, I looked old enough to be taken seriously, but young enough not to be addressed as "sir." At thirty-three, I was in my prime and held the world by the short hairs. But without Sierra, I did not consider myself a lucky man.

I ended my pity party and turned to my computer to search for young men reported missing over the past two years. Narrowing my search using age, income, and geographical criteria, I came up with a short list of missing men, but it did not include Shane Danning. He's not yet in the system, I guessed.

The men on my short list all had been in their early to late twenties and resided in either one of L.A.'s high rent districts or in Orange County. All had been located safe and sound.

I leaned back in my swivel chair. I didn't see a pattern; it seemed the young princes of Los Angeles hadn't become the victims of a serial nut job—not at the moment, anyway.

I knew finding and sifting through all the young men with missing person files would turn into a clusterfuck of mythical proportions. And those data would not necessarily reflect all the unreported and unidentified tween and teen runaways living and dying on the city's streets.

My "due diligence duties" required that I duplicate what the Missing Persons Unit's investigators had already done, and look into anything new I might stir up in the weeds. I'd begin all of that tomorrow after I talked with Captain Flynn.

Scott Davidson knuckled my office door. I looked up. "Finished?"

"Yes." Davidson crossed my office and passed me his application.

His penmanship was as precise as the lettering on an architect's blueprint. *Anal retentive much?*

Davidson lived near Bakersfield. "You don't have a Los Angeles address."

"Not yet," Davidson said. "Is that a deal-breaker? You can reach me on my cell anytime—it's the phone number on my application."

"That works." I set his application under my desk's leather pad and stood. "My business partner will contact your references and get back to you in a few days."

Following the handshake, I watched him leave.

Hope and I employed retired law enforcement officers as temps when we needed them, but temps can never take the place of permanent, full-time employees. Davidson could become a strong prospect if everything on his application checked out—that, and if the former deputy quit giving Hope the creeps. Zodiac Killer, my ass.

I turned to the windows facing the building's parking area and watched Davidson as he flipped through his ring of keys, slid behind the wheel of an old GMC pickup, and drove away. Memorizing the Jimmy's tag, I went to the keyboard and sent Hope Whitman, finder of all things great and small, a message to check on the registered owner of the pickup truck, and contact Davidson's employment references.

I'd done all I could do on the Danning case until tomorrow morning. I had a friend dropping by my house for dinner and a beer or two. I began shutting down the office.

CHAPTER THREE

Extreme Gaming

Jud Tucker, Sunset Strip, Monday, April 30

The "Steele & Whitman Investigations" block letters on the office door's frosted glass had told me what I'd already known. But I saw myself as a *semper paratus* man, always forewarned and forearmed.

Shit, I hadn't seen Clint Steele since his parents' double funeral about ten years ago. I shook my head and chuckled. "Oh, the sins of the father," I said out loud.

Wanting to do a quick reconnaissance, I'd trailed the world-famous Diana Danning gash into Steele & Whitman Investigations.

Now standing in the parking lot, I took my time picking through my ring of keys, sensing Steele had me under surveillance. Turning my back to the office windows, I unlocked my truck, slid behind the wheel, and drove away.

At the first stoplight, I drummed my fingers on the steering wheel. For my latest killing game, I decided to recruit only one player: gumshoe Clint Steele.

Steele looked too young to know his ass from a hole in the ground. But I sensed a clear and present danger right beneath his likable tough guy façade. Once I forced him into my new extreme game, he'd keep me on my toes. I'd bet the ranch on it.

But then, I liked my extreme gamers to have some fight in them.

CHAPTER FOUR

Mercury in Retrograde

Clint, The Flats, Beverly Hills, Monday, April 30

I entered my house from the garage, pulled off my shoes, then dropped my car fob, home and office keys, wallet, and pocket change into the hall table's ceramic bowl. I heard Ian's bare feet running. "DADDY!"

Dodging me, Ian shoved his feet into my dress oxfords, snagged the car's fob, and announced, "I bet if I wear your shoes I can reach the gas pedal and go for a drive, Daddy."

Before he planted his forehead into the wall with his first step in my shoes, I swept him into my arms and held him to my chest. My size sixteens dropped onto my socked feet—frigging painfully at that. I plucked the fob from Ian's fingers before he made a break for the garage. I kissed him on the cheek. "Did you have a good day?"

"No, look!"

The back of his right hand sported a Muppets Band-Aid. I affected a gasp. "What did you do, buddy?"

His face turned serious—tough to pull off, having lost his two front baby teeth.

"I did-ent do it. The kitty scratched me. I cried."

Heathcliff, our red Maine Coon, peeked around the laundry room's doorjamb. Cats always seem to know when you're talking about them. The twenty-eight-pound tom swaggered into the hallway, sat on his haunches, and began washing his face. Cats…you can't help but love them. Their litter boxes, not so much.

Frowning at Heathcliff, Ian turned his big, expressive blue eyes back to me. "I think you should put him in time-out."

I lowered Ian to the floor. He walked with me to the kitchen. "I'm certain Heathcliff didn't mean to scratch you—unless you were pulling his tail again."

As Stella unloaded the dishwasher, she narked, "Indeed, he tried to drag that poor cat across the kitchen floor by his tail like a Radio Flyer red wagon."

Stella closed the dishwasher. "I began teaching Ian some algebra basics today."

She'd worked as an elementary school teacher for thirty-five years before retiring. Thanks to Stella, Ian's writing, math, speech, and reading comprehension levels exceeded most of his peers', according to his standardized test scores.

Stella ran a hand over her white hair and checked her blouse and slacks. While in the company of a six-year-old boy, you never know what might've gotten spilled, sprayed, splattered, hacked, or sneezed onto you.

"I marinated New York strips and made vegetable kabobs for supper. Ian said he wanted a hamburger. It's all in the Frigidaire."

Viking had manufactured all my kitchen's major appliances. But in Stella's world view, Frigidaire was synonymous with refrigerator. I'd never asked her why. I thanked her for caring for Ian and getting dinner prepped.

Ian hugged Stella good-bye. She gave him a peck on the forehead. She grabbed the hand straps of today's brightly colored, monstrous granny purse. I walked her to the front door, her low heels tapping along the red oak floor.

I watched her slide behind the wheel of her Tesla. She threw me a wave and turned a one-eighty at a breakneck spin, then drove at a turtle's pace down the driveway.

I closed the door, turned, and went upstairs to the master bedroom. My little shadow followed on my heels.

I'm six-six and weigh two hundred and fifty pounds, but I balanced on one leg then the other as I pulled off my socks, slacks, and boxer briefs. I removed my tie and dress shirt.

I hung my suit and tie in my half of the walk-in closet. Sierra's clothing filled the other half. More than two years after her death, I still couldn't convince myself to donate her things.

Ian sat on the bed watching my every move, as if I might suddenly vanish as his mother had. He remembered his mom, but he'd quit asking me when she'd be coming home.

I stepped out of the closet nude, bent, picked up and tossed my socks, shirt, and underwear into the hamper. Still watching me with his big, dark-blue eyes, Ian said, "Daddy..."

"Yeah, buddy."

"When will my penis get big like yours?"

Dr. Grant Stenton, a shrink I knew, told me Ian had advanced to the phallic stage of psychosexual development. He'd be curious about his body and mine, especially the "particulars" below the belt. Doc Stenton said Ian should see me undressed from time to time. I should be casual about my nudity and teach him the proper names of male genitalia.

I pulled on stringy jean cut-offs, free balling it, then shrugged into a faded West Point Academy T-shirt. I said, "Ian, your penis, testes, and scrotum will get larger as you get older."

"Why do I gotta wait until I'm old?"

Anticipating at least one follow-up question, I had prepared myself for it. "Because your entire body gets larger as you grow from a boy, to a teen, to a man."

"Why?"

"That's how it works. You wait and see." Yes, I'd given him a cop-out answer requiring additional comments. I lifted his Dodgers T-shirt and gave him belly raspberries. He kicked, giggled, and forgot all about his and my genitals for now.

I barefooted it to the kitchen. Ian pounded down the stairs behind me.

After a yawn and a stretch, I opened the refrigerator door that I'd papered with Ian's artwork. I grabbed a Corona and a root beer from the fridge and sat at the kitchen island. Ian climbed onto the stool beside me. Pulling a short stack of adult coloring books toward us, I asked, "Which one do you want?"

"Birds, please."

That left me with trees, flowers, dogs, cats, or clowns. Considering clowns about as creepy as far-right politicians, I went with the dogs.

Ian turned to a drawing of a snowy owl. I slid his unopened root beer toward him. He bumped the can. I caught it before it went ass over tea kettle to the floor. In spite of Ian's intelligence, he remained a little boy. And throughout his continual questions, spills, stumbles and falls, I'd be there for him—time after time.

I looked up, hearing the garage door lifting. The rumble of Raoul Martinez's dual-wheeled diesel pickup sifted into the house. Raoul drove a working man's truck; no urban cowboy's shiny, tricked-out ride used primarily for extended cab tour de force fucking.

Ian dropped the crayon he was using. "Raoul is here."

"He is," I said, looking at his artwork. "Good job, son."

Ian frowned. "I don't like it."

Spoken like a true artist, I thought. After switching from children's to adult coloring books at Stella's recommendation, Ian had started lightening and darkening his colors, giving the drawing depth and perspective. Neither Stella nor I had taught him how to do it. This being Los Angeles where all the arts thrived, maybe Ian's coloring skills had come by way of something in the air or water.

With a hard-hat ring imprinted on his dark hair, Raoul Martinez stepped into the kitchen, stopped at the fridge, and grabbed a beer.

Raoul sat beside me, squeezed my shoulder, and smiled at Ian. "Hey, dude, that's a mighty fine coloring job on that owl. I should hire you to paint the interiors of my newly built houses."

Ian scrutinized him. "How much would I get paid?"

"You asked for it," I said quietly.

"Union scale when you get old enough to work," Raoul said, winking at Ian. He drank some beer, then turned to me. "Thanks for the cold one, Moose. Your brewski selections are the best of all my boyfriends."

I sipped some beer, then wrote on the top of my coloring page, *Shut your tramp mouth.*

"Daddy, what did you write to Raoul?"

I winked at Ian. "It's a secret."

"Was it something I'm not supposed to understand until I'm older?"

"Uh-huh, son." I said to Raoul, "Rough day?"

He let out a short breath. "The crew and I finished framing that custom build. Christ, two by sixes with twelve-inch centers. This house could survive an Old Testament flood."

I nodded, understanding the shop talk. When Sierra and I bought this circa 1960s two-story colonial, the term "fixer upper" made for one frigging colossal understatement. But after inspecting it, Raoul assured us it had "good bones."

Rock and Raoul Construction focused on custom houses, renovations, and masonry. I'd hired Raoul and his crew to remodel the white brick colonial inside and out.

I sometimes worked alongside Raoul on the renovations and learned a few of the finer tricks of carpentry and masonry. He and I quickly became close friends.

I plucked a wood shaving from Raoul's hair and dropped it into my empty beer bottle. "Have you gone to any auditions lately?"

He tapped my knee and said in his stage-trained voice, "I went to a cattle call last Saturday for a Shakespeare in the Park production of *Macbeth.*"

"I bet you'll get a callback." I paused, then added, "Vona has something in the pipe that may interest you."

Raoul started peeling the label off his beer bottle. "Is this a bit part where I get to be first male murder victim in the credits?"

"No, Raoul, I'm thinking you're perfect for the leading role. I'll tell you more over dinner."

Raoul chuckled and shook his head. "I got it. Don't sell Rock and Raoul Construction yet." He sipped some more beer. "What about your day?"

"Hope and I took on a high profile client this afternoon."

Raoul lifted an eyebrow. "Yeah?"

"That Hollywood royalty missing person matter," I said casually.

"Holy shit, Diana Danning's missing son?"

"Yup."

"Daddy, Raoul used a bad word."

"After dinner, we'll put him in time-out with Heathcliff," I said. "Speaking of eating, are you guys hungry?" I knew they were. It's why I'm the private investigator.

A few minutes later, I carried a tray loaded with marinated steaks, hamburger patties and buns, vegetable kabobs, and potatoes to the terrace. Raoul followed with the packed cooler. Ian began kicking the soccer ball he'd left in the backyard.

I lighted the gas grill and checked on Ian. He remained out of hearing range. I said, "Did you hear about the two terrorists' wives who went digging for food in a bombed-out bazaar?"

Raoul chuckled and shook his head.

"The older wife digs two potatoes out of the ashes and holds them up side by side." I held two large spuds side by side in my hand. "The older wife says, 'These remind me of my husband's balls.' The younger wife asks, 'Your husband's balls are this large?' The older wife answers, 'No. They are this dir-tee.'"

Raoul laughed, shooting the slug of beer in his mouth over a nearby planter of orchids. "Hot on the heels of that," he said, "where the hell do you begin on the Danning case?"

I again checked on Ian, placed the food on the grill, and closed the lid. "I'll start with the LAPD. Hal Flynn's the lead investigator."

"Great, you get to work with your cop buddy, Captain Fantastic Flynn."

I nodded while flipping the steaks and burgers. "Being a high profile case, it's no surprise it landed on Captain Flynn's desk." I began turning the meat continually.

Minutes later, I called Ian. He came running. You can call my son anything but late for dinner. I pulled everything off the grill.

We sat eating, drinking, talking, and laughing about everything and nothing of consequence. When we'd finished dinner, I pushed my plate aside. "I mentioned Vona's new film project."

"Tell me what Vona has in the pipe before I piss my pants."

"Raoul," Ian began, "if you gotta pee, you can jump into the swimming pool like I do when I'm too busy to run back to the house to use the bathroom."

I used my dad voice. "Ian, you'd better not—"

Ian giggled. "Jokes, Daddy."

My little boy would soon become a full-fledged wiseass, I told myself. I turned back to Raoul. "Vona has a film nearly out of preproduction. The budget calls for a three-month shoot, and another three in post." I gave Raoul a synopsis of the script, adding, "I believe this movie will become a holiday blockbuster. I think you're perfect for the leading role."

Raoul chewed on his lower lip for a moment. "Is this project a sure thing?"

"That's why I didn't mention it until now. Vona found investors and put up some of her and my money. That makes it as much of a sure thing as it gets in the movie biz. If you're interested, I'll try to get your foot in the door."

I handed Ian a couple of moistened towelettes. "You need to wipe your hands and face."

"Why?"

"Because you're wearing more ketchup than you ate." It was one more vestige of the little boy.

"Thanks, Moose, you bet I'm interested. I appreciate your help."

"I thought of you because Vona wants a handsome unknown for the starring role."

"Yeah, La La Land has a severe shortage of good-looking unknown actors. As mentioned, I won't hang up my hard hat right away. Thanks again for—"

"Hey, gorgeous guys! Am I crashing your dinner party?"

The voice came from the other side of the Italian cypress hedge. My next-door neighbor, Darla Wong, former sixties flower child of the Haight, now did business as Darla Love, "the Astrologer to the Hollywood Stars."

"What's up, Darla?"

She slowly climbed the ladder. Her coal black hair streaked with white, dark eyes, small nose, and thin lips appeared. One more rung, and her shoulders rose above the hedge.

A full-figured woman, Darla always wore one of her brightly colored muumuus. With rings on every finger and numerous bracelets on both wrists, she sported enough crystals, silver, and gold to disrupt aircraft communications.

She'd feng-shuied her backyard into a harmonious collection of shade and ornamental trees, exotic flowers, pebbled paths, and water that trickled over rocks into a koi pool. Apparently, good karma kept the raccoons and coyotes from eating her pricy fish. Then, fuck me sideways, Darla added a backyard aviary. I'd grown accustomed to hearing the twitters, peeps, tweets, and hoots. But I sometimes heard strange sounds that, as far as I knew, could've come from the Tookie Tookie Bird she'd conjured off an old *George of the Jungle* cartoon.

Ian ran to the hedge, smiled, and waved at Darla.

She spoke in an affected British accent, "'Ello, lit'l lovey."

Ian looked down and blushed. Darla's Asian and astrologer exoticism fascinated him.

"All righty, guys, dig it. Starting today through the middle of June, Mercury will be in retrograde. Moosie, sweetheart, do you remember what you need to do and what to avoid during any retro Mercury?"

"It's a period of bad communications, unclear thinking, and travel delays," I said. "It's a time not to make big decisions or expensive purchases. Most important, it's weeks of lies. You must question everything you're told and avoid signing big money contracts."

"Right on and groovy," Darla said. "In general, we can't get our karmic shit together during any Mercury in retro. The upcoming weeks make for a great time to reexamine problem areas of our lives and find fresh solutions. You can't fight or control what bad luck might transpire. All you can do is go with the flow, guys. Oh, and it's a bad time to begin an intimate relationship with someone. If you do, you're looking at a one-night romance."

She waved, bracelets jangling, setting off a cacophony of screeches, squawks, tweets, and whistles. She slowly stepped down the ladder and out of sight.

"Goddammit anyway," I began, "Hope and I entered into a big money contract with Diana Danning this afternoon."

"Come on, you don't believe this Mercury retrograde astrology bullshit, do you?"

I shrugged. "Whenever Darla goes out of her way to warn me about something, she's often correct."

"And it's not that you might unconsciously do careless, stupid shit, making her gloomy-doomy predictions come true."

I grinned. "You should know this line from *Hamlet*: 'There are more things in Heaven and Earth, Horatio, than are dreamt of in your philosophy.'"

"Boogah-boogah," he said.

We laughed, then we gathered the dishes and carried them to the kitchen with Ian right behind us, cradling his soccer ball. He dropped it when he stumbled onto the terrace.

We talked and worked together with the ease of longtime friends. Raoul tossed the empties into the recycle bin and took a bag of trash to the dumpster. I loaded the dishwasher.

Raoul glanced at his watch. "As your next-door witchy woman would put it, 'Oh wow, man, I gotta split.' Thanks for everything."

"You're welcome."

Ian and I followed him into the garage. Raoul and I did a one-armed bro hug, then he tousled Ian's dark auburn hair. "Bye, cute dude."

As the garage door did its slow lift, Raoul swung his six-foot frame into the truck's cab. With a final wave, he backed the dually onto the driveway.

I listened to the garage door slowly descending with its steady rattle and growl, ending with a decisive clank.

CHAPTER FIVE

Sweet Dreams

Clint, The Flats, Monday, April 30

I ran a tub of warm water with bubbles for Ian, sat on the toilet lid, and kept an eye on him while he soaked and played. I had to tell him his face and ears needed more work and remind him to wash his behind. After he dried himself, I passed him sleep shorts and a Happy Dance Snoopy T-shirt.

As we headed to his bedroom, he talked about becoming a house painter for Raoul.

"Maybe you can work for him when you're seventeen, during the summer before you start college."

"Yeah, when my penis is great big like yours."

I considered warning Stella about Ian's big-dick fixation, but she'd worked with children for decades. I supposed nothing Ian said about his penis would knock Stella out of her sensible shoes.

Pulling over a chair, I sat bedside and listened to Ian read aloud from a sci-fi novel about tween robots—a book written for ten- to twelve-year-olds. After a few minutes of perfect reading, his eyes drooped.

I set the novel on the nightstand and spent a few moments watching him sleep. I wished Sierra were here to see our beautiful child growing and thriving. I kissed him on the forehead, switched off the bedside lamp, clicked on the nightlight, and went downstairs.

I sat in my recliner with a diet soda in hand and the TV on, sometimes watching but more often spacing the marathon of eighties sitcoms. Heathcliff swaggered into the den and sat on his haunches, watching me with his large copper-colored eyes. "Come on, beast."

He jumped onto my lap and tried squeezing himself between the right arm of the recliner and my thigh, forcing me to scoot over.

Maine Coons have a lion-like mane that adds to their regal bearing.

"Did his highness finally get comfy?"

Unfazed by the staff's insolence—Heathcliff had long known I was batshit—he watched *The Golden Girls*. Or maybe it was *Designing Women*. Loud purring ensued.

In a while, I caught myself drifting. I yawned loud and long. Turning off the television, I pushed down the footrest without disturbing Heathcliff. When it came to the recliner, the beast could sleep through a gunfight in the den. I stood, crossed the room, and climbed the stairs.

Brushing my teeth, I looked in the mirror and saw my tired eyes. Since Sierra's death, I hadn't slept well most nights.

I thought I glimpsed Sierra's face in the mirror, checking her hair before heading out to the private university where she taught economics and political science. I blinked. Her visage disappeared.

I shut off the lights, stepped into my bedroom, and stretched out on my California king–sized mattress. I tossed and turned, stared into the darkness, kicked off the covers, fluffed my pillows, and cursed under my breath.

I switched on the nightstand lamp and went to the wall safe in the walk-in closet. I punched in the code. Among my guns, a roll of Franklins, important documents, and car fob, I snagged the prescription bottle and dumped two pills into my hand.

I chased them with the bottle of water I kept on the nightstand. Returning to bed, I fell into a restless sleep in minutes.

In my dream, Sierra and I lay nude in full body contact. I could smell her skin lotion, shampoo, and her natural flora scent. I heard us breathing, our hearts beating. I ran my hand over her hair as I kissed her neck, working my way down to her nipples.

The first time we'd slept together, she'd taken one look and said, "I don't know if—"

"It will fit," I'd assured her.

Our lovemaking always started with outercourse or intercrural sex. Teasing her vulva with my erect penis brought her to a screaming orgasm every time. When it came to penetration, I let Sierra ride me until we both reached a screaming, head-spinning, toe-curling climax.

The bedside telephone rang, coinciding with my night emission. Jolted awake, I pulled tissues from the box while fuzzily reading the caller ID. Shit, an unlisted number at 0218 hours.

I considered ignoring it, but thought better. A ringing phone at this hour usually meant trouble. I picked up the handset.

"Hello," I said while cradling the phone and dabbing semen out of my chest hair, which I kept closely cropped. I wiped the post cum off my glans, then grappled my half-hard cock back into my sleep shorts.

Diana Danning softly cleared her throat and used her breathy voice. "I'm sorry to call you in the middle of the night, but I thought you'd want to know right away."

"Want to know what?"

"Shane was seen in a Laguna supermarket tonight!"

"That's great news. Was it a positive identification?"

"Abso-tivly possi-llutely identified."

I knew what she expected me to do next, but I asked anyway. "Since Shane appears to be fine, do you want me to drop the investigation?"

Her voice rose. "For fuck sakes no. I still want you to find Shane and bring him home."

"You and I need a meeting of the minds on that."

"Go ahead," she said grudgingly.

"Unlike the LAPD, I can search for Shane. I'm certain I can find him, talk to him, and try to convince him to come home. If he doesn't want to return to L.A., I can't cuff him and force him into my car. Shane isn't a bail jumper, and I'm not a bounty hunter."

Diana's voice turned hostile. "You'll do whatever it takes to bring Shane home. I don't care how you do it."

She ended the call.

I briefly considered calling Diana back, then muttered, "Fuck her." I fell into a dreamless sleep.

Wide awake at 0530 hours, I put fresh sheets on the bed. I'm not one of those guys who can sleep on dried semen, including my own. I tossed the bed linens into the washer. Carrying today's clothing into the master bath, I showered and washed my hair.

Twenty minutes later, I toweled off, then brushed my teeth. Looking into the mirror, I decided to keep my scruff. I shrugged into a faded Delta Force T-shirt, pulled on butter-soft jeans with stringy holes, put on white socks, and laced up my boots. Applying a dab of product, I ruffled my hair, giving it a slightly mismanaged bad boy look.

I recalled Sierra studying me one morning after I'd similarly dressed down for work. "What?" I had asked, feigning innocence.

"I don't know about your attire."

"I'm wearing what's needed for the work I'm doing today."

"Yes, if you're working as a cathouse bouncer." Hands on her hips, she'd continued, "Hmm…that tight shirt emphasizes your broad shoulders, ripped torso, six-pack, and narrow waist. But the *pièce de résistance* is your distressed, second-skin denims. Babe, in those jeans, I can clearly see that you're huge and not Jewish."

"You think you're seeing those intimate details only because you know every inch of my body."

She placed a hand on my crotch. "Sir, I think what you're wearing can only be described as provocative."

I grinned. "Madam, on the matter of provocation, if you don't take your hand off my crank, we'll both be late for work."

We were late getting to work that morning.

This morning, I peeked into Ian's bedroom. Seeing he slept soundly, I silently closed the door.

The moment I stepped into the kitchen, Heathcliff began running in front of me and trilling his ass off about breakfast. For future reference, Heathcliff trills and does not speak in commoner cat meows. I fed his highness. Then I brewed a cup of dark roast and waited for Stella, who'd arrive at 0630 hours give or take a minute or two.

Sitting at the kitchen island, I sipped coffee, woke my tablet, and began writing interview questions.

Since Diana hadn't shit-canned me after her tantrum, the due diligence work on the Danning case began this morning. Who knew? Maybe I'd learn something new about Shane's disappearance and last night's alleged appearance in Laguna.

CHAPTER SIX

Still Not Quite Right

Jud Tucker, The Ranch, Tuesday, May 1

I pushed a handcart loaded with chicken feed and five-gallon stainless steel slop pails out of the barn, then paused to look at the old GMC parked next to my van. I'd need to sacrifice the Jimmy soon if I'd guessed the gumshoe's first few gaming moves correctly—one of which involved Steele talking with Deputy Sheriff Scott Davidson's bugfuck nuts father. Sonofabitch, I liked the old, solid, reliable, American-made pickup. They didn't build them like this anymore.

Turning my attention to the sunrise, I fired up a cigarette, exhaled the smoke out my nostrils, and squinted at another beautiful California morning.

Of the few things I loved, my ranch topped the list. My old man called it the "Million Miles from Nowhere Money Pit." But the old bastard had been such a loser, he couldn't have turned a profit off the land had he perfected a printing plate for hundred dollar bills.

I'd come into the world four months after my parents had gotten married. When I'd become worldly enough to do the math, I asked my old man about the five-month discrepancy.

"You're a honeymoon baby and born premature. That's why you're still not quite right."

At the age of six, I'd begun carrying buckets of chopped fodder to the stanchioned dairy cows while my old man and the hired hand washed udders and attached the milking machines' teat cups. Like most farm and ranch kids, I'd worked my ass off knowing I wouldn't get paid for my labors.

The hired hand started molesting me when I was seven. He'd wait until my old man went to town for supplies. He swore he'd bury me alive if I told anyone. I kept my mouth shut.

My mother called it quits when I was twelve. Dad wouldn't consider wasting money on hospitals, psychiatrists, or even medical doctors who might've helped Mom win her war with depression.

I got off the school bus one day, walked inside the house, and smelled gas. I found Mom with her head in the oven. I shut off the gas, opened all the doors and windows. I tried to wake her up, but she'd already passed away. It was what it was.

After Mom's death, my old man immersed himself in the dairy cattle, the beef herd, the crops, and the aging farm equipment that always needed repairs. His distance worked for me. Preoccupied, he didn't punch me to the ground or whip me.

By the time I was thirteen, I knew how to operate the farm's heavy equipment, how to herd cattle, how to buck bales, and how to butcher pigs, chickens, and cows. My old man put the fear of God in me on the dangers of silos, elevators, headers, augers, and PTO shafts, always ending with the same warning: "Boy, you'd best hear what I'm telling you or I'll give you a whipping you ain't never gonna forget." And by that, I knew the old bastard didn't mean a severe spanking.

Shortly after turning fifteen, I knew I still wasn't quite right. The hired hand who'd been raping me for eight years became the first person I buried on the ranch.

"Boy, it's about time you got hair on your nuts and put an axe in that old bastard's head," he'd said to me after the hired hand vanished. "All I can figure is you liked getting ass-fucked."

Maybe he'd called that one right. After all, when you know how to slaughter animals, operate a backhoe, and have a thousand acres to work with, making someone disappear forever could happen easily enough. Then again, maybe I tolerated the hired hand's molestations because I took older-male affection any way I could get it.

After graduating high school, I attended college full-time and earned a four-year degree in fire science. I got hired as a firefighter but soon returned to lectures, labs, and textbooks to become a licensed paramedic. I never returned to the ranch until the old man died.

Crushing the cigarette's cherry between the calluses on my thumb and forefinger, I stepped the fuck out of memory lane. After pocketing the butt, I moved ahead with the last of the sunrise chores.

I pulled the handcart to the chicken yard, pausing to watch the flock scratching and pecking in their own shit. I enjoyed slaughtering these filthy fucking birds, watching them make their short, final runs, blood spurting out of their headless necks.

Lifting the latch on the wire gate, I stepped into the poultry yard, opened the sack, and began filling the feeders. The fat hens would not leave a speck uneaten. I tossed the empty feed bag into the cart and moved on.

At the pig pen, four huge, snorting, squealing swine waited for me. I poured the slop from the stainless steel pails over the fence into the wooden trough. True eating and shitting machines, hogs never turned their snouts up at anything. Hell, I once watched a sow devour an old license plate. And, like the chickens, hogs never left a speck behind.

I returned to the barn and hosed out the slop pails, making certain all evidence of their former contents went down the floor drain. I headed for the house.

In the shower, I had a few minutes to think.

Yesterday afternoon, I'd almost gotten my ass busted by trailing the world famous Danning tramp into Steele & Whitman Investigations. I'd hoped to overhear bits of her conversation with the gumshoe.

But the silver-haired harridan behind the reception desk gave me the third degree and caught me off guard. Forced to think fast, I'd presented myself as Scott Davidson. Nobody could connect me to the deputy and his death. I was only an ordinary man wanting a few minutes of Steele's time.

Late yesterday afternoon, I'd tailed Steele to his house in the Flats. I parked a block away. Before long, a Rock & Raoul Construction dually drove up Steele's driveway and parked in the garage, suggesting the two men were either close friends or something else I didn't want to know about. I drove away before someone in the ritzy-titsy neighborhood noticed my old, dented Jimmy and called the Beverly Hills blues.

Last evening at home, I did some internet research. Finding Rock & Raoul Construction's website, I learned Raoul was Raoul Martinez. Using Google Maps, I found Raoul's address and a clear photo of his house, including his Ram parked in front of the garage.

Next, I caught up on Steele's cases that had made headlines. Seems he'd become one of the best at finding missing people.

After reading the articles on Steele & Whitman's successes, and my run-in with the old bag behind the desk, I'd learned never again to underestimate Steele's abilities and resources. He could become a serious problem. The stakes were too high for Steele to interfere with my plans for Shane Danning, and settling the score with his mother.

Now, dressed in suit and tie, I slid behind the wheel of my five-year-old Buick and headed to my other job. The commute would give me time to finalize my plans for my first move: a homicide that would rock Clint Steele's world.

CHAPTER SEVEN

Off on a Fucking Lark

Clint, Los Angeles, Police Administration Building, Tuesday, May 1

I found Captain Harlan "Hal" Flynn at his desk, reading the *Los Angeles Times*. I entered his office without knocking.

Flynn lowered the paper and said in his standard bug-up-his-ass tone, "As I live and breathe, if it ain't the big swinging of private dicks."

"And you know it," I said.

Flynn folded the newspaper and tossed it onto his desk.

I suppose Flynn's blue eyes, slight brogue, dark hair, and the bad-assed cop thing he wore like a discount warehouse suit made him a definite CILF to lots of people. But I'm not one of them.

For years, Flynn and I have more or less been friends, with a more or less mutual respect for each other.

Better put, we merely tolerate each other.

I went to Flynn's big green Lutheran church coffee percolator, found what might have been a clean cup, and helped myself. The black sludge smelled as if it had been reheated no more than two or three times. "Thanks for the Danning referral."

"You owe me big for that favor," Flynn said.

I sat in front of the desk and took a sip of coffee that nearly made me heave. "Diana Danning told me someone spotted her son in Laguna last night."

"Ahh, Jesus, Mary and Joseph." Flynn pulled in a long breath and let it out fast. "I told her not to jump to fucking conclusions until we could verify it was her son."

I set my coffee mug on the edge of Flynn's shit-strewn desk.

"I don't imagine you'll find too many guys out there who look like Shane Danning. With everything he has going for him in the body and looks departments, he could become the poster boy for spontaneous orgasms." I jerked Flynn's chain. "So who was spotted last night—Shane or his evil twin?"

Flynn shrugged. "The supermarket's manager is certain she saw Shane Danning in her store around 2250 last night."

"Do you consider the store manager a credible witness?"

"She's a bit of a flooze, but I think she's credible," Flynn said. "She told me the man in question paid for his groceries with an American Express card issued to Danning. He used Shane Danning's California driver's license as a photo ID."

"Can you verify the signature on the charge receipt?"

Flynn rolled closer to his desk. "The store manager swore the signature matched the handwriting on the back of the credit card. I'll know for certain when the SID criminologists get off their lazy asses and send me a handwriting analysis."

"Who leaked the Danning sighting to the media? It had to be one of your colleagues or one of the supermarket's employees."

"I don't know, but I intend to find out and lock the asshole up."

I grinned. "If being an asshole in the City of Angels were a crime, we'd need a fifty-foot-high steel fence around the entire L.A. megalopolis."

The right corner of Flynn's mouth twitched. It was his version of a chuckle.

"There's one fact I didn't include in my report," Flynn said, "meaning it didn't get leaked to the media by anyone in law enforcement."

"What fact is that?"

Flynn raised an eyebrow. "Shane Danning neither entered nor left the supermarket alone."

"Are we talking about a male or female companion?"

"Male, dark blond, brown, glasses, six-one or two, one eighty to one ninety pounds, early to mid-forties, according to the store manager."

I shook my head. "That's a great description of a fargon lot of Southern California's middle-aged male population."

Flynn nodded.

"Laguna is Sex Central for shitloads of people. It wouldn't surprise me if we have an actual Shane Danning sighting."

"Ohhhh," Flynn said, dragging out the word, "now you're telling me Danning walked away from his airline pilot career, mother, and home for sex."

I leaned back in my chair. "You and I know people go missing for everything from extended sexual liaisons to mental illnesses, bad relationships, debts, or to catch a ride on the fucking rapture flying saucer. All I'm saying is Laguna seems like a place where a young, handsome, single guy might go to relax, cruise barely covered beach bodies, then drink and fuck himself stupid."

Diana had mentioned buying Shane a new Porsche. "Did Danning drive to the Jugs & Mugs Saloon that night?"

"It appears he either walked or caught a ride to the saloon. We found his German sports car parked at his house."

I veered. "Assuming it was Danning the store manager saw, what did he buy?"

Flynn flipped past a couple of pages in the Danning file and read aloud, "Pretzel rods, chips, four cases of Killian's, and a bunch of shit from the deli."

"That tells us jack," I said.

"Bullshit, it tells me we got another rich, spoiled, west-side prince off on a fucking lark."

"If Danning blew town for sex and to party, why would he leave behind a brand-new, six-figure sports car," I countered.

"You know the brats of the Platinum Triangle couldn't care a fucking fiddler's fart less about expensive possessions."

Flynn had a point, maybe.

"The media reported two university students thought they saw Danning getting into a van after he left the saloon. One of them called the cops reporting a possible kidnapping," I said, then asked, "Did the responding officers find the eyewitnesses believable?"

Flynn shrugged. "They were about as believable as two drunk-off-their-asses college boys can be. The problem is they disagreed on everything they saw, or thought they saw."

"Jesus H, how drunk were they?"

"One of the responding officers told me the two college boys couldn't have found their own wankers with both hands in the dark." Flynn's eyes met mine as he added, "Someone shot out the streetlights along the block where Danning was either forced or willingly got into a van."

The vandalized streetlights might point to a premeditated kidnapping. "What can you tell me about Danning's ex-significant other?"

"Kristopher or Kristina Morgotti's a bawdy little cross-dressin' queen, but she or he looks clean. Not as much as a parking ticket to his or her name."

"I might agree with your conclusions: no abduction, Danning either walked or hooked a ride to the saloon, found a nice piece o' tail, and got away from it all because he could." I absently picked up the coffee mug, caught a whiff, and set it back down. "Do you mind if I do some digging?"

"Unless something else comes into the light, I'll close this case once we verify Danning's Amex signature." He shrugged. "Go ahead and earn some of that fat retainer Diana Danning gave you. And keep me in the loop."

"Consider yourself looped," I said.

Flynn closed Shane Danning's missing person file and rose from his desk chair. "Now, if you'll excuse me, I need to see a man about a horse."

He made it to the door and turned to face me, his Irish eyes smiling. "Don't you dare steal that copy of Danning's missing person file I left on my desk." He walked down the hall to the men's room.

Flynn's cooperation came as no surprise. He wanted me to do the kind of digging the LAPD was barred from doing without probable cause. I stood, slotted my thumbs in the pockets of my jeans, and checked the cubicles outside Flynn's office. All clear. I slid the Danning file into my messenger bag and headed out.

CHAPTER EIGHT

Leave a Message…Maybe We'll Call

Clint, Tuesday, May 1

Entering Steele & Whitman Investigations, I saw Hope cradling the phone while scribbling on a steno pad. Using shorthand, she could take dictation without dropping a single word. I considered such a skill damned impressive.

I wondered if technology had turned Gregg shorthand into a lost art. Did high schools and community colleges even teach it anymore? I waved at Hope and started for my office.

She pointed her pencil at me. I stopped dead in my army boots.

Hope ended the call. "Do we need to adopt a dress code? Yesterday you wore a suit and tie to the office. This morning, you come traipsin' in here looking like a Section Eight rent boy."

"I always wear the proper clothing to do the job at hand properly." Standing at parade rest, I changed the topic. "The sour look on your lovely face suggests you heard something quite untoward on the phone."

"Untoward indeed," Hope said. Her hazel eyes met my dark blues. "I checked Scott Davidson's Kern County employment reference."

"And?"

She turned to her notes. "On the job, Deputy Sheriff Scott Valentine Davidson consistently proved to be a reliable, honest deputy, who meticulously followed orders. He was a hard"—she said "hahd"—"working, punctual deputy who was motivated, demonstrated solid problem-solving skills, worked equally well independently or on a team and—"

"Hope, I think I got it. Scott Davidson's work ethic made him an HR director's wet dream." There might be something positive about

Gregg shorthand becoming a lost art, I thought. "So what the hell's the problem with the deputy?"

"The problem, Mister Grouchy smaht-ass, is Deputy Scott V. Davidson did not retire from Kern County." She paused for impact.

I waited for her to continue. "You know, Hope, as a member of the lesbian tribe, you can sometimes turn into a real drama queen. For fuck sakes, tell me the rest of the story."

"Deputy Scott V. Davidson died about two months ago from a self-inflicted gunshot wound." She slid her pencil into her silver-haired bouffant that sort of looked like a chrome beehive.

"Scott Davidson is dead?"

"That's precisely what I told you."

Given the superlatives Hope had noted on Davidson's job performance, I wondered what might have driven him to suicide. Then it hit me: the Kern County Sheriff's Department could've had two deputies named Scott Davidson.

"I can hear the wheels in your head spinning," Hope said. "The Kern County Sheriff had only one deputy named Scott Valentine Davidson."

"Your mind reading scares me sometimes." I parked one butt cheek on the edge of her shipshape desk. "Would you see if you can get a photo of Deputy Davidson from the sheriff or the DMV?"

Then I brought her up to speed on the sighting of Shane Danning in Laguna.

She wrote more shorthand. "So noted."

"What did you find on that GMC pickup I saw in the building's parking area yesterday?"

She flipped the page on her steno pad. "The forty-year-old GMC belonged to Scott V. Davidson. The registration's address is a two hundred acre farm"—she said "fahm"—"owned by Scott's father, Francis Valentine Davidson."

"And you have Francis's phone number." I knew she did.

She wrote the number on a Post-it and passed it to me. "Not for nothing, but the Kern County Sheriff tells me Francis Valentine Davidson has a drinking problem and can be a truly charming"—you know how she said it—"man to deal with."

"Sarcasm noted." I started for my desk but turned back. "Would you put together a six-pack, including Shane Danning's photo, and get his house key out of the safe, please?"

"Done." She opened a desk drawer and pulled a collection of

young men's photos lined up three per side in clear vinyl sleeves, as well as Danning's house key.

"Thanks, but your mind reading does get spooky," I said, picking up the key and the six-pack of photos.

"Don't you know from reading John Updike's novels that all New England broads are witches?" She mimicked Margaret Hamilton's Wicked Witch of the West screeching laugh. (If necessary, JFGI.)

The phone warbled. Hope pulled the pencil out of her bouffant beehive and snapped up the handset.

Seated behind my desk, I found the cell phone number of the man who had presented himself as the deceased Scott Davidson. I tapped in the phone number he'd given me. Two rings, and "This number is no longer in service. Please check the listing and try again."

I didn't need to try again. I wondered who in the hell would attempt to impersonate a dead man. Whoever this fuckrag dime-store cowboy was, he had to know the truth would come out with a single phone call.

And whoever this asshole was, he apparently liked playing games.

I punched in Francis Valentine Davidson's number. I was one ring away from hanging up when a gruff male voice with a two-pack-a-day nicotine habit and a quart or so of something a hundred and fifty proof answered the phone.

"Don't ya know what goddammed time it is?"

I considered asking him if anybody truly knew what time it is, but I thought better of it. Never go Zen when talking to a cranky alcoholic. I identified myself, then asked, "Am I speaking to Francis Davidson?"

"You with a fuckin' collection agency?"

"No, I'm a private investigator." I pushed the envelope. "Would you mind answering a couple of questions concerning your late son?"

Davidson didn't speak. But I heard the old fart's wheezy breathing. At least he hadn't hung up.

I hung in. "Yesterday afternoon, I met with a man who identified himself as Scott Davidson. He drove away in a GMC pickup registered to your late son." I paused, letting that much information sink into Davidson's calcified brain. "Do you have any idea who would impersonate Scott and why?"

"Fuck no."

Francis Valentine Davidson ended the call. I frowned at the dead connection for a moment, muttering, "Asshole."

I thumbed through Shane Danning's missing person file and found the statements given to the police on April twenty-fifth by Blake Walsh and Blaine Vogel, the university students who'd called 9-1-1 after witnessing a possible abduction on a Hollywood sidewalk.

I scanned the responding officers' reports. As is common with multiple eyewitnesses, Walsh and Vogel disagreed on almost everything they thought they'd seen.

Walsh claimed the victim didn't move when the van driver blocked the sidewalk.

Vogel said Danning froze for several seconds, started to run, and stumbled. The driver caught him, pinned his arms behind his back, and frog-marched Danning into the van.

Walsh stated with certainty the driver stretched his arm across Danning's shoulders and walked him to the van's passenger side door.

With the streetlights out, Vogel could not positively identify the van's year, color, make or model. He thought the vehicle might've been a dark-colored, late model Ford. He could not see the tag.

Walsh could not guess the year, make, model, or color of the van. But he thought the tag included either a "V" or "W," either a "3" or an '8," and a definite "9."

Fuck me sideways, so much for the accounts of eyewitnesses, I thought. I continued reading, hoping I might pluck a dime or two out of the bullshit.

Neither Walsh nor Vogel could give a complete description of the van's driver. Walsh thought he was about five feet ten inches tall. Vogel said he was six-three or four and might have weighed around three hundred pounds.

Walsh and Vogel had seen Danning in the Jugs & Mugs Saloon on the night of April twenty-fifth. They agreed on Danning's description: twenty-seven to thirty years old, about six feet two inches tall, a hundred eighty to ninety pounds, and dark hair.

"He's one of the sexiest men I've ever seen," Vogel told the cops, "but he blew us off when we smiled at him."

Neither of the eyewitnesses knew his name at the time.

I yawned, stretched, and turned the page.

One of the responding officers had pulled her flashlight and walked the block, stopping when she spotted a man's wallet near the curb.

Pulling on gloves, she retrieved and opened the black leather wallet. She found no cash, no credit cards, no driver's license; only Shane Danning's FAA pilot certificate and a government issued photo ID. The officer instantly recognized Danning's face and surname.

I looked up from the file. Since Danning's wallet held only

his pilot creds, the eyewitnesses may have seen a mugging that escalated into an abduction once the van driver read and recognized his victim's Hollywood royalty surname. Then again, it was possible with the streetlights not working on that block, the eyewitnesses saw a premeditated kidnapping.

I supposed there were those possibilities, or Danning had gotten picked up by a friend, and his wallet had slipped out of his hip pocket when he stepped off the curb.

Sometimes a guy who went clubbing would slip his cash, a credit card, and driver's license into his front pants pockets and leave his wallet at home.

I checked the file for Walsh and Vogel's phone numbers. Roommates, they had given responding officers what looked like a landline. University students who didn't give their cell numbers seemed strange to me.

I called the students' landline and leaned back in my swivel chair.

Two rings…four rings…six rings…and the voice mail answered. "A pleasant hello. You have reached Blake and Blaine's mental help hotline. Please leave a message…maybe we'll call."

I hung up. I needed a face-to-face with these boys.

The copy of the missing person file included the phone number of Shane Danning's ex, Kristopher/Kristina Morgotti. I also needed a face-to-face meeting with the cross-dressing gossip columnist.

But I'd give Morgotti a call when I was about two blocks from her house.

CHAPTER NINE

Closed-Toe Wedges, Antique Swedish Clogs, and Shitkickers

Clint, Tuesday, May 1

There's a neighborhood in the Hollywood Hills not far from southern Laurel Canyon called Mount Olympus. Here, the neo-glam mansions are as over the top as the area's name.

Turning onto Janus Drive, I pulled to the curb and called Kris Morgotti and told her I'd be arriving soon with some follow-up questions concerning Shane Danning.

It took me less than two minutes to find Morgotti's address. I parked in the circular drive and stepped into another shimmering, blue-sky Los Angeles morning.

Skirting a fountain, I loped to the white manse's double doors flanked by potted dwarf lemon trees. I pressed the bell, faintly hearing the bongs from within. I wondered whether Kristina or Kristopher would come to the door.

I got Kristina Morgotti in her bare feet. Standing about five feet nine inches tall, she wore a white silk blouse, a light gray skirt hanging a gnat's ass above her knees, and a blue blazer with heavily padded shoulders à la Joan Crawford (JFGI).

Kristina said in a dusky voice à la Tallulah Bankhead (JFGI), "I didn't expect you to arrive so quickly. I'm working. What the ever-loving fuck do you want?"

I smiled at her.

She gasped. "OMFG! That square chin and those twin dimples could break a girl's heart."

She gave me an unabashed down-up, stopping and holding midway.

I shyly shuffled my feet and started to introduce myself.

She flapped one of her manicured hands. "Sweetheart, I know who you are." She opened the door wide. "I told the police all I could recall about Shane, and nearly everything about our relationship. I can't imagine what you think I might add to that wretched tale."

I'd bet the cross-dressing Queen of Snark knew a hell of a lot more about Danning's disappearance than she'd told Captain Flynn. I smiled. "I've a few follow-up questions. May I come in?"

She stepped aside. "Get in before I change my mind and slam the door in your handsome face."

I wasted no time in getting my ass inside.

Looking down, Kristina Morgotti gasped again. "My goodness, Grandma, what big feet you have."

I whispered a laugh. "You know what they say, Ms. Morgotti...big feet, unusually large...shoes."

Kristina smiled. "Before you take another step, please remove your unusually large...shitkickers."

Standing on one leg, then the other, I unlaced my combat boots, not shitkickers, and dropped them one at a time onto the entry hall's black marble floor. I gave the gossip columnist an imitation earnest look. "Would you like me to take my socks off too?"

"You can keep your socks on—for the time being."

I followed her down the entry hall into an open great room with thick white carpet and black leather furniture. Impressionist oil paintings hung on the walls.

The mansion stood on a promontory. A wall of floor-to-ceiling glass provided a spectacular view of mountains and ocean. Apparently, innuendos, suppositions, and simply making shit up paid well.

"Please sit down," Kristina said, settling herself on a sofa.

She crossed her long, shapely legs. If I hadn't known better, no one could've convinced me that Kristina was a Kristopher.

I sat in the armchair straight across from Kristina. I pulled out my tablet and checked my notes. "You've heard someone spotted Shane in Laguna last night."

Morgotti shrugged. "That's old news. I posted a report about Danning's sighting on my *Hollywood Nights* website around one thirty this morning."

Sometimes the gossip grapevine worked faster than the internet, telephone, and tell-a-cop. Rumor had it Morgotti paid police snitches for information about stars' embarrassing misdemeanors and criminal busts. Or so I'd been told by a cop.

"In my *Hollywood Nights* archives, I've a photo of producer-director Vona Steele standing beside you at a black tie fundraiser. You're fabulously photogenic, but seeing you in the flesh...shit, that shot did not do you justice."

"Thank you," I said kind of shyly. Never mind I'd willfully, intentionally, and with malice aforethought arrived dressed like a brazen boy tart to catch Morgotti's eye. Her flattery suggested I'd hooked said eye.

"I usually know everything about all the industries' leaders and their family members. You, however, have kept under my radar since your lovely wife's tragic accident." Kristina looked directly into my eyes. "Neither my photographers nor I have spotted you out on the town in ages. I'm dying to know what you've been doing with yourself."

"That's easy to answer. Between my job and my single parent status, I don't get out much anymore."

Kristina gave me another dismissive hand wave. Then she took the offensive. "You did an abrupt about face on your military career. When you became a private eye, we at *Hollywood Nights* wondered what motivated such a drastic change in occupations."

"There's no secret to that either. I'd completed my mandatory military service in exchange for my free West Point education, then I mustered out of Delta Force." My smile showed lots of teeth. "Miz Morgotti, if you don't mind, I came to ask questions, not to answer them."

Morgotti winked garishly, à la Rona Barrett (JFGI). "But I saw you get out of that shiny black sports car. A ride like that plus your surname points to work in TV, music, or films, not taking photos of cheating spouses and searching for someone's lost cat."

"My partner and I don't handle missing pet or cheating spouse cases." A chuckle rumbled in my chest. "As to my car, you're asking about my old Dodge?"

I didn't mention I had to win a bidding war at a Valley garage that restored classic sports cars to buy my ten-cylinder, six-speed, limited edition 2004 Mamba Package Viper.

She sighed. "Since you're not willing to talk about your shiny ride, let's shift gears. No pun intended." Kristina leaned closer. "The grapevine says Steele Productions has something huge in the pipe. You must have your fingers in that project."

"As Steele Productions's silent partner, I'm not directly involved in the company's projects and day-to-day operations." I glanced at my tablet notes. "According to LAPD Captain Hal Flynn's file, you and Shane had a chance meeting and the two of you exchanged phone numbers. Take it from there, please."

"If you insist." Kristina shook her head, smiling at her memories of her first date with Shane. "I didn't expect to hear from him ever again. I almost fell out of my closed-toe wedges—no wait, they were my antique Swedish clogs—when he called and asked me to have dinner with him. I pounced on his invitation like a mongoose on a cobra. Who the hell wouldn't? According to Tinsel Town gossip, I knew I'd get an unforgettable fuck and maybe some Diana grist for my *Hollywood Nights* mill."

"Did you get one, both, or *nada* on your first date?" I asked.

"I got a fabulous fuck from Shane, but fuck-all about Diana. While we were dating, he never said anything negative about his mother." Kristina winked. "Shane's a loyal Mama's boy."

"Did problems with Diana lead to your and Shane's split?"

Morgotti chortled. "Heavens no. We didn't run into Mama problems, because whatever Diana demanded, Shane got right on it."

I nodded, but kept my poker face. "Tell me more about your relationship with Shane."

"For such a hot man, you ask a fucking lot of questions." She stopped to think. "Shane often told me he wanted to find one person for a long-term relationship." Kristina's voice turned rueful. "Christ, I've had enough one-night romances to know a player when I see one."

"But your relationship lasted about six months."

Kristina folded her well-turned legs beneath her. "Yes, like a doe-eyed starlet, I kept hoping Shane would settle down."

"You wanted a monogamous relationship."

"Hell yes, that's what I wanted. Shane's an intelligent, sexy, funny, and colorful man who knows how to use that big prick of his to the maximum." She smiled sadly. "But in his mind, monogamy is a board game where you buy property, pay rent, and get your ass thrown in jail."

I looked straight into Morgotti's eyes. "Did Shane tell you about his indiscretions?"

"In roundabout ways. He'd call me while he was getting a sloppy blow job or when he was screwing someone else." Turning to look out the wall of glass, Kristina fell silent.

"Sorry to hear that." I could see Danning's indiscretions hit Morgotti hard. But it all sounded Hollywood ordinary to me.

I considered ending the interview, but decided to take another run at Morgotti. "It seems you'd accepted Shane's playboy ways. What finally ended the relationship?"

Kristina turned from the tall windows to face me. "If you want the dirt, what would you say to a quid pro quo?"

I leaned closer to Morgotti. "I'm listening."

She looked straight into my eyes. "I want you to pull out that monster cock of yours and fuck me. Then I'll tell you the rest of the Shane Danning saga." She winked. "It's something I've told no one."

Kristina had my attention. She'd apparently committed at least one lie of omission in her statement to Captain Flynn.

And I'd never slept with a beautiful cross-dresser with a rich, dusky voice that damn near had me dropping my jeans.

But I leaned toward her and said, "Here's my counter offer. Sex is off the table, but tell me why your and Shane's relationship ended, and I'll persuade Vona to give *Hollywood Nights* certain first-print rights to Steele Productions's upcoming film project." I grinned. "This movie will be huge."

"Excellent!" Morgotti cheered, clapping her manicured hands. "Can't blame a girl for trying for the big package, pun intended." She exhaled a breath. "Okay, I'll take negotiated first-print rights to the film and tell you what ended my relationship with Shane."

"We have a deal."

I needed to give Diana the reason why Shane went AWOL on her, his home, and a career he loved. Maybe Morgotti had the answers. I waited for her to drop a dime on her ex.

"Shane's indiscretions didn't end our relationship."

I settled back in the armchair.

"Shane came into a sizable trust when he turned twenty-five."

"I know." I'd read about the trust in Flynn's file notes.

"He pissed away his monthly trust dole on clothes, electronics, and other toys. At some point, he added casino weekends with models and celebrities he wanted to fuck. For the record, I wasn't one of them."

"So noted."

"When we met, I didn't know about Shane's gambling addiction."

Holy shit, I'd heard something new. Captain Flynn didn't mention anything in his notes about Danning allegedly having a gambling problem. Maintaining my nonchalance, I asked, "California or Nevada casinos?"

She answered without hesitating, "Both."

I crossed my right ankle onto my left knee. "Did Shane mention taking on some high-interest loans to support his habit?"

She let out a long breath. "It's possible, but I'd like to believe Shane knew enough to stay away from the loan sharks." She looked at the floor. "His gambling losses had him pawning almost everything he owned, except his car and some furniture. I asked him to consider rehab. He told me he didn't have a problem with gambling."

I nodded.

"We split over two months ago. I remember because it was Valentine's Day." She once again looked out the wall of glass before speaking, finally saying, "Anyway, on Valentine's Day, he asked me for a five thousand dollar loan. He said he'd landed a second job and could pay me back within a month." She shook her head. "I knew he wanted a gambling stake, and I refused. We argued, he brushed past me and unintentionally knocked me on my ass. I told him we were finished. He packed his duffel, and walked out, slamming the door behind him." She again smiled sadly. "End of another Hollywood love story."

"Did you see or speak to Shane after you threw him out?"

She shook her head. "Not once."

I asked if she knew where in Laguna I might find Shane.

"I've no idea about Laguna. When Shane and I wanted sun and surf, we went to Malibu." She looked down her nose and spoke like a snooty socialite. "On Malibu, Mommy Dearest has a stunning manse and a private beach."

Kristina slid her feet to the floor and stood. "You'll forgive me, but I've a column to finish writing."

I stood and crossed the great room. I pulled on and laced up my combat boots, not shitkickers, and thanked Kristina Morgotti for her time.

"If you ever change your mind about my initial offer, give me a call."

"Your number's in my cell." I extended my hand but changed my mind. I hugged her.

I slid behind the wheel of my Dodge, knowing one thing for certain: There was more to Shane's disappearance than a "fucking lark."

Chapter Ten

Disparate and Desperate

Clint, Hollywood, Tuesday, May 1

I parked on the street in front of Shane Danning's single story wood frame house. His new Porsche remained in the carport—dusty but not missing any parts as far as I could tell. I got out of my car and did a quick recon.

At first glance, the exterior of Danning's house looked all right, if your idea of all right wasn't highly defined. Removing my sunglasses, I saw fissures etching the driveway's pavement. The lawn needed watering. The house bore a patina of age and neglect from roof to foundation.

I slid the key into the front door's lock and had to jiggle the goddammed thing for about thirty seconds before the deadbolt slid home. I stepped inside.

The musty scent of an old house enveloped me. The hardwood floors needed sanding and a few coats of varnish. The walls hadn't been painted in years.

The only son of a Hollywood legend lived in a dump like this? I knew airline pilots' salaries barely put them above the federal poverty line. But hell, consider the prestige of flying seven miles up at almost five hundred miles per hour in a huge tin can with wings, sophisticated electronics, great big engines, and everything. Maybe Shane lived in a house that could've been condemned because he was trying to prove he could make it on his own with a trust fund and his prestigious but low-paying career.

Bullshit. Nothing felt right about Shane Danning—his disappearance, reappearance, disappearance, his abandoned sports car, his alleged compulsive gambling, his sad house, fucking *nada*. I turned left, took one step into the living room, and stopped.

I suppose I could say Danning liked minimalism and eclectic furnishings. The living room included a love seat Shane could've picked up curbside. He had no coffee or end tables, no lamps, and no overhead lights. Kristopher/Kristina Morgotti told me Shane had pawned most of his possessions to support his gambling habit.

She'd also said Shane claimed he'd landed a second, high-paying job. Could've fooled me. To his credit, Shane had kept what looked like about a seventy-two-inch flat screen TV mounted above a low slung Italian mahogany cabinet. Disparate and desperate, I thought. I moved along.

In the dining room, two novels, a short stack of magazines, a tablet, and an empty coffee mug topped a card table. A folding aluminum chair had been pushed back from it.

I picked up the tablet and pressed the home button to wake it. Shane had powered it fully off. The scanner wouldn't recognize my fingerprint to turn it on. I slipped the tablet into my messenger bag.

I briefly considered borrowing Shane's copy of *Pilot Buddies* magazine to share with Hope, but I changed my mind. One should never dick-taunt a lesbian ex-cop who'd spent time on the bomb squad.

In the kitchen, mail covered one counter. Flipping through it, I saw what looked like unopened bills, among sales flyers and other junk. In the cabinets, I found three boxes of plastic cutlery, a stack of paper plates, and two ceramic mugs. I unplugged the off-brand coffeemaker, the kind that could melt down with no provocation and possibly set the house on fire. The stained kitchen sinks didn't hold stacks of dirty dishes—only because he hadn't much that needed to be washed. In a cupboard were bachelor's staples of marinara sauce, pasta, and coffee. He'd packed the freezer with Lean Cuisines. Two containers of Greek yogurt and a half gallon of milk, all past their use-by dates, were on the fridge's top shelf. Bottles of water and soft drinks filled the door's bottom shelf, but no beer. Danning didn't appear to have a problem with alcohol.

In the bathroom, damp towels that had been dropped on the cracked linoleum floor gave off the funk of mildew. Danning kept a bottle of designer body wash in the shower. Men's toiletries lined the counter. He stored little in the medicine chest: razor, shaving cream, toothpaste, toothbrush, and aspirin, but no prescription drugs. He didn't seem to have a problem with pharmaceuticals either.

The house had two bedrooms, one with nothing in it but a herd of dust buffalo. The master bedroom's full-sized mattress and box springs were stacked on a frame without a headboard. I pulled back a corner of the top sheet and found nothing but clean bedding. A chest of drawers held socks, underwear, and T-shirts.

The bedroom closet included pilot uniforms, designer dress and casual shirts, slacks, and a half dozen pairs of stressed jeans, costing several hundred bucks each. Gifts from Diana, I guessed. Four pairs of uniform and five pairs of casual footwear with nothing stashed in any of them filled the shoe rack. On the upper shelf, I found three empty pieces of designer luggage.

I raked a hand through my hair. For fuck sakes, most college students had more shit crammed into their dorm rooms than Shane Danning had in his entire house.

Heading for the front door, I stopped and retraced my steps to the living room. I knelt and began opening the Italian mahogany cabinet's doors and drawers. Shane owned about fifty DVDs and a DVD player/recorder. I opened the DVDs and found the appropriate disc in each jewel case.

And he'd kept an old RCA VHS player/recorder and about two dozen videotapes.

Checking the videocassettes, I found no adhesive tape or tape residue, suggesting nothing had been recorded over the movies. I looked inside the videotape boxes.

In the bottom of the *Boogie Nights* box, I found a flash drive. I took it, along with Shane's tablet, stepped outside, and locked the door—more key jiggling required.

I headed for Hollywood's Jugs & Mugs Saloon, the dive in which Shane Danning had last been seen.

Chapter Eleven

Danny Boy

Clint, Tuesday, May 1

At this hour of the morning, the Jugs & Mugs Saloon had one patron: a young man reading at a table near the bar. He wore a UCLA T-shirt that hugged his muscular chest and biceps. He looked sexy as hell in a boyish kind of way—maybe twenty or twenty-one. Shit, make that eighteen or nineteen.

Our eyes met. Standing, he took three steps and placed a hand on my shoulder, stopping me. "Hi, I'm Dan. Do you have time to join me for a drink?"

It wasn't the most clever pickup line I'd ever heard, but he looked extraordinarily innocent and sincere. I hated to turn him down. Christ, I'd gotten hit on twice today before 1100 hours. I guess I still had a little of it left in me, whatever it might be.

I smiled. "Sorry, I'm working." I handed him my business card. "In case you ever need a private dick." Yes, it sounded kind of trampish, but he'd hit on me first.

Dan read my card, then took his hand off my shoulder. He looked at me as if I'd pointed my Glock at his head. He flicked the edge of the card before slipping it into a hip pocket of his tight-fitting jeans. "I'll give you a call," Dan said.

I made a beeline for the bar.

"What can I get you?" the bartender said in a baritone voice.

I ordered his best water. He set a twenty-buck bottle of thawed glacier ice on the bar. I pointed at Dan, who had his nose in a book, and asked the barkeep to pour him another.

Dan's drink of choice was Diet Sprite from the tap, no ice. Watching as the bartender served Dan his fresh soda, I decided he definitely had the looks of an all-American frat boy sans the tendency to drink too much.

Dan held up his fresh drink and smiled his thanks.

I nodded at him, then turned my attention to the tall, barrel-chested bartender. I introduced myself and pulled out my private investigator creds.

The bartender scanned my license but didn't raise an eyebrow. "Ron Kitson," he said. "I'm the owner."

We shook hands.

He leaned closer to me. "I suppose you're here about Shane Danning."

"Yes." I sipped some water, and pulled out my tablet. "Were you working last Wednesday night?"

Kitson nodded without having to think about it. "When you own a bar, you're working most days and nights."

"Then you saw Shane Danning in here last Wednesday night." I'd made it a statement, not a question.

Kitson let his beefcake arms drop to his sides. "I was tending bar, and I served Shane last Wednesday night. He's a regular. Never causes problems, never gets drunk, and never needs a tab anymore."

"You used to open a tab for him."

"The pilots union must've gotten crew members decent raises," Kitson said, chuckling. "I used to carry Shane's tab for weeks, sometimes months, but not anymore. He always has plenty of cash lately, tips good—a great customer and one helluva nice guy."

I juxtaposed Kitson's statements beside the shithole Shane lived in and next to Kristina Morgotti's claim that Shane asked her for a large loan.

The facts about Danning, as I'd been told, baffled me. Maybe he'd gotten lucky at one of the casinos. Sure, and at any moment pigs could fly out of my ass. Too many things about Danning did not compute, including his alleged compulsive gambling habit.

"You say he has plenty of cash when he comes in here."

Kitson winked at me. "Shane's one of those lucky bastards with plenty of cash these days and more than his fair share in the good looks and great body departments. A lot like you."

The bartender caught my brief look of surprise.

He raised both hands. "I meant that as a compliment, not a come-on."

"Roger that," I said. Given Danning's Hollywood good looks, maybe his alleged second job involved whoring himself by way of an escort service. "Do you recall how much Danning drank last Wednesday night?"

Kitson wiped the already clean bar with a damp rag. "He drank one beer."

"He had one beer?"

"You know he's an airline pilot, and they get surprise urine tests."

I nodded.

"Shane always stops at one beer. He doesn't drop by to drink himself stupid." His chuckle rumbled deep in his chest. "He comes in here huntin' pussy or pecker. It never takes him long to find either or both."

"Did he leave with anyone last Wednesday night?"

Kitson shrugged. "I noticed people smiling at him. One couple seemed to capture Shane's attention. But I'm certain he left here alone shortly before midnight." He smiled, showing perfect white teeth. "Then I had both eyes on an exchange student from Vienna, or so she told me." Kitson warmed to his topic. "Man, she was fine and jonesin' for a man of my persuasion." He shrugged. "Guess there ain't too many people of color in Austria."

I put one hand over my mouth, bent, and yawned hugely. I thanked Roy Kitson for his time. Then I finished my twenty-buck bottle of water. "Please get Dan another drink." I dropped some bills on the bar and smiled bye-bye at Danny boy.

I needed help from my longtime best friend, the man whose grasp of technology ran second to no one's.

I called Mars Hauser.

CHAPTER TWELVE

Blue Money

Clint, Hauser Security, Tuesday, May 1

I parked in front of Mars Hauser's two-story, beige stucco office building. Stepping onto the pavement, I let loose with a yawn that went all the way to my toes.

Sporting a designer suit and a bulge under his left arm, a security guard whom I knew only as Alesandro approached me, seemingly from out of nowhere.

"Don't tell me my Greek magnificence has tuckered you out already," Alesandro said.

"Yes, your Greek magnificence shit has become tiresome." Then I yawned again.

"Let's go, sleepy boy. The big boss man awaits you."

I followed Alesandro into Hauser Security's bland building with its bulletproof, signal-defense glass. I knew the way to his office, but Alesandro escorted me.

I entered Mars's corner office. Alesandro silently closed the door behind me. Marston "Mars" Hauser stood and grinned. Our handshake became an all-out backslapping hug.

Mars and I have been best friends for about fifteen years. We'd been West Point barracks mates all four years due to our broad shoulders, muscular bodies, and heights (his six-five and my six-six), which demanded longer, wider, heavier-duty bunks than those issued to other cadets.

Mars's loose blond curls, two-day stubble, cut-offs, vintage T-shirts, and flip-flops, which he always kicked off once he was seated at his desk, redefined office casual.

On paper, Mars's company did business as Hauser Security, but he did not offer his services to corporations or the general public. His classified assignments came through various intelligence agencies, from orders that often originated at 1600 Pennsylvania Avenue.

Mars and his thirty-member crew used cutting edge technologies to analyze data and to conduct cyber warfare and/or cyber black ops against adversaries of the United States. Outside of the office, Mars Hauser's hobbies included portrait sketching, paintings in oils, and breeding prize-winning orchids. I saw him as a riddle concealed in secrecy wrapped in contradiction.

I took a seat in the leather chair fronting Mars's paperless desk and stifled a yawn. My eyes drooped.

I saw Sierra standing beside him.

"I've always been fond of Mars. And you know Ian adores him." She winked at me. "I love his Puckish charisma, and he's so nice to look at. I bet he'd be fun to come home to."

What the hell? Sierra and I never had this conversation in the past. I looked at her. *You ended two sentences in prepositions. Did you trip and fall into the solecisms circle of hell?*

"You're becoming a regular laugh riot." She looked straight into my eyes. "Seriously, sweetheart, I think you should make a paradigm shift with your next spouse and take a walk on the dude side."

This was definitely not a past conversation.

I shook my head at her visage. *Mars and I have a bromance going. We love, admire, and respect each other without sex.*

"You know relationships needn't remain linear."

I wish I hadn't told Sierra Mars and I used to bonk each other as well as women during our West Point years.

Mars leaned back in his executive chair. "What can I do for you, Moose?"

I snapped out of my daydream and pulled Shane Danning's tablet from my messenger bag. "I found this powered off, and I know this model is fingerprint protected. Can you crack it?"

Mars chuckled. "Is a frog's ass watertight?" He ported the tablet, clicked twice, and the wall of programs appeared.

I shook my head. "Hoser, you've got magic fingers."

He handed me Shane Danning's unlocked tablet. "Do you have anything else you'd like me to get my magic fingers on...or maybe around?"

I didn't take his flirtatious comments seriously. I handed him

Danning's flash drive. "I found this cleverly hidden. I'm guessing it may need a password."

He slid the drive into a port and scanned one of the three monitors on his desk.

A couple of keystrokes later, a warning appeared on the monitor. "The following films are intended for adult audiences only. Please store your files accordingly."

Mars paused it.

"You amaze me."

"It's nothing but hacker skullduggery 101." He grinned. "I suspect we've some porn afoot. Or maybe merely ten inches. Do you want to check it out?"

Pornography bored me senseless. But if it was nothing more than fuck films, why had Shane password protected the flash drive and gone out of his way to hide it? My curiosity got the better of me. "Let's give it a look." I moved my chair behind Mars's desk and sat next to him.

The production company's name, *Bicurious Fantasies*, appeared on the screen, followed by the film's title: *Ass Bandit I: Lady Poldtranes Unlocked and Sir Knightly's Big Surprise.*

"Shit, this sounds deep," I said with all due sarcasm.

A medieval bedchamber with blazing torches attached to the stone walls and a suit of armor standing in a corner appeared on the monitor. A buck naked Sir Knightly entered, followed by an almost nude Lady Poldtranes. Her strawberry-blond hair covered her back and ass. Sir Knightly unlocked her chastity belt and let it drop to the floor. They kissed and fell onto the canopied bed.

"I know boob jobs didn't exist during medieval times," Mars said, "but what about canopied beds?"

"Hoser," I said again using Mars's West Point moniker for Hauser, "it's porn—you'll probably see a waterwheel-powered vibrating dildo." I nudged him. "Hark! Prepare thine self for brilliant dialogue."

"Suck that cock," Sir Knightly said. "Finger those hairy balls."

I yawned. "Why does porn always use 'that' and 'those' instead of 'my' in reference to male genitalia? Is there a spare penis and another pair of balls somewhere in the room?"

Mars chuckled. "Christ, Sir Knightly's bush hides most of his dick. Maybe he should find a waterwheel-powered electric razor."

The Ass Bandit, wearing only a black domino mask, made his entrance through the bedchamber's *meurtrier*. "Away, thou lily-liver'd, one-inch worm'd boy," he said to Sir Knightly.

"What?" Mars said.

I nudged Mars. "Holy shit, plagiarized Shakespearean dialogue regarding Sir Knightly's microdick."

Ass Bandit locked the chastity belt around Sir Knightly's face. Then he ripped the sheet and bound Knightly's hands and feet.

"Oooh, you brute! Rip the sheets!" Mars said.

Ass Bandit kneeled between Lady Poldtranes's legs. "Oh, thou art fair, m'lady."

"Ass Bandit has a porn star's big dick, but he couldn't have made Linda Lovelace (JFGI) gag on it," I said.

It's only the camera angle and the lighting, I thought, but then I leaned toward the monitor to get a closer look at Ass Bandit's face. His eyes went from dark brown to blue to violet. I asked Mars to reverse the flash drive fifteen seconds.

He did.

It hadn't been my imagination. The camera angle, lighting, and the black mask brought out Ass Bandit's violet eyes—the same color as his mother's.

Lady Poldtranes's moaning and screaming reached a crescendo. Then the Ass Bandit went at Sir Knightly hard and for a long time. The brave knight shrieked like a twink.

I asked Mars to fast-forward through *Ass Bandit* one. The flash drive contained *Ass Bandit* films two and three, each about thirty minutes long with differing fantasies and gender combinations. We fast-forwarded through those.

Maybe Shane Danning's gambling losses had made him desperate enough to moonlight as a porn star. I knew this particular adult film producer had a reputation for paying his stars well and always made his actors' health and safety on the set a priority. Shane Danning's stardom verified bartender Roy Kitson's claim that Shane seemed to have plenty of cash these days, not to mention Shane's assertion to Kristina/Kristopher that he'd landed a second job and could quickly pay back his/her $5000 loan.

But why hadn't Shane taken the path of least resistance and asked Diana for financial help? I paused. The simple answer was Shane enjoyed having a porn star moonlighting gig. I put the flash drive and tablet back into my messenger bag and thanked Mars for his help.

Mars slid his bare feet into his flip-flops and walked outside with me. Alesandro followed, standing out of hearing range. Mars and I shook hands.

He didn't let go of my hand. "If there's anything else I can help you with, anything at all, give me a call."

I exhaled a laugh. "You might want to think twice before offering your assistance. This case gets stranger by the hour."

"My offer stands," Mars said. "You know we'll always be brothers in arms."

I slid behind the wheel, started my car, then powered down the driver's side window. "Thanks again, Mars. You've my apologies for the porn."

Mars grinned. "I'm a nerd, but not a prude." He placed his hands on the window frame and leaned toward me. "Looking at you in profile, you should consider becoming a porn star."

"I think you need new glasses or contacts."

"Well, I am past due for my annual eye exam." He paused. "If you don't need my help with your investigation, call me anyway. It's been a couple of weeks since we've gotten together."

Some bonding with my best friend sounded great. "Check your schedule and text me the dates you have open."

"Count on it." Mars tapped the Viper's roof and started back to his office.

I watched him walk away.

Then I pulled my cell and called the Laguna Stop & Save—the supermarket where Shane Danning and his companion made an appearance last night.

CHAPTER THIRTEEN

Some Old and Some New

Clint, Laguna, Tuesday, May 1

I worked my way onto the 5. About an hour later, I merged onto 133 South.

Last night's two hours of sleep had caught up with me. I had the air-conditioning cranked and the radio blaring to keep myself awake. I exited onto Forest Avenue.

I smiled, recalling that summer day during our first year of marriage when Sierra and I'd come to Laguna for some sun, sand, and surf. Yawning largely and loudly, I rolled to a stop at a red light.

Call numbers began blurring across the radio's digital display. The scan stopped on a classic rock station playing Lynyrd Skynyrd's "Free Bird" (JFGI).

I saw Sierra in the passenger seat, looking gorgeous in a black bikini. She'd sung a line of the Skynyrd song, then she'd said, "Everyone needs a little rockabilly hoochie-koo from time to time."

"Sho nuff," I'd said.

The light changed. The driver in the Mercedes convertible behind me held down the horn. I jerked awake and drove away.

Sierra turned in her seat and looked at the driver of the Mercedes. "Why do you suppose so many women driving luxury convertibles think they must become bottle blondes and get their breasts enhanced?"

More new dialogue, I thought. I answered her rhetorical question with, "It's an American sociological mystery requiring years of empirical investigations, data gathering, and critical analyses."

I tried to concentrate on driving, but kept glancing at the now empty passenger seat. I needed to talk to Dr. Grant Stenton about my hallucinations. They'd become increasingly common. I'd dubbed them memory echoes. But what did I call our new conversations?

I chuckled at the young women and men in swimwear walking along the sidewalks. With all the cleavage, tush, basket, and muscle scenery, the local chamber of commerce could post signs designating Laguna as the ass-end-crash capital of California.

I almost drove past the Stop & Save. I downshifted and swerved into the parking lot.

Then I rolled into an empty slot, shifted the Viper into neutral, and put on the parking brake. Leaving the engine idling and the AC blasting, I closed my eyes—only for a few moments. Or that's what I told myself.

As I slept, Sierra looked at the supermarket. "Another joyless big box store. I hope the person who invented this retail concept doesn't have other things on the drawing board."

This was another new conversation. I kept my eyes shut. If I opened them, I knew Sierra wouldn't be sitting beside me.

Sierra's voice brightened. "Did I ever share my thoughts with you on America's supermarket caste system?"

In my mind, I shook my head.

"In our theoretically egalitarian society, there are three classifications of supermarkets coinciding with the working poor, the middle class, and those privileged few who are either too wealthy to be of much use or unconscionably rich and truly worthless."

"And whenever you're shopping, always look for the union label, comrade," I thought.

Sierra pinched my cheek. "That's funny. Now pay attention. On the top of the supermarket heap are the bright, color-coordinated extravaganzas with floors that shine like polished glass. These supermarkets always price everything at or above the MSRP and never put anything on sale since such enticements are considered unnecessary and *trés gauche* by their customers. These supermarkets employ smiling, All-American youth to double bag your groceries, then they'll schlep them out of the store and into the trunk of your luxury car. Do you have any questions so far, handsome husband?"

I shook my head.

"Then we have the less glossy but always clean, well-stocked supermarkets with friendly associates who know an artichoke from a zucchini, a portabella from a shiitake, and their asses from their elbows.

These supermarkets offer weekly specials, and the checkers assist you in bagging your groceries, but you must wheel your purchases out of the store and load them into the trunk of your late-model Sonata, Fusion, or Suburban."

"Dr. Wilkenson-Steele, may I assume you're going somewhere with this lecture?"

She tapped my cheek with her fingertips. "We're almost there. At the rear echelon, hind tit, ass-bottom of the pile are the untouchables such as this Stop & Save. In here, you'll find discolored and cracked linoleum floors, water-stained ceiling tiles, high prices, packaged products way past their use-by dates, and malodorous smells in and around the meat, deli, and dairy coolers." She waved her hand toward the store. "Ohhhh, Clint darling, you do not want to go in there. This dump could give you food poisoning from breathing the air."

I jolted awake, inhaled a long breath, and slowly let it out. No one sat in the passenger's side seat.

I killed the engine, grabbed the Danning file, and stepped into Laguna's Mediterranean-like heat and ocean air.

The Stop and Save's automatic doors didn't work. With the scrape of metal across metal, I pushed my way into the store.

I saw her standing behind the customer service counter. Her heavy makeup and flaming red dye job might suggest she'd been around the block enough to have worn a rut in the sidewalk. I watched her reading a tabloid, licking her index finger to turn the page.

I stood in front of her.

She looked up at me, lifted her thin, drop-dead-red lipsticked lips, and said in a whiskey and cigarette voice, "My, my, my. Look at you."

I smiled, triggering my dimples. "May I speak to the manager?"

"Honey, I'm her." She extended her hand—the one with the finger she'd been licking.

I shook it. She didn't let go of my hand.

"Larena White," she said, letting my hand go and closing the tabloid. "I don't suppose a tall, sexy devil like you wandered in here looking for a job." She smiled. "I'd hire you on the spot and have you sweating in two minutes."

"I'm not looking for work." I set my private detective creds on the counter's cracked Formica. "We spoke on the phone about an hour ago."

Larena pushed my creds back at me. She winked brashly. "Oh, my. A private dick. What can I do you for?"

One more double entendre, and I'd heave up my testes.

I opened the Danning file, pulled out the photo six-pack, and slid it across the counter. "Have you seen any of these men?"

I waited while Larena eye-fucked each pic, then tapped a ruby red talon on the shot of Shane Danning. "Saw this one last night and scanned his groceries." She smiled and shrugged. "Over the past few days, there's damned few alive that ain't seen a picture of Shane Danning somewhere."

"Did Danning come in here alone last night?" I knew he hadn't, but when interviewing an eyewitness, I never asked a question I couldn't answer.

"No, he came in with a fortysomething man. And yes, they left together too." She pursed her thin lips in thought. "Ya know, after I talked with the cops last night, I got to thinking Shane Danning might be related to the guy he came in with."

"What made you think they might've been relatives?"

She shrugged. "They reminded me of two guys that had known each other for a while, like an uncle and nephew, or maybe first cousins. Or they might be real good buddies." She winked, putting a lot into it. "If ya know what I mean."

I nodded slightly. Her perfume started to make my eyes burn. I slid my sunglasses back on as a shield before I went blind. She continued along a similar line.

"I suppose the older man could be a friend of the family."

I put the photos back into the file. "Can you describe the older man?"

"Lord love a duck, I surely can." Larena cackled. "My eyes stayed on both of those sexy devils."

I kept quiet as she gave the same description of the unknown man I'd read in Danning's missing person file.

"Hell's bells, I wondered if Shane Danning's buddy might be a movie or TV star," Larena said.

"What made you think that?"

She shrugged. "His good looks and self-confidence."

Having heard enough of her bullshit theorizing, I veered. "Do you take American Express in here?" I knew she did, but hadn't seen the usual credit card decals on the double doors.

"Honey, we'll pretty much take anything you slap down on the counter. We gotta, what with the tourists we get from New York City, Cisco, Seattle, and Asscrack, Wisconsin."

"Did you see what these two men were driving or get a tag number?"

"Hell no. The only glass in this brick box is the in and out doors. You gotta stand right in front of them to see the entire parking lot."

With Shane Danning's Amex card being monitored, a police cruiser had been dispatched to the supermarket before the ink had dried on the receipt. For what it was worth, the police couldn't have missed catching Danning and his companion by more than two minutes.

Larena had repeated what I'd learned from Danning's missing person file: No one working last night had seen what make or model of car Danning and the fortysomething man had driven into the parking lot; No one had been able to see the tag; no one had known in which direction the two men had gone when they'd driven away—nothing, *nada*, zero, frigging zip. Shit.

"Did either Danning or his companion appear drunk or on drugs?"

Larena cackled again. "Honey, did you fall out of a cross-country bus a few moments ago?"

I only smiled.

"Ain't nothing unusual to get people in here that's had a few drinks, smoked, dropped, shot, or snorted a little something. I hardly notice the fucked-up customers anymore unless they're barely able to stand." Larena's lips curved into something like a smile. "I only noticed how either one or both of them gorgeous guys I saw last night could leave their shoes under my bed anytime."

I'd bet Larena White could chug beer like a frat boy, wouldn't hesitate to tell a California Highway Patrol officer to kiss her ass, liked to eat wieners right out of the package, and could've beaten Minnesota Fats (JFGI) in three out of four games.

"Oh honey, I forgot to tell you the older man wore pricy designer glasses."

I sighed inwardly. Expensive optics around here were as common as animal shit in a zoo. I switched gears. "Did Danning appear under duress or coercion?"

"Do you mean was Danning with the older man against his will?"

"Yes."

Larena shrugged again. "I don't think so."

"I've got one more question. Are there video cameras aimed at the checkout lanes, doors, and the parking lot?" I knew there weren't. But sometimes eyewitnesses told cops one thing and other people something entirely different.

She snorted. "Surely do, hon, but they ain't worked for the past four or five years." She flashed a sad smile. "The corporation has its priorities. This here rat hole ain't one of 'em."

I pulled a business card from my shirt pocket, added my cell number, and slid it onto the counter. "If you see either Danning or his companion, or both of them coming in here together again, would you let me know right away?"

"Sure thing, hon, if it'll bring you back again."

I thanked her for her time. Then I sensed her eye-fucking me all the way out the door.

I unlocked and opened the driver's side door to let out some of the interior's blast-furnace heat. It's the downside of owning a black on black car in Southern California. But it's a Mamba Package Viper, goddammit! Dodge only manufactured two hundred of them, and they all came in black on black with red accents. One must somehow persevere.

I started the Viper and turned the AC up to the freeze-your-nuts-off setting.

Out of nowhere, I sensed that Raoul needed my help. I started to call him. I paused, thinking, call him and tell him what? I slipped the cell back into my pocket.

I heard Sierra say, "Clint, sweetheart, you're about to give me hives. Don't analyze a simple matter to death. Raoul needs you tonight. Call him and say you're taking him out to dinner. Tell him it's mandatory, not optional."

I'd heard something new again.

Even if Raoul didn't need my help, it had been a long day in the private detective mines. Some dinner, a beer, and conversation with Raoul sounded like a fine idea.

But I first called home and asked Stella if she could babysit this evening. Not a problem. Stella had a room of her own in my house, where she kept several changes of clothing. A lipstick lesbian, she also kept enough toiletries and cosmetics in there to stock a Walgreens store.

I asked to talk to Ian. He's young enough to be thrilled hearing someone wants to speak with him on the phone.

"Hey, buddy," I said.

Without preamble, Ian asked, "May I go swimming?"

I told him he could. I'd begun teaching him how to swim when he was three. At six, he swam like a dolphin.

"Can Heathcliff swim?"

"Yes, but don't let him in the pool's chlorinated water." Heathcliff, as with most Maine Coons, wouldn't think twice about jumping into the tub with you while you're taking a bath.

He then asked if he could give himself a haircut. I sighed inwardly.

"No, son. Let me speak to Stella, please."

I said to Stella, "I assume you heard."

"I did, and you can assume I'll keep both eyes on the boy."

Then I called Raoul.

CHAPTER FOURTEEN

Less Than Stellar

Jud Tucker, Mystic Canyon Casino, Tuesday, May 1

Standing behind one-way glass fifteen feet above the high stakes poker tables, I watched a four-member card-counting team at work. Two college boys kept table-jumping and making significant changes in their bets based on signals from their spotters.

The two spotters, a pair of young, big breasted, short skirted blond babes, signaled the college boys when a shoe got hot and when to hold while simultaneously keeping the pit boss preoccupied. I shook my head in disgust at the pit boss's negligence.

But the team looked healthy and in their early twenties. On the black market, their hearts alone would go into six figures. And their kidneys, livers, corneas, and lungs would become other gold mines, not counting everything else in and on them with a market value.

After another lucrative organ harvest over the weekend, only three prisoners remained in captivity. A single pair of the card-counting team would make a full house.

But taking them off the floor would have all four team members making one hell of a scene when security approached them, capturing the attention of all the players at the high stakes tables. I'd never get away with abducting any of them. I returned my attention to the problem at hand.

We casino directors considered one gambler counting cards a nuisance—until he or she started taking too much of the house's cash. But we objected strenuously to teams of counters with winning systems.

I'd tell my idiot pit boss to radio a pair of guards, then escort the card counters to my assistant director's office. They'd be questioned and photographed. After checking and copying their photo IDs, all four of the assholes would find themselves blacklisted at casinos across North America.

I radioed pit boss Tom Andrews.

"Yes, Mr. Tucker."

I described the team. "Pull your eyes off those spotters' tits and twats, radio two security guards to support you, and bring all four of them to my assistant's office now."

Busted, Tom Andrews's face reddened. "Copy."

I watched Andrews and two security guards approach the card counters. And yes, all four of them raised hell.

They would never know how lucky they'd been, getting taken away from the tables, I thought.

Since I'd promoted Tom Andrews three months ago, he'd proved himself a less than stellar pit boss. A twenty-seven-year-old former Army MP, Andrews had the brawn and some of the brains for the job, but he sure as shit couldn't control his roving eyes and rabid libido.

I'd considered firing him, but none of the casino's execs wanted to deal with a disgruntled former employee's lawyer. More to the point, a former employee who'd served his country honorably and was working full-time while taking college courses part-time.

Considering all my options, I decided I wouldn't need to demote or fire Andrews. He'd told me that he lived alone.

And I had his address on file.

CHAPTER FIFTEEN

Faraway Eyes

Clint, West L.A., Tuesday, May 1

I watched Raoul lock the front door of his renovated Craftsman, then fleet-foot it down the porch steps to my car. He slid onto the passenger's seat.

"Thanks for taking me up on my last-minute dinner invitation," I said.

"As though my social calendar were packed to the nuts," he said.

I pulled away from the curb. "You're a talented, handsome Cuban American actor and a successful contractor. After knowing you for over five years, I still don't understand why you live like a monk."

Raoul grinned. "We're opposite sides of one coin. You're alpha, and I'm omega. It's my role to keep your ass baffled."

"Speaking of ass, when the hell did you pull these alpha omega roles out of yours?"

"On the day you hired me to remodel your colonial." Raoul laughed and chucked my chin. "You're gaping."

I yawned hard.

Raoul raised his voice. "Get into the far right lane or you'll cruise past the frigging restaurant."

I didn't miss the turn. I did chirp the tires. And got honked at by the tool who'd been riding my bumper.

Inside Fat Boy Benjie's Gourmet Burgers, we found an empty table for two close to the kitchen's swinging doors. Our waitress appeared. We each ordered a Fat Boy burger with the works, fries, and a beer.

Raoul's good looks, green eyes, athletic build, and perfectly aligned teeth, either the result of genetics or an upscale orthodontist, turned heads when he walked into a room. I knew the film and TV industries well. Raoul would, sooner rather than later, become a star. My thoughts got interrupted as the waitress brought our drinks.

I sipped some beer.

So did Raoul. He set his pilsner glass on the table. "Whoever invented beer should be canonized and adored by all."

I thought I saw Sierra standing behind Raoul. Then I believed I heard her speak my name. I closed my eyes. When I opened them a few moments later, she hadn't disappeared.

Her form brightened as she tousled Raoul's hair. "Don't you love this managed mess look he has going with his mop?"

I'd heard another new comment, not an echo of an old conversation. I didn't reply.

Raoul patted his hair down. "Someone must've opened the kitchen's door to the alley." He stared across the table. "Clint... CLINT...*CLINT!*"

I jerked awake. Lifting my beer, I looked at Raoul over the rim of the glass, my face a study in innocence. "Yeah?"

"Moose, you got that faraway look in your big blues again."

"Sorry, my mind wandered."

What the hell else could I say? I'd slipped into dreamland again. I wondered if it was my insomnia or some type of mental breakdown. Maybe it had something to do with my abstaining from sex for over two years. Maybe it was a combination of all the above.

I stopped pondering as the waitress slid our dinner plates on the table, cracked her gum once, and asked, "You gentlemen need anything else?"

"No, thanks," I said.

Raoul smiled at her and shook his head.

She jetted off, leaving a minty-fresh vapor trail in her wake.

"Del, my agent, wants me to audition for a national TV ad for a new line of men's grooming products," Raoul said. "I told him I needed to think about it."

"For fuck sakes, what do you need to think about?"

"I'd speak a couple of lines while standing in a shower shampooing my hair."

"C'mon, it's not as though you're doing a porn shoot. TV viewers will see you from your chest up, and imagine the rest of you."

Raoul chuckled. "Well, the commercial's something damned close to porn."

I raised an eyebrow.

"Del said there'll be a one-frame nude shot of me in the ad."

"Ahh, the old subliminal message trick. You wait and see. The product will fly off the shelves, and people won't know what motivated them to try something new." I raised my brows. "And you'll become an overnight TV ad sensation."

Raoul exhaled a laugh. "My psychiatrist father would fall out of his golf cleats should he learn my fame began with TV viewers getting a flash of *la verga y las pelotas*."

I laughed. "Your cock and balls aside, have you heard from your parents?"

"I don't hear from Mom and Dad. They let me alone as long as I keep my humble carpenter's career and my queer-assed acting ambitions out of Cleveland."

Raoul had grown up in the Cleveland suburb of Pepper Pike, in a Catholic household with five brothers and two sisters. All of Raoul's siblings emailed, texted, and called their youngest brother regularly—his parents, not too often.

Raoul ate a couple of fries, then bit into his burger. He chewed, swallowed, and chased the grease with a swig of beer. "Mind if I ask a personal question?"

"Go ahead."

"I've been wanting to ask you when you knew for certain you were bisexual."

"I knew I liked both girls and boys by the time I'd turned eleven. But I didn't test drive my bisexuality until I got a little older."

"How much older?"

A chuckle rumbled in my chest. "At sixteen, I sometimes let the college varsity quarterback next door fellate me, while also playing fuck master to my father's twenty-six-year-old female production assistant."

Raoul raised an eyebrow. "You had two adults going after your sixteen-year-old prick? Can you say statutory rape?"

I shrugged. "What can I say? Both of them had noticed I was awfully large for my age."

Raoul grinned and shook his head. Then he took a swig of beer.

We continued eating, talking, and laughing with all the comfort and camaraderie of close friends.

Glancing to my right, I saw Sierra sitting at the bar, winking at me and lifting a tumblerful of scotch in a toast. I rubbed my eyes with both hands and looked again. She'd disappeared.

"Buddy, you got that faraway look in your eyes again. What's wrong?"

I forced a smile. "Nothing's wrong. I thought I saw someone I used to know sitting at the bar." I checked my watch. "It's time I get home, hug my little boy, and relieve Stella." Knowing the menu and the prices, I set cash on the table plus a tip.

We shot the shit as I drove toward Raoul's neighborhood. Seeing flashing lights ahead, we fell silent.

Fire trucks, EMT vans, and LAPD squad cars formed a barricade along the street.

A cop I knew stood nearby, watching a crowd of rubberneckers. Killing the engine, I stepped out of the car with Raoul right behind me.

Raoul's beautiful Craftsman had been reduced to one wall and mounds of smoldering rubble. Strips of clothing, paper, pieces of furniture, cabinetry, major appliances, wiring, and everything that fills a home lay scattered along the block. A smoke and dust haze still hung overhead as firefighters hosed down hot spots.

LAPD officer Ella Parson approached us. "Steele, I know you don't live here."

Raoul introduced himself and handed her his Class A commercial driver's license. "Officer Parson, it's my house. What the hell happened?"

She studied Raoul's CDL, glanced at him, then shifted her stance to something more relaxed. "One of the firefighters said it looks like a natural gas explosion."

Raoul's shoulders dropped. "Was anyone injured?"

"Was anyone in your house?"

"No," Raoul told her.

"That's good news. Some of your neighbors' homes sustained damage, but everyone is fine."

"All that's important is nobody's injured or dead." He gave Officer Parson a hopeful look. "How about getting my car?"

She handed his commercial driver's license back to him. "You're lucky the detached garage butts up to the alley. After you speak to the fire investigator, it's my guess you can get your vehicle and leave," Parsons said.

Raoul forced a smile. "Moose, you don't need to wait around. After I get my car, I'll check into a hotel."

"The hell you say." I put my arm across Raoul's shoulders and led him to my car. "You know I have a five-bedroom house. You've only got what you're wearing, your pickup and car. You're welcome to stay at my place and regroup."

I saw Raoul frowning, trying to think beyond the smoke and rubble that had once been his house and home. "Thanks, but I couldn't impose on you."

"We're friends. It's no imposition. *Mi casa es su casa.*" I squeezed his shoulder, then dropped my hand. "I'll give you the time and space you need to put your life back together."

Raoul looked at his feet, lifted his head, and tried to smile. "Thanks, Moose."

CHAPTER SIXTEEN

Dirty Deeds

Jud Tucker, Tuesday Night, May 1

With my degree in fire science and my firefighting training, I know how to extinguish a blaze. I also know how to start one without leaving a trace of evidence.

Arsonists using accelerants often get caught. But I use what's naturally there at the scene. The old meter on the rear of Raoul Martinez's house made it child's play to increase the gas pressure, causing the pipe's welds and joints to crack, and the leaking gas to explode. It took me a couple of minutes to turn the renovated Craftsman into burning chunks of rubble. That, and blackened pieces of Raoul's body. Hey, natural gas disasters happen all the time.

But that had only been dirty deed *numero uno* for the day.

I'd also been trained in the usage and effects of all types of pharmaceuticals. I can knock someone out for hours with an IV injection, or I can kill my captive. Firefighter-paramedic, man, what a great calling.

Now at 2330 hours, I waited in the dark near Tom Andrews's crumbling bungalow. Distant headlights appeared in my van's side view mirror. I stepped onto the cracked sidewalk and silently closed the door. I squatted out of sight beside the right front fender. Tom Andrews parked his pickup in his bungalow's carport and killed the engine.

Walking along the driveway's grass line, I saw the dome light come on as Andrews opened the driver's side door and stepped out of his pickup. I let him get as far as the tailgate before I Tasered him. His keys and knees dropped onto the driveway's concrete. I'd set the weapon to cause neuromuscular incapacitation, as well as some agony—only because he'd been such a fucking pain in my ass.

I pocketed his keys. Andrews lay on his back, unable to speak or move. But his eyes followed me. Holding a penlight in my mouth, I slipped the needle of a syringe loaded with a fast-acting barbiturate into the major vein in the crook of his arm. He fell unconscious in about twenty seconds.

I cuffed his hands and ankles, and loaded him into the back of my van.

I drove away.

CHAPTER SEVENTEEN

Turn the Page

Clint, Santa Monica, Wednesday, May 2

When Grant Stenton was twenty-one, a quarterback sack in the final minute of a university home game changed his life forever. In a heartbeat, he went from a blond, blue-eyed NFL draft prospect to a blond, blue-eyed person with paraplegia.

Twenty years later, Grant owned a successful psych clinic and had a beautiful wife and an adorable two-year-old toddler.

I tapped on Doc Stenton's open door and returned his smile.

I crossed Grant's office and sat in the chair fronting his desk. With the exception of emergencies, I knew people sometimes waited weeks for an appointment with one of the therapists, psychologists, or psychiatrists at Grant's clinic. "Thanks for squeezing me in."

Grant smiled. "I usually don't see patients on Wednesdays. I let people assume I join my brethren and sistren on the links."

I laughed at his joke.

Grant's voice turned as soft as a summer night. "I'll always make time for you."

About three years ago, Grant's wife became the victim of a stalker. I caught the asshole en flagrante delicto, strong-armed him into an alley, backed him against a dumpster, and pressed my Glock under his chin. I told the fuckwad if he ever came within five hundred feet of Mrs. Stenton again, he'd neither see me nor hear the crack of my kill shot.

He pissed his pants.

And he left Mrs. Stenton alone. Sometimes an overt threat and a piece of Austrian weaponry work wonders in influencing douchebags.

"Do you need a profile?" Grant said.

"No, this one's personal," I said.

"What's on your mind?"

"I've never told anyone what I'm about to tell you."

"All right."

"On a rainy February evening, I was reading in my recliner while waiting for Sierra to get home from teaching a night class. Ian had fallen asleep on my lap. I vaguely heard the paperback I'd been reading thump onto the floor."

Grant dipped his head.

"I woke up, hearing Sierra's voice. I saw her kneeling beside me. She picked up my paperback and set it on the recliner's armrest."

"I see."

I paused, shaking my head. "Grant, I know I saw and heard my wife that evening as clearly as I'm seeing and hearing you now."

Grant moved his head a fraction of an inch.

"Sierra told me while on her way home, the driver of a Hummer veered into her lane and hit her car head-on. Then the doorbell woke me."

Grant's soft blue eyes didn't leave mine.

"I opened the door to a couple of Highway Patrol officers. I let them tell me what I already knew."

"I see," Grant said.

"Ever since Sierra's death, I dream of her most nights." I shifted in my chair. "These dreams go beyond sight and sound. I smell the skin lotion she always wore to bed. I feel her warm body pressed against mine. We make love. I know I'm only dreaming, but it all seems so goddammed real."

"Yes," Grant said.

"I don't know, maybe these dreams are a byproduct of the prescription sleeping pills I take."

"Which sleeping pills are you taking?"

I told him the name of the pharmaceutical. "I've had chronic insomnia since Sierra's death. Even with the pills, some nights I get three or four hours of restless sleep, other nights, around two... sometimes less."

"While sleeping, have you ever woken gasping for breath?"

"No. About a year ago I spent a night in a sleep clinic with electrodes stuck all over my body. I didn't get a diagnosis as to the cause of my insomnia, but I learned I didn't have either sleep apnea or narcolepsy."

"You're having pleasant dreams of Sierra," Grant said.

"Yes. Dreams are one thing. What concerns me is I've started seeing, hearing, and talking to Sierra while I'm awake."

"Talking...as in conversations?"

"Yes, but these talks are echoes of conversations she and I had in the past." I paused to choose my words. "As of yesterday, I began having new conversations with her." I gave him a couple of examples. "Have I gone screaming at clouds insane?"

Grant tilted his head slightly. "What do you think?"

I almost flinched from my friend going all shrink on my ass. But then, that's why I wanted to talk to him. "I'd like to believe I'm sane. I don't think I'm seeing and talking to Sierra's..." I shut up.

"I'm no expert in the field, but I believe parapsychologists use the term 'apparition,'" Grant said.

I leaned closer to Grant. "Whether awake or asleep, do you think it's possible I'm seeing and talking to Sierra's apparition?"

"Parapsychology as a science has always been robustly disputed. But proponents have vigorously defended their research data and conclusions." He smiled. "You're an educated, well-read, open-minded guy. I'm only an ex-jock with too many diplomas and a few licenses." He shrugged. "I can't deny the possibility that some people possess sixth senses, giving them either clairvoyant gifts, or precognitive capabilities, or the ability to see apparitions." He sighed. "The skepticism comes with fitting these phenomena into our limited understanding of the universe."

Looking at the floor, I nodded.

"You mentioned not sleeping well, and seeing vivid images of Sierra both day and night. Do you sometimes fall asleep for a few seconds either while at work, or during a conversation, or while driving?"

"Yes to all three."

"Extreme daytime sleepiness and micro sleeps may be the first symptoms of several medical conditions."

"Such as?"

"Bacterial or viral infections, or a chronic illness such as rheumatoid arthritis, anemia, or congestive heart failure. I think a physical exam and blood tests are in order to eliminate those illnesses." He looked at me firmly. "What we must not ignore is extended periods of sleep deprivation can result in hallucinations. It's been over two years since Sierra's accident, correct?"

"Two years, two months, and five days."

"I see you're still wearing your wedding band."

"Yes." I saw no reason to mention I didn't want to take it off my finger because I missed my wife every day.

"Most psychologists and psychiatrists agree that people go through five phases of grief following the death of a loved one: denial, bargaining, fear, anger, and finally acceptance. Which phase best fits how you feel right now?"

"I think I've gotten beyond most of my anger." I raised my voice, "*Even though some fuckhead saw nothing wrong with texting while speeding along a two-lane highway on a rainy night.*" I forced myself to calm down and lowered my voice. "He's found guilty of manslaughter, gets a two-year sentence, and is paroled after serving seven months. I'm still furious at that brainless sonofabitch for leaving Ian motherless and me without my best friend, lover, and the love of my life." I pulled in a long breath and let it out slowly. "I also felt some anger toward Sierra for teaching a night class that wasn't her responsibility."

"Oh," Grant said.

"She agreed to fill in for a colleague who often challenged her comments during faculty meetings, forcing her to back the bastard against the wall with empirical data. Sierra used to say university politics is so vicious because the stakes are so low." I paused at length, finally saying, "I keep what remains of my anger to myself."

"Anger turned inward can result in depression, which feeds insomnia. Do you think you're depressed?"

"No…maybe…shit, I don't know."

Grant said, "Only you know whether you're depressed, and only you know the reason or reasons why." He sat motionless, looking directly at me. "As an educated guess, I'd say you may have a mild form of depression that can be treated with talk therapy."

I realized I'd gotten a "specific suggestion" from Grant. It's only one of the clever skills taught in *The Big Book of Shrinkology*.

"Since Sierra's death, have you felt that you're living or existing?"

"Is there a difference?"

Grant, the clever doctor, had handed me a couple of things to consider. He was on a roll. "I'm sensing you're under a great deal of stress," Grant said.

"I guess."

Grant dropped his pen onto his notebook. "I think you need to take at least a week off from work. You can go on short sightseeing trips or stay at home doing things you enjoy. Sit in the shade and read, take your son to Disneyland, work in your gardens. Would you give a week or ten days to yourself while we begin your daily talk therapy sessions?"

"I can try." I considered all that this task would encompass, finally saying, "I'm afraid Sierra's death put a gaping hole in my heart that will never heal."

"Which philosopher said something like, there is no truth, only perception."

"Socrates, Goethe, Descartes, and Nietzsche all had slight variations on the truth-perception theme," I said.

"Maybe what you're seeing as a gaping hole in your heart is a matter of perception?"

I shrugged.

Grant inclined his head slightly. "You know, Sierra will always, always hold a spot in your heart."

I looked at my feet.

"Try seeing Sierra's love as a gift she left you that you can treasure as long as you live," Grant suggested.

Sir Grant the Clever had given me more specific suggestions.

For the first time in over two years, I let myself cry.

I finally wiped my eyes, took a long breath, and let it out. I'd known for a long while I needed to get beyond my grief and start living again. The time had come to turn the page.

After leaving the clinic, I stopped by the office and told Hope I'd be on vacation for the next seven business days.

She slid her pencil into her silver bouffant. "You're way past due for a vacation." She smiled. "You're like the son Stella and I never had, and we love you dearly. But we've been worried about your endless grieving."

She rose from her chair, came around her desk, and hugged me. "While you're out of the office, either feed the kitty or give some trick a hot beef injection. Better yet, aim for both."

Hope returned to her keyboard. "Least said, soonest mended. Now get the fuck outta here."

I'd learned long ago to appreciate Hope's candor.

CHAPTER EIGHTEEN

The Thing with Feathers

Clint, The Flats, Saturday, May 12

Around 1040 hours, I sat in the sunshine, reading an espionage novel while keeping one eye on Ian and his buddy, Sage, as they yelled and splashed in the pool.

I looked up as a mockingbird began singing its repertoire. It reminded me of a work of literary genius. Not *To Kill a Mockingbird*, which reads like a Truman Capote novel. I'd long thought if Capote hadn't written it, he'd edited it with a heavy hand.

No, I'm thinking of Emily Dickinson's "Hope Is the Thing with Feathers." I recalled the opening lines:

> *Hope is the thing with feathers that perches in the soul,*
> *And sings the tune without the words,*
> *and never stops—at all.*

No matter how tough, painful, or surreal life gets, hope always dwells within us.

Instead of defining my life as a result of Sierra's death, Doc Grant had gotten me thinking along the hope, expectation, and courage lines.

And I'd started getting six hours of sleep most nights. The clouds had begun to break. I saw my life as a great new beginning.

But when it came to hope and courage, Raoul deserved a gold medal. He'd lost his house and everything in it. The fire inspector believed a defective gas line made the pressure rise, causing pipes to crack. The gas water heater, gas dryer, gas kitchen range, and two gas-fueled fireplaces simultaneously exploded, not to mention making his neighbors simultaneously shit themselves.

Adding insult to injury, Raoul's agent wouldn't return his calls. Likely cause of the radio silence: Raoul declined the men's grooming products commercial that would've given every viewer a millisecond look at his junk. He'd simply shrugged. "Tinseltown agents can become such unforgiving assholes. Hoo-fucking-ray for Hollywood."

Raoul hadn't linked his misfortune to, as he'd put it, "that retro Mercury gloom and doom horseshit" pitched by my astrologer neighbor. Hell no, he'd told me it had been nothing but great luck we had gone out for dinner at Fat Boy Benji's the evening his house went up like a NASA rocket.

Raoul's homeowner's insurance would cover his losses. He'd arranged for the rubble of his house and its contents to be hauled away in dump trucks and the lot bulldozed. He'd begun designing his new home.

Through it all, Raoul hadn't become frustrated and hadn't lost his optimism. And I'd helped him capture his dream of a film career.

I'd spent last weekend putting Raoul through his theatrical paces, shooting stills and videos, coaxing the best out of him as if I were a director, while capturing him in optimal angles, lights, and shadows like a studio cinematographer. I'd learned a thing or two about the movie biz by cutting my teeth watching great actors, directors, and technicians practicing their crafts.

Once I finished editing Raoul's new, high resolution digital portfolio, I would stop by Steele Productions to show Aunt Vona the star of her next blockbuster.

And during one day of my vacation, I'd bagged all of Sierra's cosmetics and toiletries and tossed them into the dumpster. Next, I placed her clothing, shoes, and purses in lawn and leaf bags.

I asked Raoul if he'd mind hauling it all to Goodwill. He understood my need for some time alone and asked Ian if he'd like to come along. He didn't need to ask twice. Ian loved going for rides in Raoul's big diesel pickup truck.

What had been *our* walk-in closet had become *my* walk-in closet. I now had enough room for my casual and dress clothing; all perfectly spaced, separated by colors, and neatly hanging. *Anal much?*

I boxed Sierra's books, CDs, and DVDs to donate to any library willing to take them. I gathered her awards, letters, cards, yearbooks, and diplomas, and stored it all in the Saratoga trunk in the attic. I hoped her personal and professional mementos would one day give Ian a better understanding of his mother and her accomplishments.

I kept Sierra's wedding band and engagement ring with my cuff links and tie tacks where I could see them each day while I got dressed. Then I turned the final page, so to speak, and removed my wedding band from my left ring finger. I placed all three rings in their original boxes and set them in the back of my safe.

Someday, Ian might want to give his mother's engagement ring to his fiancée. And the new couple might wear our wedding bands. Hope is indeed the thing with feathers.

But until that day came, I would occasionally open those ring boxes to remember, to weep, and to smile.

Then I'd closed the walk-in closet doors, leaned against them, and felt centered for the first time in a long while.

CHAPTER NINETEEN

Uncle Martian

Clint, The Flats, Sunday, May 13

Ian squealed and took a run at Mars Hauser as he stepped into the kitchen. He caught Ian mid-leap and held him to his chest.

"How you doing, Boo-boo?"

"I'm fine, Uncle Martian."

At the age of three, Ian pronounced "Marston" as "Martian." He could now say Marston, but he stuck with the misnomer.

Raoul had gone to his warehouse to inventory supplies with Katie, his right-hand crew boss. I didn't expect him back before midnight.

Mars had caught me sitting at the kitchen island, working on Sunday's crossword. I put down the pen as Mars took the stool beside mine, holding Ian on his lap.

The three of us spent the day in the So Cal sun, playing catch and dodgeball, swimming, and going through a large bottle of sunscreen. We ate burgers and hot dogs for lunch and had barbecued chicken for dinner. For all intents and purposes, we had a family Sunday.

By 2030 hours, Ian's eyes had begun to droop. I didn't get an argument when I told him he needed to get ready for bed.

Showered and in his pajamas, Ian asked, "When my penis gets big, will I get hairy legs like you and Uncle Martian?"

I sighed inwardly. "Yes, son, without a doubt." I kissed him on the cheek and told him I loved him.

"I love you too, Daddy." He hugged me.

He'd fallen asleep before I turned on the nightlight.

Mars and I sat at the poolside table, shooting the shit and drinking beer. I occasionally glanced at the nearby audio-video monitor. Ian remained sound asleep.

Mars sipped some beer. "When you get your lazy ass back to work tomorrow, where do you pick up on the Shane Danning case?"

I set my bottle of beer aside. "A couple of days after Shane was seen in Laguna, Captain Flynn closed his missing person file." I checked the monitor. "Needing a fresh trail to follow, I'll wait until someone spots Danning again. It's merely a matter of time."

Shane didn't need to call, email, send a letter, or unloose a courier pigeon to his mother. He had the right to hide his address and phone number from anyone he chose, including Diana. With no evidence of foul play and no ransom demand, the LAPD couldn't invade Shane's privacy by tracking him down.

But I could hunt Shane down and ask him to go home. I might turn on the charm, but I would not cuff him, force him into my car, and take him to his mother.

I lacked a piece or two in the matter of Shane's disappearance, and my curiosity would spur me on. I wanted to know what motivated him to vanish like smoke, briefly reappear in Laguna, then disappear again.

Noticing that Mars had fallen silent, I knew he was reliving a memory. I lightly kicked him under the table. "What's on your mad scientist tech nerd mind now?"

"I was thinking about the time you and I got a weekend pass, went to Manhattan, and got our asses abducted by those twin sister cops."

I exhaled a laugh. "We met them in a bookstore, they started chatting us up." I again kicked Mars under the table. "Then they opened their bags, showed us their guns, and ordered us to follow them." I laughed. "They took us to their apartment, and damned near had us bare-assed naked before the door finished closing." Smiling, I shook my head. "We each could've gotten a dishonorable conduct dismissal."

"Well, shit, they swore they were single. How the hell did we know they were estranged from their husbands?"

"Christ on a crotch rocket, the way they went for our cocks and goddammed screamed their pretty asses off, I thought they hadn't gotten laid in years," I said.

Mars gave me a barefooted kick under the table. "I could understand your cop's squeals. I always felt as if you'd split me in half each time we fucked. It became our dating game. The two of us and two women, then you and I later on."

"As bisexuals, we gave credence to the adage about dating West Point cadets: The odds are good..."

"But the goods are odd," Mars finished. "I miss the close, personal relationship you and I shared at the Point." He paused. "Do you think we could go back to the way we were?"

"Now that your ass is single again, I wouldn't mind." I drank some beer.

"Before we get started, I'll need to use some toys for a while," Mars said.

"I read about something that will neither split you in half nor have you walking funny for days," I said.

Mars lifted one eyebrow. "And what would that be?"

I glanced at the child monitor. Ian still slept peacefully. "Stand up and drop 'em."

Mars's shorts hit the pool deck. It sounded as if he had keys, Swiss Army knife, metal-jacketed Zippo (someone might need a light), lip balm, iPhone, nail clippers, and about ten bucks' worth of change in his pockets. No matter how metro-hip handsome his looks, in one way or another, he's always a nerd.

"Do you have a condom in one of those pockets?" I asked.

He bent, dipped two fingers into his right rear pocket, snagged a condom packet, and opened it with his teeth. He rolled the condom on.

I told Mars to close his eyes.

Standing face-to-face, I held a fist to my mouth and made the sound of a radio squawk. "Mars probe, this is Houston."

Mars squawked. "Copy, Houston."

I squawked. "Prepare for docking."

Then I began docking (JFGI) him.

"Wow, that's softer than any vagina I've ever had my dick in. How come we never tried this before?"

"I recently read about it. Ain't the worldwide web a wondrous thing."

Twenty minutes later, Mars said, "Moose, can you dock me again?"

I did.

CHAPTER TWENTY

Can't Find My Way Home

Shane Danning, The Ranch, Monday, May 14

When I was fifteen, Mom sent me packing to one of London's exclusive prep schools. I met my roommate, Robert, the day before classes started.

Robert's bearing and locution tagged him as a member of the British aristocracy—the penniless but proud Fifth Earl of Krotchrotten Downs, or something like that. I was a Hollywood princeling whose mother owned a twelve-million-dollar Palisades Beach mansion in the People's Republic of Santa Monica. My roommate and I became fast friends.

Robert always had deep pockets, never mind his family didn't have a pot to piss in or a crumbling castle window out of which to throw it, or so he'd told me. When I asked him about his monthly allowance, he snickered. "You Yanks may be the world's best shoplifters, but we Brits long ago turned picking pockets and purses into an art form."

He let me observe him at work in London's crowded squares, packed tourist spots, and tube stations. He taught me some of the tricks of his trade in exchange for sex. Don't be shocked. Or, as Robert would've put it, "Do try to carry on." After all, we attended an all-boys' school while our pubescent hormones were running wild.

I'd never needed to use the specialized skills Robert had taught me until this morning, when everything for a breakout from Jud Tucker's private prison fell into place.

Tom Andrews, casino pit boss turned kidnap victim, and I had slapped together a basic escape plan. I would pick the prison key from a guard's pocket, subdue him, hijack some wheels, and get the fuck off the Ponderosa.

We'd a few flaws in our plan. First and foremost, we didn't know our twenty; that is, we didn't have a frigging clue where the fuck we were. Our abductions had happened at night, and each of us had been drugged senseless before Jud Tucker brought us to his slave ranch and private prison.

But shit, I navigated the wild blue yonder by flight instruments and the seat of my pants while flying four hundred and eighty miles per hour at thirty-six thousand feet. During his military service, Tom had driven in Middle Eastern deserts without signage. We could, damn it, determine our location once we got outside the prison's windowless walls. Roger that.

We knew Tucker kept only one guard on duty Monday mornings. And this Monday's bull had been wanting to get his hands on me since Tucker caged my ass.

When he unlocked my cell this morning, I was lying on my bunk faking sleep, and wearing only boxers with my dick hanging out the fly.

While the bull gazed at my junk, I picked his pocket. Then I subdued his ass, bound his wrists behind his back with his T-shirt, tied his ankles with his jeans, and gagged him with his socks. I waggled my cock near his bull face. Yeah, I can sometimes turn into a bit of a douche.

Then I got dressed and unlocked my cell with the bull's master key.

Tom Andrews was dressed and ready to run when I unlocked his cell. We jogged toward the prison's only door.

I hoped either Andrews or I could get law enforcement into this private hell before Jud Tucker returned. Failing that, I knew the young bull bound and gagged in my cell would be dead before dark. I didn't want to be responsible for his death, but I suspected he wouldn't be the first of Tucker's guards and prisoners to vanish.

Outside the cinderblock prison, Andrews and I each did a three-sixty, trying to get our bearings. The morning sun pointed us east.

A large two-story white house, probably Jud Tucker's, stood not far from us.

But we didn't need shelter. We needed transportation. We ran for the barn.

A heavy padlock kept us from opening the barn's solid wood sliding doors. Peering through cracks between the barn's boards, I saw a tractor, grain truck, van, and an old GMC pickup.

"Tom, buddy, I believe we found the transportation mother lode."

But we couldn't even work our fingers between the slight gaps in the padlocked wooden doors.

"That old GMC looks solid enough to drive through these thick doors without denting the bumper," I said. "We need to find another way into the barn."

"What about keys to that Jimmy?"

"We're on a working ranch. We'll find the fucking keys either in the ignition or behind the sun visor. If I'm wrong, that pickup is old enough to start by hotwiring it."

Looking for another barn entrance, Tom and I ran along one side of the building—nothing but solid wood, except for the door below the roof's peak where hay bales were loaded into the loft.

We loped to the back side of the barn, slowed, and stopped, spotting another pair of double doors sans a padlock. To get to them, we needed only to climb over a six-foot-high barbed wire fence.

Andrews put his foot on the fence. His ankle touched a wire, and the current jolted him backward about ten feet.

Tom landed flat on his back. Kneeling beside him, I couldn't find a pulse. He didn't appear to be breathing. I began CPR. After about every two minutes, I stopped the chest compressions and exhaled a breath into his mouth. After twenty minutes of CPR, Tom's heart hadn't started beating, and he still couldn't breathe on his own. One look at Tom's eyes, and I knew he was dead. I sat cross-legged beside his body.

I held a degree in aeronautical engineering and flew jet aircraft. Such sophisticated machinery ran on fuel for the engines...wait for it...and electricity for everything else. Maybe I knew more than the average Hollywood princeling about electrical currents. Touching high voltage hurts like hell, but isn't necessarily deadly. It's the amperes that result in electrocution.

Tom Andrews probably died of ventricular fibrillation from a current of 110 to 220 volts at a fatal 100 to 200 milliamps. He'd likely been dead before he landed on his back.

I heard the crunch of gravel under tires.

Chapter Twenty-One

Gaslighted

Clint, Monday, May 14

On my first day back to work, I read the *L.A. Times* with my feet up on my desk, drank coffee, returned calls, drank more coffee, and replied to a backlog of emails. Then I pulled the newspaper out of the recycle box, tackled the crossword puzzle, and drank some more coffee.

Finished with all that, I checked the time. Shit, I'd gotten less done before noon than most people didn't do all week at work.

To celebrate, I took Hope to Mousseau and Frank for lunch and cocktails. We talked, I sipped one beer, and Hope got half in the bag on several margaritas. Before she started singing and dancing on top of the table, I guided her back to my car and got her strapped in.

Back at the office, I let her sleep lunch off while I focused on Danning's tablet, which was no longer locked, thanks to Mars Hauser. What a guy.

Shane's email inbox had five unopened messages: a couple from Diana and the other three from cabin attendants who wanted Shane to fuck them. He had nothing archived, *nada* in the trash, and nothing sent. Apparently, Shane didn't bother with his email. I couldn't fault him for that.

I found around fifty nude photos in a file saved as "Playtime Pics." I recognized a few faces, including a young, married, morality-preaching conservative network news reporter, a hugely popular rock band's lead singer, and a city councilwoman with Shane taking her in the front and another man taking her in the rear. That Shane boy did get around.

Being forced to investigate so much nude flesh put a hellacious strain on my eyes. It's a dirty job, but someone had to do it.

Home by 1730, I sat with Ian at the kitchen island, where we talked and colored.

Raoul made it home in time to join us for the evening meal. I grilled fresh salmon and asparagus spears dipped in melted butter. We ate poolside.

"Raoul, are you really Daddy's boyfriend?"

Ian's question came from Raoul's smart-assed comment about my having the best brewski choices of all his boyfriends. Children seldom forget anything they hear.

"Let's see," Raoul said, "your dad and I are boys, and we're friends. I guess you could call us boyfriends of sorts."

"If you're boyfriends, then why don't Daddy and you sleep together?"

"You keep asking for it," I mumbled to Raoul. "Ian, Raoul and I are friends, as you and Sage are friends. We're not suitors or dating or steadies or boyfriends who sleep together. Do you understand?"

Ian shook his head. "I don't get it. Sage and I are friends, and we sleep together when I stay overnight at his house and when we have a sleepover here."

Oh, the innocence of children. "When you're six-year-old boys, you can get away with sleeping together. That sort of companionship will likely mean something else when you get older."

"Yeah, when my penis gets big like yours," Ian said.

About to laugh his ass off, Raoul covered his mouth and pretended to sneeze, saying softly, "Fok-choo!"

At 2126 hours, I lay on top of my bed in sleep shorts, flipping through a spyware catalog. My eyelids drooped. Thanks to Doc Stenton's talk therapy, I'd been granted a reprieve from two years of insomnia. I switched off the bedside lamp.

My cell phone vibrated.

It didn't take clairvoyance to guess the caller's name.

"*Clint, I need your help!*"

Diana sounded about a sneeze away from hysterical. I slipped out of bed and dropped my feet to the floor. "What's wrong?"

"Someone keeps calling my private line and doesn't speak when I answer. I'm certain it's a man. I can hear him breathing." She sobbed, then said, "He's called four times in the past half hour."

Four hang-ups in thirty minutes didn't sound like some fuckwad repeatedly punching in the wrong phone number. Being her private line, it seemed likely she knew the caller.

"You don't recognize the caller's number?"

"No."

"Do you want me to drop by, check things out, and sit with you for a while?"

"God, yes, thank you."

She gave me her address.

I checked the child monitor. Ian was fast asleep. I got dressed, pulled my car fob, house key, and my Glock out of the safe, slid my phone into my front pocket, and headed down the hall to Raoul's bedroom.

Raoul sat at the desk, poring over his company's books. I tapped on his partially open door.

Raoul looked up from his laptop. "Yeah, Moose."

"I need to leave for a while." I told him about Diana's frantic call. "Would you keep your ears open in case Ian wakes up and gets out of bed?"

"Not a problem." Raoul grinned, stood, and stretched. "I have to mention this sounds like the oldest male lure in the female tackle box." He snapped his fingers. "Did Diana say anything about her mansion's gaslights dimming and hearing footsteps overhead?"

He'd spoken about one of my favorite old movies, *Gaslight*. "Sometimes you're a real LMFAO-fest." I shook my head, but smiled while doing it. "I'll be home in a couple of hours, maybe sooner."

Diana lived in what Angelenos call the Birds Neighborhood, due to streets such as Whippoorwill, Wren, Pheasant, and other pleasant-sounding fowl names.

High above the Sunset Strip, this Hollywood enclave is known for its panoramic views and privacy. More movie, TV, and music celebs reside here than in Beverly Hills, making it one of the wealthiest hoods in all of LA-LA Land. It's also one of the safest, due to the attentive, head-thumping private cops on patrol around the clock.

I knew Diana had gotten frantic over nothing. A single call to the security service would've had the entire rent-a-cop hordes storming her castle walls. I'd known all along what she wanted—a package from the dick delivery man. I'm not as unsophisticated as I may sometimes appear.

I turned onto Partridge Drive, stopped outside Diana's gates, and powered down the driver's side window. I pressed the call button.

A dark-colored SUV rolled up and parked within an inch of my bumper. Fuck, the Gestapo had arrived.

A man who reminded me of a fuglier Hulk glowered at me. Then he shined a Maglite in my eyes.

"Lower that Mag before I shove it so far up your ass your face will glow like a jack-o'-lantern."

He pointed the powerful flashlight down slightly. I handed him my PI creds. His lips moved as he read.

Diana's disembodied voice came through the call box speaker. "Thank God you're here."

"Are you talking to me, Ms. Danning, or do you know this man?"

Diana's voice turned clippish. "Yes, I know him. Thanks, Tank, you can leave."

The private cop returned my PI license, mumbled something about getting lucky tonight, and returned to his SUV.

"I'm going to check the grounds," I said to Diana. "Don't open fire if you see a flashlight beam bobbing around."

"Please be careful. Someone may be out there."

A less than zero chance of that, I thought.

The gate swung open. I parked in the circular drive fronting the mansion, checked that I'd chambered a round in case some tool did get past the rent-a-cops and the gate, and slid my Glock back into its tension holster.

Diana had the grounds glowing like Times Square at Christmas. I killed my Maglite. Although the chances seemed slim that anyone was out here, I checked anyway. Only doing my job, ma'am. Finding no one lurking behind any of the trees, bushes, statuary, shrubs, tennis court, in or around the pool house, I worked my way to the front of the mansion and climbed the marble steps to a pair of carved doors.

Before I lifted the knocker, Diana opened one of the double doors, rushed me inside, slammed it shut, and threw the locks. Melodrama, what great foreplay, I thought.

Wrapped in a blue silk robe, Diana hooked her arm in mine and ushered me along the manse's marble entry hall. We made a turn into the media room. I sat at the bar.

Diana filled two short tumblers with a pricy single malt she served neat. I watched her stir one drop of water into each glass. I never would've pegged her as a scotch connoisseur, a discovery that got me thinking I could fall even more madly in lust with this woman.

She sat beside me and proposed a toast to a pleasant night.

We clinked glasses and sipped some great single malt. "Have you gotten any more hang-ups?" I could hear her saying, "Not since I called you."

"None since I called you."

Close enough. "Good."

It could be someone was watching her house, but I didn't mention it. "The caller must be someone you know. Either that, or some geek hacked into your cell service provider's database."

"I suppose either of those is possible," she said vaguely. She fell silent studying my chest. "Raw power literally rolls off you." She looked at my face. "And, darling, you're a chip off the old blocks."

"Pardon me?"

She said, "You inherited your father's deep voice, dark blue eyes, lips, square chin, smile, and dimples. Then you have your lovely mother's dark hair, black eye lashes, high cheekbones, and olive skin."

I gave her a quick smile.

Diana brightened. "Did you know your father discovered me?"

Those who'd achieved Hollywood-legend status love to share their discovery stories. "Yes, I've been told Dad spotted you in a coffee shop." The story had become a piece of Hollywood lore along the lines of the industry reporter who'd discovered Lana Turner (JFGI) drinking a Coke at a Hollywood soda fountain.

"I was late for my bookkeeping class," she began. "I decided to skip it and stop for a cup of coffee." She smiled fondly. "I was sitting at a table, drinking a double latte when your father spotted me. He introduced himself, then told me he'd never seen a young lady as lovely as I."

"How old were you?"

"Fifteen. Anyway, he handed me his business card. Being a recent Seattle transplant, I knew little about the film industry; I hadn't heard of either Liam Steele or Steele Productions."

She sipped some scotch, then shook her head, smiling. "I figured this handsome but forward man might be a porn director."

I laughed. Dad would've shit bricks if he'd known what Diana initially thought of him.

"But this Liam Steele gave off an earnest, confident vibe. A bright red aura surrounded him, telling me he was passionate, competitive, sexual, robust, and successful."

I'd never noticed my father's aura, but I didn't scoff. She'd characterized Liam Steele to a T—well, my father and all other movie directors. It would not have surprised me to learn Diana regularly consulted with my next-door neighbor, Darla Love.

She swirled her scotch, then took a sip. "Your father and I talked in the coffee shop, and he met with my parents about a week later. Liam sent me to the best acting, voice, and dance teachers. He hired tutors, and I earned my high school diploma."

Under the bar's lighting, her violet eyes changed to dark blue, then deep brown—the same way Shane's eye colors changed in his porn films.

"I was seventeen when Liam released *Invisible Threads* and launched my film career."

She smiled at me.

I smiled back.

Sometimes, a man might miss a woman's subtle signals. But my job required me to interpret body language and read the emotions of others. And right here, right now, I didn't have my head up my ass. She wanted me to take her on a long, sweaty Pecos Bill ride.

Wordlessly, she took my hand. We walked up the grand staircase.

In her bedroom suite, Diana shrugged out of her robe and let it slide to the floor. She looked exquisite in clothing, but in the nude, she was a work of art.

In the military, I'd learned how to dress and undress posthaste. I got buck naked in about twenty seconds.

She gave me an up-down look. She reached into the nightstand, where she stashed what looked like a drugstore's selection of condoms and lubes. She handed me a Durex XXL. "I've waited a long while for a man who could wear one of these."

Her comment prompted me to check the condom's expiration date. It was goddammed close. But I'd risk it. I ripped open the package between my teeth and gloved up.

We kissed tenderly, almost hesitantly at first; then I began kissing her like I fucking meant it. She responded in kind. Our hands ghosted over skin.

From this point, I needn't draw you a picture. I'll mention multiple orgasms on her part as I followed her slower, harder, faster, deeper commands. With all the bed rocking, moaning, screaming, and yelling, I half expected the fuglier Hulk to come crashing through a bedroom wall.

Later, we lay face-to-face, our legs entwined, both of us catching our breath in a drained, sweaty postcoital glow.

She traced my lips with a forefinger and spoke softly, "Liam was hung, but sweetheart, you are prodigious."

A man's mind freezes after swashbuckling sex. When I finally replied to Diana's comment, I said something fucking brilliant. "What?"

"I was sixteen when your father and I first made love."

Gobsmacked by her revelations, I looked into her eyes questioningly. She didn't turn away.

Fuck me sideways, but I'd never known about Diana and my father's sexual relationship. I felt like one of the Kennedy brothers, who allegedly shared Marilyn and other lovers with each other. And with Joe.

"I make no apologies," Diana said. "Liam's the only man I ever loved, respected, and adored with all my heart." She paused. "Our affair lasted right up to Liam and your mother's deaths. I still miss him every day. I've never regretted a moment we spent together."

My father cheated on my mother for years, and I never had a clue. But I'd seen my mom and dad infrequently throughout my youth and teens. The last four years my parents were alive, I'd lived on the opposite coast at the USMA, also known as West Point. I suppose Mom knew. I've been told the wife is seldom the last to know. An offspring's knowledge of such matters was optional.

I calmed my ass down. Knowing Diana had been married more than a few times, I had one question I needed to ask. "Who is Shane's father?"

"Paternity is often dubious. Maternity is the only certainty. I'm Shane's mother, and that's all anyone needs to know."

She'd answered my question. I'd nothing more to ask.

"No matter how much you look like your father, and no matter how much I enjoyed making love with you, I feel absolutely foolish thinking I could recapture the magic with you that Liam and I shared. I shamelessly used you."

"No, we used each other."

In a while, her deep, steady breathing told me she'd fallen asleep. I slipped out of bed.

Invading her master bath, I flushed the used condom down the toilet. Yes, it took a few flushes—plus using the plumber's helper I found in one of the cabinets under the sinks. I stepped into the shower.

Ten minutes later, I looked into a mirrored wall and felt bad about Diana's broken dreams. Hers and my own.

I got dressed and showed myself out.

CHAPTER TWENTY-TWO

The Morning After

Clint, Steele & Whitman Investigations, Tuesday, May 15

I made it to the office by 0840 hours. "Diana Danning phoned," Hope said. "She wants to speak with you. I checked your calendar and told her you'd be available at nine thirty."

I stopped in front of Hope's desk. "Did Diana say what she wanted?"

"She received a ransom demand in the wee hours of the morning."

I'd expected a heart-to-heart call from Diana about last night's romp and run. But a ransom demand—what brave new shit was this?

Shortly after Shane's appearance in Laguna, Captain Flynn closed Danning's missing person file. I'd decided to take a laid-back approach in my search for Shane. Had I missed something critical by setting aside my work following his disappearance-reappearance-disappearance acts? I let out a long breath. It was time to whip it up and do the job Diana hired me to do.

"Did Diana tell you what the kidnapper said?"

Hope passed me a transcription of her shorthand notes. I scanned the page.

Looking up at Hope's monitor, I saw a full body shot of a man in uniform. "I take it you tracked down a photo of Deputy Scott Davidson."

"Of course I did."

I took another look at the deputy's photo. "I wonder why that dime-store cowboy tried to pass himself off as a dead man. He had to know we'd learn the truth about Deputy Davidson's death with a single phone call." I looked at Hope. "Didn't you wonder about that?"

Hope sighed. "Well, hell yes, I didn't wonder too. Whaddaya, retahded?"

Translation: Certainly, I also wondered about that. What's the matter with you? Are you a person with a developmental disability?

"I used my old badge number to get fax copies of the official reports on Deputy Scott Davidson's suicide. I stuck them on your desk," Hope said, pulling the pencil out of her beehived hair before answering the phone.

I started for my office. Before Diana arrived, I wanted to read the official reports Hope "stuck" on my desk.

I dropped into my office chair to peruse the lead investigator's findings at Deputy Davidson's death scene.

I put the cop talk into plain English as I read.

On February twentieth, Deputy Scott Valentine Davidson arrived at the Windbag Saloon at approximately 2240 hours. Davidson had dinner, a single glass of beer, and talked with several acquaintances. At approximately 2335 hours, Davidson paid his tab and departed.

Around 2340 hours, patrons heard a gunshot near the Windbag Saloon's parking area. The bartender contacted the police.

Responding officers arrived on the scene at 2347 and saw an adult male lying supine, parallel to a GMC pickup parked in the southeast corner of the Windbag Saloon's lot. Responding officers could not find a pulse, nor did the victim appear to be breathing. CPR procedures were initiated.

An EMT crew arrived OTS at 2350 hours; repeated attempts to resuscitate the victim failed. Time of death was recorded as 2359.

A current California driver's license identified the victim as Scott V. Davidson. OTS evidence indicated the cause of death was an apparent self-inflicted gunshot wound to the head. A 9mm S&W semiautomatic was found 11.8 inches from the victim's right hand. A single shell casing was recovered 4.6 feet from the body.

Police Investigator L. Roberts had signed the report.

I next thumbed through the medical examiner's autopsy report. Scott Valentine Davidson was forty-four years, nine months old, six-one, 174.7 pounds with dark blond hair and hazel eyes.

Preliminary findings indicated Davidson was in perfect health. With the exception of an appendectomy scar, no other identifying marks were found on the body. No prescription or illicit drugs were detected in his bloodstream. His blood alcohol level was .01.

The cause of death was extensive head and brain trauma resulting from a 9mm hollow point bullet. Stippling surrounding the entry wound on the right temple indicated the weapon was fired at close range, as might have occurred in a suicide. Gunpowder residue on Davidson's right hand might further indicate the gunshot wound was self-inflicted. No prints were lifted from the 9mm shell casing found at the scene.

I leaned back in my desk chair. Gunpowder residue tests consistently proved unreliable at best, and could not be construed as conclusive evidence of suicide. Davidson could have spent some time on the department's firing range that day or a week ago. Also, the explosion of gasses in a fired gun generally destroyed any partial or latent fingerprints that may have been on the shell's casing. On the surface, it appeared Deputy Davidson had taken his own life.

Or maybe someone had taken his life from him. There were some things missing—an irregularity or two that stuck out like a warthog at a cat show, I thought.

For instance, why would Davidson climb into his pickup to get his gun and step back onto the parking lot to shoot himself? He could've done the job inside the cab.

Davidson's low blood alcohol level also nudged me. Wouldn't a guy planning to kill himself get at least halfway drunk? The BAL told me he drank one glass or bottle of beer. Maybe fear of the bartender asking for his keys and calling a taxi could've kept the deputy sober, but not likely.

Statistically, about twenty-five percent of those who commit suicide leave a note. Men write something more often than women. Why didn't the lead investigator's report mention a suicide note or the lack of one?

"Am I interrupting you?" Diana said from my office door.

"No, come in." I stood and met her halfway to my desk. I removed her star-going-incognito sunglasses and saw she'd been crying.

I handed her a tissue and let her cry on my shoulder. I wrapped her left hand under my right arm and helped her to a client chair. I sat beside her.

Diana wore no makeup. She'd pulled her hair into a loose chignon. Multiple strands had strayed from the knot. She'd dressed in walking shoes, jeans, and a short-sleeved blouse. The sadness in her eyes almost made me flinch.

"Diana," I began in a gentle tone, "repeat what the caller said."

She let out her breath and began speaking in a beaten voice, "He said he wants five million dollars for Shane's release." She stiffened. "I told him I'd need a little time to pull together that much money. I begged him not to harm my son and asked to speak to Shane. The kidnapper hung up."

Again, she cried.

I'd set a box of tissues on the edge of the desk. She pulled out a couple, wiped her eyes, and dabbed her nose. Her shoulders slumped, and she leaned back into the chair.

"I know this is difficult for you, but please try to bear with me."

She nodded slightly.

I held her left hand in both of mine. "Can you tell me anything about the caller's voice?"

"What do you mean?"

"I'm asking about cadence, inflection, choice of words, American or non national."

"He had a deep, masculine voice...definitely American." She paused for a few moments. "He spoke almost gently, as if he were a counselor or a minister. He didn't sound angry."

"That's great, Diana." I knew I was pushing it but I went ahead. "Could you estimate an age from his voice?"

"Neither youthful nor elderly. I'd guess early to mid-forties."

"Did you hear anything in the background such as a TV or radio, running water, an engine or traffic noise?"

Diana held perfectly still for several moments. "I heard absolutely nothing in the background."

Being a ransom demand for the return of her son, a pile-driver could've been operating ten feet from the caller and she might not have heard it.

"Do you recall anything else the man said?"

"He said he staged the Laguna shopping trip to prove Shane was still alive. He warned me not to call the police or FBI."

I could've guessed she didn't contact Captain Flynn. The wealthy didn't always involve law enforcement following the kidnapper's ransom demand. Statistically, the odds were better for a kidnap victim's safe return when directives were followed to the letter without the involvement of the cops or the feds.

Diana quietly cleared her throat. "The kidnapper expects your participation in Shane's release. If you refuse to help, or if one of us calls the cops, no one will ever find my son's body...nor yours. The caller said to wait for further instructions." Diana again dabbed her eyes. "Will you please help?"

"Yes."

"Thank you. You know, I didn't answer your question last night about Shane's father."

I'd wanted a sibling or siblings all my life and didn't want to wait for Diana to tell me. "Shane is my half brother."

She looked into my eyes. "Yes."

I briefly considered the many things I could say about a brother and family ties, but I kept quiet about all that for now. Someone had kidnapped Shane. Finding my half brother became my only priority.

"Hope Whitman, my business partner, will come to your house and install a digital recorder on your phone lines."

"That's fine. I only want my beautiful boy back."

Diana slid her sunglasses on and stood to leave. She leaned on me as I escorted her out of my office and down the hall.

Hope sprang from her chair and pulled Diana into her arms. Diana's shoulders shook.

"Don't cry, dear. Everything's going to be all right. Clint and I will see to it."

"We need a digital recorder on all of Diana's phones as well as all of mine."

Hope nodded and dismissed me with a wave of her hand. "Go on now. Let us girls have some tea and tears alone."

CHAPTER TWENTY-THREE

Two Deuces

Clint, Tuesday, May 15

Leaving the ladies to their tea and sympathy, I walked outside to my car, pulled out my phone, and called Captain Flynn. I caught him at his desk.

"Captain, can you do a late lunch?"

"Why? Are you looking for an escort to a quiche-tasting gala? Or maybe a bodyguard for the grand opening of a new dance club?"

I chuckled. "So bicurious, yet so homophobic. What's a handsome Irish American fence-straddling cop to do?"

"In a pig's ass I'm straddling anything. Why the hell do you want to meet for lunch?"

"It's called information sharing." I unlocked my car while listening to Flynn's whining about his never-ending duties. He finally named his latest greasy-spoon-from-hell discovery.

"I'll meet you there around 1330 hours." I slid behind the wheel and headed for Westwood Village.

I rolled to the curb in front of a shell pink stucco California bungalow with a tile roof. The windows gleamed in the sunlight. The lawn looked like a putting green, shaded on two sides by a perfectly clipped hedge. A pair of colorful, hand-thrown pots filled with lavender and pink impatiens decorated the stoop. I damned near rolled my eyes over the MX5 Miata Sport parked in the carport. The two young men living here didn't need a JumboTron announcing which team they played on.

I climbed the steps and pressed the doorbell. The chimes played the opening notes of the Village People's "YMCA." This pair of college boys had to be the bane of upscale and uptight Westwood.

A dark-haired young man wearing cut-off jeans and a faded Nirvana T-shirt opened the front door. He greeted me with the blank stare of his generation.

He was either incredibly brave, fucking stupid, or stoned out of his mind to open the door to a stranger without the chain in place. I smiled winningly. "I'm Detective Steele, working with the LAPD on Shane Danning's disappearance."

I got no response. I pushed ahead. "Are you Blaine Vogel or Blake Walsh?"

"I'm Blake. Blaine hasn't pulled his lazy ass out of bed yet."

"I need to speak to both of you. May I come in?"

Blake shrugged and swung the door open wide.

I stepped into a nicely furnished living room, sat on the black leather sofa, and checked my surroundings. Two male university students living under the same roof with no stacks of books, no athletic gear, no beer can pyramids, no pizza boxes, and no overflowing ashtrays. The place neither smelled of dirty sweat socks, nor garbage, nor doobage. The fuck?

Before Blake could make a move at getting his partner out of bed, Blaine Vogel came thumping down the stairs wearing nothing but bright orange, red, and yellow boxers.

He stopped at the bottom of the stairs when he saw me.

He leered. "Well, hello. I'm guessing you're not here handing out copies of *The Watchtower*."

Blake moved to stand beside his partner. "This is Detective…"

"Steele," I finished.

"Yeah, that," Blake said. "He's with the LAPD."

Blaine ran his fingers through his dark-haired bed head. "No shit? I take it you're an investigator."

I only smiled.

Vogel adjusted his loud boxers to accommodate his morning wood and sat in a leather armchair that matched the sofa. "Don't you LAPD investigators usually work in pairs?"

"Budget cuts," I said. "Besides, you guys don't look too dangerous to me." I smiled. "Mr. Vogel, it's evident you're not packing anything."

Blake Walsh snickered.

Blaine Vogel sneered and adjusted his boxers again. "I suppose you've got some more questions about what we saw that night."

I pulled my tablet from my messenger bag and waited, openly scrutinizing Walsh and Vogel's eyes and body language. They appeared calm and relaxed.

Blake perched on the arm of Blaine's chair. Both young men looked at me in expectation of my first question. I made them wait while I read my tablet notes.

"You live in a quiet, upscale neighborhood. As university students, how do you swing it financially?" I looked steadily at the young men.

Blake broke the silence. "Blaine's dad owns rental properties all over Los Angeles and Orange Counties."

"I get the place rent-free from Dad as long as I maintain my four-point GPA," Blaine said. "Blake and I will both start law school this fall."

I smiled. "It doesn't come much better than that. I read the sworn statements each of you gave the responding officers regarding Shane Danning's disappearance. The two of you didn't agree on anything you saw that night." I looked directly at them. "Investigators always focus on conflicting statements, and you two gave the LAPD an ass-ton of them."

Blaine returned my stare and shrugged. "Fuck, dude, Blake and I had gotten tanked that night." His tone turned edgy. "What did you call them? Conflicting statements?"

I nodded without breaking eye contact.

"Besides being drunk off our asses, it was fucking dark along the block where Danning got picked up."

Blake nodded in agreement.

My voice turned skeptical. "Still, you clearly saw Shane Danning."

Blake and Blaine shared a glance. Blaine said, "At the time, we didn't know he's the son of a movie star." He wore a randy grin. "Danning gave us a come hither smile in the Jugs & Mugs Saloon. Then the fucker blew us off. We followed him out, hoping he might change his mind about a three-way."

I looked up from my note taking. "Did either of you talk to Danning that night?"

They told me no in unison.

Blaine grinned. "We didn't need to talk to him. Merely looking at that hot dude turned me and Blake into lusting fuck pigs."

"What the hell's this line of questioning about?" Blake said. "After he was spotted in Laguna, everyone knows Shane Danning's alive and well."

I didn't mention the new development in the Danning case. I did lean closer to Vogel and Walsh. "You thought Danning might have gotten abducted. One of you called 9-1-1. Then you gave the responding officers conflicting statements on almost everything you saw. That bothers the hell out of me. People lie to cops all the time."

Neither Vogel nor Walsh spoke.

"Is there anything you told the responding officers you'd like to amend? Maybe there's something you saw but remembered later," I added.

Blaine shook his head.

"Uh," Blake began, "maybe one thing."

Blaine narrowed his eyes at his partner, but only for a second.

"Go ahead," I urged.

"It hit me the next day, while Blaine and I watched *Fortune and Men's Eyes* on DVD."

Blaine leaned closer to me. "I like the prison shower scene where Rocky rapes Smitty, making him scream and plead like a little girl. Dude, that's nothing but fucking hot. Ever see that movie?"

"I've seen it." I also saw Blake pinch Blaine's glans before stuffing his partner's stiff prick back into his flashy boxers.

Blaine scowled. "That fucking hurt."

Blake frowned and punched his partner hard in the arm. "I meant it to hurt. Quit being a whining little bitch. Anyway, that shower scene made me realize something."

"What's that?"

"Danning didn't yell for help—not even when it looked to me like the bigger man overpowered him." Blake shrugged. "It's all moot, since we know Shane Danning's fine."

I sighed inwardly. *You're going nowhere with these two deuces. It's time to fold.* I stood to leave. "Thanks for your time."

Blake Walsh and Blaine Vogel's eyes met in a silent exchange.

Vogel smirked.

Walsh sneered.

I showed myself out.

Chapter Twenty-Four

A Presence That Wraps Around You

Clint, Tuesday, May 15

While parked at the curb in front of Vogel and Walsh's shell pink bungalow, I called Raoul. I heard the sounds of nail guns and a table saw when he answered.

"So tell me, did you get laid last night?" Raoul said.

"A gentleman never speaks of such things."

Raoul chuckled. "You did!"

I changed the subject. "You're on the path to your first starring role. I can feel it."

"Thanks, but I'm on the path to wondering whether I have what it takes to make it in the film industry." Raoul laughed. "I keep asking myself whether I want to continue chasing what's likely nothing but a pipe dream."

"Don't ever stop chasing your dream. I called to tell you I'm taking your brand-new, high-resolution portfolio to Vona's office."

Raoul thanked me. "You know what they say around here: Carpenter is only another word for a wannabe underwear model."

"Hmm, never thought of that. Maybe—"

"Jenson, for fuck sakes, where's your hard hat and safety glasses?" He returned to our call. "Moose, I gotta have a chat with the new guy before I'm filling out worksite accident reports for the next ten years. I'll see you tonight."

I tossed my phone on the passenger seat and pointed the car toward Century City.

Thanks to the family business, I'd heard all the Hollywood folklore, including the story behind the Western Los Angeles neighborhood called Century City.

After several box office flops, culminating in the millions-over-budget bomb *Cleopatra*, cash-strapped Twentieth Century Fox sold a hundred and eighty acres of studio backlots to a commercial developer. Century City rose from Fox's ashes and offered some of the most costly office space in Southern California.

I turned onto Avenue of the Stars and rolled to a stop in front of a glass tower. A valet greeted me by name as I got out of my car. In the lobby, I stepped into a private elevator that shot me to the top floor.

Designer furnishings and original oil paintings by SoCal artists decorated Steele Productions's reception suite. Kenny, an actor wannabe from Miami, talked into a phone headset as I neared his desk. He winked at me and pointed down a long hall, letting me know that Vona Steele had sequestered herself in her sanctum sanctorum.

Outside of Aunt Vona's closed office doors, her executive assistant, Devin McLean, sat at his desk keyboarding. He'd come to work wearing a light gray suit and a regimental tie. Devin's hair had begun to silver at the temples, but his dark eyes still had a Burt Reynolds gleam in them.

While Dad directed films and played all the Hollywood games and Mom planned, coordinated, and conducted charity events for all the right causes, Devin had been my standby father. He picked me up and hugged me as I did my toddler pratfalls while he babysat me during office hours. He taught me how to swim, ride a bicycle, pitch a baseball, throw a football, shoot hoops, and how to defend myself. He guided me along my adolescent rites of passage leading to adulthood: uncut male hygiene, using a straight-edged razor without shaving my face off, how to knot a neck tie and a bow tie. He gave me driving lessons. He attended my high school graduation. Devin didn't turn judgmental when I told him I liked both genders. He listened. "Then you'll get the best of both worlds," he'd said. A former Marine Corps sergeant, Devin encouraged me when I told him I'd been thinking about applying to West Point.

Devin stood and stepped around his desk, smiling warmly. He and I did a bro hug.

"Great seeing you." He fingered the sleeve of my jacket. "Looks like James Lewis tailoring."

"It is." I looked Devin over from head to toe. "But you're still the one man in this building who always looks as if he stepped off the cover of *GQ*." Devin McLean's physique completed the package.

I grinned at Devin as a muted thump and splat seeped through Vona's office doors. "She's reading screenplays," I said.

"Affirmative." Devin picked up his desk phone and told Vona I wanted to speak with her. He dropped the handset back in its cradle and winked at me. "I suggest entering with due caution."

After a ten-second delay in thumps and splats, I pushed my way into Vona's office. The opening door shoveled the tossed scripts into a pile.

An L-shaped mahogany desk dominated the huge corner office, backdropped by floor-to-ceiling glass offering a spectacular view of the Pacific.

Aunt Vona stood with open arms as I approached. Dark-haired, svelte, and six feet tall, Vona Steele turned heads when she entered a room. But it was her poise that held every Tom, Dick, and Mary's attention.

We hugged and exchanged real, not air, cheek kisses. I took a seat in one of the soft leather chairs fronting the desk. Vona sat several inches higher, enabling her to look down upon her visitors. But being tall myself, that old movie mogul trick didn't work on me.

Vona's eyes met mine. "What's on your mind, Clint?"

I got right on it. "Have you found Peter Remington?"

Vona sighed. "As I've told you more than once, you're the perfect man to play Peter Remington."

I shook my head. "I've watched some of the best and the worst actors at work. I recognized years ago that I fell under the latter category."

"Bullshit," Vona bellowed. She lowered her voice. "You're a talented actor. It comes with being a successful private detective." She frowned. "Why must you be the only person in all of goddammed Baghdad who doesn't want the starring role in a major motion picture."

I smiled. "Appreciate your offer, but I've found the perfect male lead for your Remington project."

The original Peter Remington TV series had been a huge hit in the late fifties and early sixties. Private investigator Remington was a beatnik who spent his time hanging out in coffee houses with his dreamy but dazed girlfriend, smoking doobage, and unwittingly solving crimes. The new Peter Remington would be young, blond, metro hip, and deadly.

I stood, then sat on the edge of Vona's desk. "Look, I know an all-around great actor who's the perfect man to play Peter Remington."

"What's his name?"

I told her.

She pondered the name for several seconds. "I believe I've heard talk of his stagecraft."

"Then do yourself a favor and test Raoul. Del Kendal is his talent agent."

"Are you sleeping with him?"

"With Del Kendal?"

"Don't be a smart-ass."

Ignoring the pejorative, I kept my voice in neutral. "Raoul's a friend. He and I aren't sleeping together. Never have, never will. Even if I were, what's that got to do with anything?"

"You believe this Raoul Martinez, a friend of yours, is perfect for the lead in a multimillion-dollar motion picture. What if I disagree?"

"You told me you wanted a fresh face for the lead. Test Raoul for the part." I shrugged. "If you love him, sign him. If not, wish him luck and send him packing."

I passed a flash drive to Vona. "Take a look at our Peter Remington."

She slid the flash drive into a port and opened a series of stills I'd shot of Raoul. She nodded without speaking.

"Raoul Martinez has the looks and voice for the big screen," I began. "He moves with a masculine, seductive grace that's not affected. Most important, he has the solid acting skills and those ineffable qualities of a star." I sat without uttering another word.

Vona watched my videos of Raoul for almost four minutes—an eternity for producers-directors. She met my eyes. "He's strikingly handsome and sexy." She turned back to the monitor. "You're right. Raoul has presence that wraps around you, and Jesus H Christ, the man can act." She smiled. "You did some great cinematography here, by the way." She fell thoughtful for several seconds. "All right, I'll ask Devin to contact Del Kendal and arrange a screen test."

"You won't regret it," I said.

CHAPTER TWENTY-FIVE

All in One Nasty Package

Clint, North Hollywood, Tuesday, May 15

I drove past the pub several times before spotting the dimly lighted "B ER" neon sign above the door. With its pair of boarded-up windows, the place looked like a crack house closed for repairs.

Spotting Flynn sitting at a corner table, I crossed the pub and slid onto a red tuck and roll booth that could've once been the bench seat from a fifties-era Coupe de Ville (JFGI). The cracked vinyl reeked from decades of accumulated methane that, with a single static spark, might level the entire block.

"Is this shithole someone's idea of Irish shabby chic?"

Flynn scowled. "The owners focus on beer and food, not the goddammed décor. Quit your bitching."

Flynn had ordered drinks before I'd gotten here. A pint of stout awaited me. I peered at a shape in the foam. "Did a cockroach fall off the ceiling and land in my beer?"

"If you'd gotten your ass here on time, you would've seen a lovely carving of a harp in the foam." Flynn shook his head in disgust. "You could get the shit beaten out of both of us traipsing in dressed like a frigging male supermodel. In case it escaped your flighty attention, we got construction workers left and right in here."

"No one in this dump cares a fiddler's flying fart less about my suit and tie." I drank some beer and wiped the foam off my upper lip with the back of my hand, flipping the suds onto the floor. "There, was that gauche-butch enough for you and your construction boys galore, or should I add a rampant belch?"

"Only if you can say the entire alphabet before the end of your belch."

That Flynn, what a tool.

The waitress appeared and rattled off today's special. "We gotta aged eight-ounce beef steak smothered in a lovely brown gravy—comes with garden-fresh peas and fluffy mashed potatoes."

The special being cheap, Flynn ordered it. I asked for the fresh garden salad, no dressing.

Flynn took a pull of beer. "You come waltzing in here dressed to the fucking nines and order a salad. You won't be happy until we gotta fight our way out the fucking door."

"Did you often get beaten up by the neighbor kids when you were a child?" I glanced around and let out a rumbling chuckle. "You only need to follow me to the door, princess. I can hand any guy in here his ass." I turned serious. "Diana Danning received something like a ransom demand around O Dark Hundred hours today."

Flynn leaned toward me. "What the hell d'ya mean by 'something like a ransom demand'? Either it was or it wasn't."

"The male caller demanded five million bucks for Shane's release, but he didn't specify how, when, and where the ransom needed to be delivered."

"Did he say anything else?"

"He warned Diana not to call anyone in law enforcement, or she'd never see her son again." I shrugged. "He said she'd get more instructions later."

"If Danning got kidnapped, it must've happened after he was seen in Laguna. Shit, I'd wager he's still shacked up, and someone's trying to profit off his lark."

I gave Flynn a noncommittal shrug.

The waitress served Flynn his mystery meat, instant mashed potatoes, and canned peas special. My fresh garden salad consisted of wilted iceberg lettuce, one cherry tomato with a gray spot, and a hint of shredded carrot.

I checked the bottom of the salad for insect remains and/or rodent droppings. I found a curly black hair. I shoved the plate aside and sipped some beer.

"You've heard *nada* about a ransom demand."

With his mouth filled with mystery meat, Flynn frowned at me.

"Let's say someone did kidnap Shane," I opened. "When the story gets leaked by a cop, and you know it will, Shane Danning gets dead."

I didn't mention whoever called Diana this morning also threatened my life if the cops or the feds got involved. "Imagine the shitstorm the brass will drop on your head if the missing son of a Hollywood legend is found dead because of some cop's big mouth." I silently counted to five. "If you want me to look into Danning's alleged kidnapping and the ransom demand, let's go balls out—deputize me."

Flynn swallowed his mouthful of meat from an unknown source, sipped some beer, then said, "I'd planned to do that."

Flynn fished through several pockets, pulled out a badge case speckled with lint, and slid it across the table. "You're deputized," he said. "Even though you're official, don't get caught doing anything I got to explain to the brass."

"*Moi?*" I said with mock annoyance.

"Talk with me before you make a move."

"You know I will." I dusted off the badge and pocketed it. I glanced at the bill, stood, and pulled cash off my money clip. "Been real. I'll be in touch."

"Wait a goddammed minute. I got something for you," Flynn said.

"Don't say you got me something like a gift subscription to *Vatican Digest.*"

"Shut your gob and sit down. There's a reason I deputized you that has nothing to do with Danning's alleged kidnapping and half-assed ransom demand."

I dropped back onto the tuck and roll.

Flynn leaned closer and lowered his voice. "Two weeks ago, a twenty-seven-year-old man disappeared. His girlfriend reported him missing."

Flynn had my attention. "What's the missing man's name?"

"Tom Andrews, a pit boss at Mystic Canyon Casino."

"Christ on a crotch rocket, we might have a Tom Andrews–Shane Danning connection."

Flynn cocked an eyebrow. "Do we now."

I told Flynn about Danning's alleged gambling habit.

"And when were you planning to tell me about this?"

"I said he *allegedly* had a habit. I can't verify it. Besides, gambling didn't become relevant until you told me about the missing pit boss. What's Tom Andrews's physical description?"

"Six-two, one hundred and eighty pounds, dark brown, hazel. I got a photo of him. He's a good-looking man."

Flynn passed me a file he'd kept beside him. I opened it and saw the photo of Tom Andrews. I thought him handsome in a self-assured, I'm-too-sexy-for-my-jockstrap sort of way.

I read Flynn's fact sheet on Tom Andrews: military honorable discharge, full-time employment at Mystic Canyon casino, and part-time university student.

I turned the page. Tom Andrews clocked out at 2310 hours on May first. Casino cameras showed him leaving employee parking about five minutes later. Credit card charges indicated Andrews stopped for gas and fast food not far from his house.

I looked at Flynn. "Why did Andrews clock out ten minutes after the end of his shift?"

"What ten minutes?"

"Andrews clocked out at 2310. His shift ended at 2300. Assuming he's a nonexempt wage-earning employee, he likely would've clocked out at 2300, give or take a minute or two."

Flynn shrugged. "How the ever-lovin' hell should I know? Maybe he took a shit, then changed out of his uniform while still on the clock. Maybe he chatted up a working girl at one of the casino's bars, then spent a few minutes in the men's room interfering with himself. You're fretting over nothing."

I shrugged. "Maybe."

"Talk to Andrews's supervisor if those ten minutes bother you."

I shook my head. "You know how secretive casinos are about everything, including personnel matters."

Flynn leaned back on the bench. "Andrews drove home and parked his pickup in the driveway." He held up a hand. "Before you ask, the interior of his house looked neat and orderly. We found no evidence of a forced entry and no apparent burglary. Andrews's luggage and clothing were in the bedroom closet."

I looked directly into Flynn's eyes. "After Andrews parked his pickup, someone must've grabbed him between the driveway and his house."

"That's what it looks like."

"Did any of Andrews's neighbors see or hear anything?"

Flynn looked at me steadily without speaking.

I shook my head in disgust. "What I figured."

If Shane Danning had a gambling habit, it didn't take Columbo (JFGI) to see his potential connection to Tom Andrews. It could be a coincidental link, but private investigators don't believe in coincidence. Except when it is.

But if there was a tie, how in the hell were they linked? One worked for a casino, while the other allegedly spent a lot of time sitting at the poker tables losing his ass. I didn't see a nexus there.

I turned my attention back to Flynn. "We can assume Andrews would have driven away in his pickup had he blown town on his own volition. You mentioned Andrews's girlfriend reported him missing. I take it she's not a suspect."

"She has a strong alibi for the night Andrews disappeared."

I squinted at Hal. "Yeah?"

"She's a registered nurse. On the night Andrews disappeared, she worked from 2300 hours to 1100 hours the following day, verified by her supervisor, coworkers, and the timed notes she wrote in her patients' charts."

The nurse seemed innocent. But how many other girlfriends did Andrews have? His cocky looks suggested he might have been involved with more than one woman, I thought. "Did you speak with Andrews's boss?"

"A couple of Mystic Canyon PD uniforms talked with him. Andrews's boss didn't add anything to what we already knew," Flynn said.

"And you couldn't push Tom Andrews's boss. It's not your case, not your jurisdiction, and you didn't want to step on any of the local cops' toes," I said.

Flynn smiled.

I smiled back, understanding what Flynn hadn't said. I could question anyone, anywhere about anything. The downside being, even though deputized, some people would realize I was out of LAPD jurisdiction and wouldn't hesitate telling me to take a flying fuck at the moon.

"The name and direct line number of Andrews's boss is in the file I gave you."

Tom Andrews's boss was named Jud Tucker. I closed the file. "You and I know men are usually abducted only for ransom, torture, rape and/or murder. Do you think we might have a serial kidnapper, rapist, pathological sadist, and killer rolled into one nasty package?"

"Yes," Flynn said calmly, "we may have such a monster on our hands."

A few minutes later, I unlocked my car and slid behind the wheel. Shane Danning and Tom Andrews's cases looked strikingly similar. Their vehicles were both left behind, no immediate ransom demands, and no apparent reasons for their disappearances. Then we had the potential gambling link—Shane Danning allegedly loved poker too much, and Tom Andrews worked as a pit boss at the largest casino outside of Vegas. But that's only a coincidental link. The real connection appeared to be their kidnappings.

With random serial felons being the hardest to catch, finding connections between the killer's victims could make an arrest far easier. The Tom Andrews–Shane Danning link and the similarities in their disappearances might be our first breaks in both cases.

CHAPTER TWENTY-SIX

Turn Around

Clint, The Flats, Tuesday, May 15

I got home shortly after 1730 hours, pulled off my dress oxfords, and let out a breath. Heathcliff lay curled up and sleeping in the hall table's ceramic bowl—the bowl where I used to drop my wallet, car fob, pocket change, and house key. I scratched behind the big cat's ears. Heathcliff purred without waking.

Ian came charging down the hall, waving a small envelope and yelling, "*Daddy, look what I got!*"

Heathcliff jumped to the floor, then hauled ass to parts unknown, his ears back, his bushy tail straight up and flicking.

I picked Ian up and hugged him. "May I see the envelope, please?"

Ian handed me a birthday party invitation from his friend, Sage Pruitt. "Wow, your first piece of postal service mail. That's cool."

Ian's missing two-front-teeth smile showed such joy that my heart broke a little bit. I hugged him again.

"I wanna go, Daddy."

Stella came down the hall, wildly colored, monster purse in hand. "Ian, make your sentence a request, not a demand, and use proper English."

Stella never cut the boy any slack. She waged a one-woman war to slow the dumbing down of Americans. I loved her for that. But I didn't remind her that she called all refrigerators "Frigidaires," every lunch was "dinner," and every dinner was "supper." She would forever keep her Midwestern figures of speech. I would forever keep my goddammed mouth shut about them.

"May I go to Sage's birthday party, please?"

"That's excellent, Master Steele," Stella said.

"Yes, you may," I said.

Stella finger-combed her hair. "There's a chicken noodle hot dish in the Frigidaire for supper. Put it in the oven at 350 until it bubbles, or in the Radarange for two minutes, stir, and cook for another minute or two."

"Will do," I said. Shit, I'd forgotten that, in the world according to Stella, a casserole was a hot dish, and any microwave oven was the original Amana Radarange.

I checked the time and date of the party. The invitation included a phone number to RSVP. Yes, it seemed a bit pretentious for a little boy's birthday party. But the Pruitts lived in one of the Hills's most affluent neighborhoods. Yes, degrees of privilege exist in them thar hills.

"We need to get Sage a birthday gift," I said.

"Daddy, let's go now," Ian said.

"Let's behave like gentlemen and walk Stella to the door first."

Ian wiggled out of my arms and dropped to the floor, barely missing my socked feet. He grabbed Stella's free hand. "It's time for you to go home."

Stella's eyes met mine. We both grinned. "Men are such pigs," I said.

Stella winked. "It's a peculiarity of the male tribe."

After seeing Stella off, I went upstairs to put on casual clothes, my little shadow following on my heels.

After meeting with Flynn in that shithole pub, my clothing probably reeked of last Friday's fish fry and yesterday's boot socks. My suit went into the dry cleaning bin. I pulled on faded jeans and shrugged into a blue T-shirt, then sat on the edge of my bed to make a call.

With Tom Andrews's file open beside me, I punched in the direct line to Mystic Canyon Casino's security director, Jud Tucker. It being late in the day, I didn't expect Tucker to pick up his desk phone.

"Security," a male voice answered the phone.

"Jud Tucker?"

"Yes."

I identified myself. Then I said, "I'd like to ask a few questions about Tom Andrews."

"Call the Mystic Canyon cops."

He ended the call.

The fuck? Why wouldn't Jud Tucker, the surly bastard, want to offer his assistance in finding the casino's missing pit boss?

I slipped the phone into my hip pocket, smiled at Ian, and gave his face, hands, and clothing a close appraisal before we headed out—still clean. "Ready to go shopping?"

My phone vibrated. Checking the number, I answered the call.

Raoul sounded elated. "I've got a screen test tomorrow morning. Thanks for your help."

"I didn't do much."

"Bullshit, you got my foot inside the door of Steele Productions, something my agent hasn't been able to do over the past five years."

"That's great news," I said. "Ian and I need to make a run to the mall. I'll see you this evening." I almost ended the call before saying, "There's a chicken noodle casserole in the refrigerator for dinner. Warm it up and help yourself."

I dropped my phone onto the bed. Ian lunged for it. I grabbed it first.

Ian roared like a dinosaur and jumped on my back. Both of us laughing, I let him wrestle me to the floor. In a flash, my little boy would be a tween. In a blink, he'd be starting college. Turn around, and he'd be a young man heading out the door to start a life of his own. While I still could, I hugged him and kissed him on the forehead. "Let's go, buddy."

We went to the Beverly Hills mall where every floor had stores bearing designer names. Looking for Prada? It's right here at a store named Prada. Want Diesel jeans? Your ass is covered at the Diesel shop. Looking for Gucci, Armani, Burberry? It's all right here in stores bearing the designers' names; those clever bastards. Want a barista-brewed coffee? There's even a Starbucks here. But where the hell isn't there a Starbucks within pissing distance?

I never step into a mall until I know what I want, where to get it, and whether it's in stock. How the hell did we manage before the days of smartphones? Ian and I made our way to a store called Brand Name Toys & Games. The wily bastards.

A slender, mid-thirties woman with dark auburn hair and deep brown eyes approached us. Her name tag identified her as Shawn. "May I help you gentlemen find something?"

"You're pretty," Ian said.

Ian usually smiled bashfully at women and might say hi while looking at his feet. But I understood his comfort with this stranger. Shawn's hair color matched Sierra's dark auburn to a T. Her svelte build and the way she walked reminded me of Sierra. She and Shawn almost could've been sisters.

Shawn looked amused. "Why, what a handsome charmer you are." She looked from Ian to me and back. "I can see this man's your father. So, where did you get that handsome auburn hair?"

"From my mama. She died."

Following the winds of that dark cloud, Shawn glanced at me. I nodded. She bent and gave Ian a quick hug. "You sweet boy, I'm sorry about your mother, but I can see your father loves you dearly."

Shawn stood and forced a smile. "Would you like to browse, or may I help you find something?"

I told Shawn what I wanted. "It's for a six-year-old boy."

Shawn led us to the radio-controlled model cars. "These are age appropriate."

"Do you think Sage would like a Ferrari?"

Ian nodded enthusiastically. "Daddy, if we bought two cars, me and Sage could race them."

I didn't correct his grammar. Stella did enough of that. I could cut him some slack and spoil him a little too.

"Which one do you want?"

"The Mustang, please."

"Good choice, buddy. That's the one I'd have wanted." He'd picked a 1968 Mustang Shelby GT500. It's a dream car of mine.

"We'll take these two," I told Shawn, and I asked her to gift wrap Sage's red Ferrari.

At the counter, I handed her plastic money. Her warm, slender fingers touched mine as she took my Centurion card.

It had been nothing but a casual touch comparable to a handshake. But I liked it. I liked it a lot. My shameless prick tweaked. And that's only because she reminds you of Sierra, I told myself.

With Sage's gift beautifully wrapped and ribboned, Shawn slid her business card across the counter. "I own the store. If you have questions about these RC model cars, give me a call. I know how every toy I carry works."

I returned my Centurion plastic to my wallet and pulled out my business card, placing it in Shawn's hand. "In case you ever need my assistance."

She read the card and looked up with an expression that flowed from surprise to bemusement. "Thank you, Clint Steele."

I smiled and flirted. "My son's almost right. You go beyond pretty. You're beautiful."

Ian and I left Shawn's toy store. I needed to get my son home to feed him Stella's Frigidaired, Radarangeable chicken noodle hot dish. That, and I wanted to get my half-chubbed prick out the door before someone noticed.

As we got into the car, my phone vibrated. I checked the number. It was the Stop & Save supermarket in Laguna.

"That man I saw with Shane Danning left the store about a minute ago. But he didn't have Danning in tow this time," Larena White, store manager, said. "I don't know if he's important anymore, since everyone knows Shane's alive and doing good."

"That man you saw remains a person of interest." I told Larena White I'd be at her store in about ninety minutes to talk with her.

Then I called Mars Hauser.

Ian and I found Raoul sitting at the kitchen island reviewing his company's latest balance sheet and income statement. "Would you mind keeping an eye on Ian while I make a fast trip to Laguna?"

"Not a problem, Moose. I'm in for the evening."

Ian opened his mall bag. "Look, Daddy got me a Mustang. Wanna play race car with me?"

"You can play after dinner," I said.

Raoul had reheated Stella's chicken noodle hot dish in the oven. Its mushroom-soup haze hung in the air. I spooned some of the casserole onto a plate for Ian and warmed it in the microwave.

I hugged Ian, thanked Raoul, and headed out the door.

CHAPTER TWENTY-SEVEN

Talisman

Clint, Tuesday, May 15

About to turn onto the street, I saw my next-door neighbor, Darla Love, "Astrologer to the Hollywood Stars," running toward me, waving a red scarf. I powered down the window.

"Man," Darla gasped, "I'm glad," she gasped, "I caught you," more gasping, "before twilight."

I asked her why.

Her breathing slowed. "I don't want to freak you out. Well, maybe I need to scare the ever-lovin' shit out of you, man."

"Why's that?" I said, expanding on the "why" theme of our conversation.

"You know Mercury's still in retro. Your horoscope for this evening warns that you're in danger."

"Oh?" I said, but thought, What's new about being in danger? We live in Los Angeles.

"Hold out your hand, man," she said firmly.

I hesitated, uncertain whether she'd drop a tarantula or an asp in my hand.

"Your hand, man," she demanded.

I surrendered my left hand. She placed a circular crystal about the diameter and thickness of a quarter on my palm. I held it up to the westering light and saw shifting flashes of colors like those in a prism, but moving and changing as if it were alive. I looked at Darla. "What is this?"

"It's a talisman. Put it in your pocket, and keep it there tonight."

Again, I hesitated.

She yelled, "*Do it, man.*"

I slid the talisman into my pocket.

"Keep your eyes on the shadows tonight." She headed home, mumbling, "Now I feel better."

Sometimes, an encounter with Darla felt like a trip into Rod Serling's *Twilight Zone* (JFGI). That, or a bad acid trip. I drove away, watching my rearview mirror until I reached the end of the block.

Mars Hauser lives in a multilevel house constructed of glass, steel, and stone located in a Beverly Hills neighborhood of curving streets, tall hedges, black iron gates, exotic backyard gardens, and what Mars calls "a homeowners association run by fucking Nazis."

His was the only dissident voice to be heard at HOA meetings; e.g., "What do you mean I needed to get an architectural modification request form approved before I replaced my central AC unit? I had the same brand of air conditioner installed in the same spot. Take your paperwork, roll it up tightly, and slide it up your ass!" Or one of my other favorites: "Who the hell's whining that I'm hogging all the butterflies and hummingbirds because I grow too many flowering plants that attract them? Someone in here needs to get a full-time job." And so on, and so on.

I rolled to the gates. They opened, Mars slid onto the passenger seat and set his messenger bag on the floor. "Okay, Moose, whom or what do you want me to sketch?"

"I need a sketch of a person of interest in the Danning case."

He lifted one eyebrow. "This sounds serious."

"Serious as antibiotic-resistant syphilis."

We kvetched about the drivers who thought they could get ahead by continually changing lanes in the slow-and-go rush-hour traffic. I finally worked us onto the 5.

"You've got to see my *Epiphyllous Oxypetalum*," Mars said.

"That's the orchid cactus with huge, white flowers."

"Eleven inches long, five wide flowers. They have an incredible scent. The cactus blooms every night around 2400 hours."

"I'd like to see it in all its glory," I said.

"Welp, get your ass over to my place and take a look." Out of left field, Mars asked, "Are you dating anyone?"

"No." I chuckled. I didn't mention my bonk with Diana. It hadn't been what I'd call a date. I saw it as a one-time trick, served with pricy single malt. I said, "How about you?"

"There's been no one for me either. A couple of assignments kept me out of circulation for a while, and April had me tied up in divorce court for six months."

"Remind me: Wasn't April wife number four?"

"Nah, five," Mars said.

I didn't laugh at my best friend's marriage misfortunes. I didn't find schadenfreude amusing. I said ponderously, "Someone suggested I take a walk on the dude side the next time I get married." I didn't mention that Sierra had made the suggestion in Mars's office.

"That's my plan. Women and I don't seem to play house together real well." Mars blurted, "Maybe you and I need to negotiate a big package deal, pun intended."

"We can talk about that." He'd caught me off guard.

But I didn't almost drive past the Stop & Save.

CHAPTER TWENTY-EIGHT

Best Laid Plans

Jud Tucker, Laguna, Tuesday Evening, May 15

"Lookie what we got here," I said aloud as I watched Clint Steele slide from behind the wheel of his car.

I'd watched the trollop behind the customer service counter pick up the phone as I'd pushed my way out the supermarket's door. Steele hadn't wasted time getting here after the manager called and told him she'd seen me again. People behave so fucking predictably, abducting them almost becomes a brainless endeavor. It only takes patience.

"Goddammed motherfucking sonofabitch!" A brick shithouse of a man with one of those queer messenger bags got out of Steele's car on the passenger's side.

I'd planned to take Steele out of circulation tonight. But no fucking way could I subdue in a public parking lot two men with the height, build, and musculature of NFL linebackers. One must always recognize one's limitations.

I started my van, pulled out of the parking lot, and headed home. So much for best laid plans.

People-hunting required tactics, strategies, luck, perseverance, patience, and sometimes, more than one attempt.

And I didn't mind playing games with Steele a while longer.

CHAPTER TWENTY-NINE

Déjà Voodoo

Clint, Laguna, Tuesday Night, May 15

As Mars and I pushed through the doors, I saw Larena White, the Stop & Save's manager, standing behind the customer service counter reading a tabloid. I noticed something new. Larena's hair had gone from flaming red to black. And she'd added black eyeshadow.

Stopping by the shopping carts parked some distance away, I nodded toward her. "So, Hoser, whom does she remind you of? Actor and character's names, movie title, and a line from the film." It was an old game of ours.

Mars discreetly looked at Larena White, turned toward me, and smiled. "She kind of looks like Gloria Swanson as Norma Desmond in *Sunset Boulevard*." He quoted, "I *am* big! It's the pictures that got small!"

We bumped fists.

As we approached the customer service counter, Larena White simultaneously eye-fucked both of us. I thought it kind of impressive in a sad sort of way.

At the counter, I made the introductions and pushed ahead. "Do you have a quiet place where we can work?"

"Surely do, hons," she said with a wink. I expected her false eyelashes to get stuck on the thick layers of eyeliner. They didn't.

Mars and I followed her up a narrow wooden staircase, then into a small office with an Army surplus gray metal desk. Mars opened his messenger bag and pulled out a sketch pad and pencil. I stood behind Larena and watched two experts at work—a keen observer of man flesh and a masterful artist.

Mars had brought books of heads and facial features, but he didn't need to use any of them. In response to his questions, Larena provided the shape of the man's head, then described in detail, his forehead, hairline, brows, eyes, nose, lips, cheeks, chin, and ears. Mars effortlessly sketched the facial features following Larena's precise descriptions of a man she'd only seen twice.

Mars asked about tattoos and scars.

"No ink I could see," Larena said while studying the drawing, "but he has faint acne scars on his cheeks and forehead. I'd guess a plastic surgeon did some sanding, because they're barely noticeable."

Mars added faint acne scars.

"That's awful close, sweetheart." Larena studied the sketch some more. "Try making his nose a little thinner and his bottom lip a tad plumper."

Mars made the changes.

"Lord love a duck, that's him!"

Stepping forward, I glanced at the sketch, then did a double take. The fine hairs on the back of my neck tingled. I'd met this man in my office. He'd called himself Scott Davidson.

I thanked Larena for her help. Mars and I left the store without speaking.

I started the Viper. "Can you scan this sketch and find him on the Web? I need his name."

Mars fastened his belt. "It might take me a little time. I'll tell my computer to sketch him twenty years younger. I'll find him and his name for you." He leaned closer. "Moose, you know we'll always be brothers in arms."

"Always," I repeated.

CHAPTER THIRTY

Chasing Rabbits

Clint, Bakersfield, Wednesday, May 16

This morning, traffic on the 5 moved with a calm, steady grace. It does not happen often anywhere in the City of Angels. I exited onto North 99, accelerated the Viper to eighty, and stayed in the fast lane. Settling back for the drive to Bakersfield, I let my thoughts wander.

Diana had enjoyed our sexual liaison as much as I had, or so we'd let each other know with all our moaning, screaming, and yelling. She'd hoped to recapture a lost love. But other than looks, my father and I had nothing in common.

Christ on a Harley, after learning I'd slept with my deceased father's mistress, not to mention the mother of my half brother, I felt as if I were the main character in a Joyce Carol Oates novel.

I passed a line of eighteen-wheelers. The miles clicked by. The landscape became increasingly flat and bleak.

What about the ransom demand for Shane Danning's release? This twist did not fit the case's known facts. I'd considered what I knew was true about Shane Danning's disappearance, then developed theories that quickly became as useless as spit on a sidewalk.

The solutions to perplexing cases are somewhere in the details, and the obvious answers usually proved correct.

I needed the name of the middle-aged cowboy who'd come to my office, identifying himself as deceased Deputy Scott Davidson before he made an appearance with Shane Danning in the Laguna Stop & Save, then dropped by the supermarket alone early yesterday evening. Whatever his name might be, it didn't take a Rhodes scholar to deduce this middle-aged "dime-store cowboy," as Hope called him, played a part in Shane Danning's disappearance. It was the obvious answer. And probably the correct one.

I was headed to Bakersfield with some questions about Deputy Scott Davidson's suicide. Although it was a long shot, I'd brought Mars's sketch hoping the lead investigator of Deputy Davidson's death might know the dime-store cowboy's name.

I glanced at my empty coffee mug and considered making a stop for a refill at the truck plaza ahead. I barreled past the exit. I swept my right hand over my short hair.

Tuned into a throwback rock channel on satellite radio, I sang along with Jefferson Airplane's Grace Slick.

Glancing to my right, I didn't see Sierra sitting in the passenger's seat, saying, "Stop...my ears...they burn," as she used to do when I'd try to sing. Now that I was sleeping decently, my imagined sightings of Sierra and memory echoes had stopped haunting me.

Goddammit, but Grace Slick could belt out a song.

The miles rolled by.

Eventually, the traffic got heavier and slower. I signaled and changed lanes.

I glanced at the gas gauge.

The GPS babe started mouthing off.

Some tool driving a Fiat cut me off near the first exit to Bakersfield.

The nagging GPS babe told me, "In 1200 feet, take the next right." To shut her the hell up, I didn't miss the turn. I thought her voice acquired a dash of bitchiness whenever she needed to say she was recalculating.

I found a vacant spot in visitor parking.

Most law enforcement officers would sooner get beaten senseless than share information with a private investigator. After all, we civilians were major fuckups in most cops' minds. I'd first turn on the charm with BPD Investigator Larry Roberts.

Roberts kept me cooling my heels in the waiting area for five minutes before showing me to his desk. I sat without flashing my badge to remind him that Captain Flynn deputized me.

A fiftysomething department lifer, Roberts sported a large gut and a big nose webbed with burst capillaries. He smiled like a hyena before it rips out its prey's throat. "Your LAPD buddy, Captain Flynn, asked me to talk with you about Deputy Davidson's suicide. What do you think I can add you don't already know?"

I began by telling Roberts I'd come across the deceased deputy's name while working another case. I pulled a copy of Mars's sketch from my messenger bag and slid it across Roberts's desk. "Do you recognize this man?"

He glanced at the sketch and looked up with a what-the-fuck expression all over his fat face. "I've never seen him before," Roberts said. "What the hell made you think I'd know him?"

"I knew it was a long shot you might know his name. I'm guessing this unidentified man may have been a friend or acquaintance of Deputy Davidson, and may live in or around Bakersfield."

I veered from the sketch and began with the information I'd read in Roberts's death scene report. He answered my questions with either single words, or nods, or headshakes. Roberts wouldn't give me his insights on the investigation, nor any personal comments about fallen deputy Davidson. But I took another run at him.

"Your report didn't mention whether the deputy left a suicide note."

Roberts sneered. "Why the fuck are you asking me about a suicide note? Davidson didn't leave anything at the scene but his body, his gun, a shell casing, and his goddammed old pickup truck." Roberts glared at me. "I didn't think twice about not finding a note. Fact is, I would've thought it fucking strange if Davidson had written one."

I tried to conceal my growing annoyance with this arrogant, condescending sack of shit. Still, disdain edged my voice. "As to the death scene, didn't you find it fucking strange, to use your words, that Deputy Davidson shot himself in the parking lot instead of inside his pickup's cab?"

"It's a waste of my fucking time, and yours too, sonny, sitting here trying to second-guess the whys and why-nots of someone who offed himself." Roberts stood, ending the interview.

I started to leave, then turned around. "I'll ask Captain Flynn to contact your commander if I think of anything else I need answered." I took my leave.

Returning to my car, I headed out of the city for a talk with Francis Valentine Davidson, the deceased deputy's father.

I turned off a county road onto a rutted gravel lane bordered on both sides by weeds. Parking in front of a wood frame farmhouse in need of paint and a couple bundles of roof shingles, I made a wild-assed guess that routine maintenance had gone by the wayside since Deputy Davidson's death.

As I stepped out of my car, a white Samoyed with dark eyes bounded down the porch steps. I didn't freeze in fear of getting bitten. The dog trotted toward me wearing the Sammy smile.

The dog stopped, sat, tilted his head, and sized me up. In a few moments, he began to pant. I whistled. The Samoyed trotted over, allowing me petting, patting, and squeaky-voice talking time. I dropped my hand. The dog barked playfully.

"What's wrong, Lassie?"

The Samoyed whined, then let fly a bark that became a brief howl.

"Oh no, did Timmy fall off the barn roof again?"

The dog barked.

"Shut the fuck up!"

The man's phlegmy voice sounded way past pissed. He opened the screen door and hawked a wad onto the porch. He let the door slam shut. "Who the fuck are you?"

The Samoyed dropped his tail between his legs and cowered beside me. Crouching, I patted the dog's head and neck, noticing that the dirty white fur had silver tips. Beneath his coat, I thought the dog felt underweight.

I stood and badged the old man. "Are you Francis Davidson?"

"Who the fuck wants to know?"

"Clint Steele. Somebody stopped by my office about two weeks ago driving a GMC registered to Scott Davidson. Did you sell your late son's pickup or did somebody steal it?"

"Not that it's any of your frigging business, but yeah, I sold that junk pile after Scott died. I didn't have use for it, or nothin' else of his."

Francis Davidson was as big an asshole in person as he'd been when I called him about two weeks ago. And I found him about as welcoming as that fuckhead Investigator Larry Roberts. Maybe it's something in the water, I thought. I petted the dog's head, then climbed the two steps onto the porch, avoiding the wad of phlegm. "The truck's registration and plates are still in your son's name."

"I signed over the title. I don't give two shits what the buyer did or didn't do after he paid me cash and hauled the pickup outta here."

Davidson turned slightly. I saw a wheel gun in his left hand. A cigarette smoldered between the index and middle fingers of his right hand. He's a southpaw, I thought.

He'd come to the door wearing nothing but boxers. From five feet away, I could smell his body odor coated in one hundred and fifty proof sweat.

I took a step back. "Do you recall the name of the person who bought Scott's GMC?"

"You one of the fuckin' city or county cops?"

"I'm with the LAPD," I said.

He sneered. "You're a little outa your jurisdiction. Get the fuck off my property and stick your nose in someone else's business."

I tried another approach. "I'm not convinced your son shot himself."

Davidson smiled maliciously. "Is that right? How well did you know Scott?"

"I never met your son. Scott's name came up in another matter I'm investigating."

Davidson laughed. "Bullshit! You lie like a cheap fucking rug." He hacked another phlegmy cough but didn't spit this time. "I'd bet you got to know my boy real good after he pulled you over in that flashy car of yours."

Had he suggested his son Scott had been gay or bi? It might explain Investigator Roberts's half-assed investigation of the deputy's death. But in the paramilitary world of law enforcement, Scott would've likely kept his same-sex preference so far back in the closet a cave explorer couldn't have found it. If Scott Davidson had been gay or bi, it would be damned near impossible to verify unless a former lover stepped forward, and that wouldn't likely happen. Davidson's partner, if he had one, probably also worked in law enforcement.

"Give me the name of the person who bought Scott's pickup."

Francis Davidson let out a wheezy breath. "The buyer called himself Ray J. Johnson."

Fuck my luck. If Francis Davidson wasn't lying, the buyer might've taken his alias from the old Ray Jay Johnson shtick (JFGI). He might've as well used John Smith, or John Doe, or Jesus H Christ.

"Before you ask, I don't remember Johnson's address or phone number, if he ever gave them to me." Davidson scratched his balls with the gun's barrel while simultaneously lifting the cigarette to his lips.

This one's a real multitasker, I thought. Bet he can fart and chew gum at the same time too.

"I got paid cash for the truck and didn't ask Johnson no questions."

I held Mars's sketch close to the screen. "Is this the man who bought your son's Jimmy?"

Davidson squinted at the sketch then said, "Never saw him before."

"Thanks for your time." I started to leave. The Samoyed sat with puppy dog eyes at the bottom of the porch. I turned back to Davidson. "When did you last give this dog fresh water and food?"

"If you're worried, take Scott's fuckin' mongrel with you before I shoot him."

I met the old man's rheumy eyes. "You're joking."

"No I ain't," he said.

"You need to know I won't give the dog back if you change your mind."

"Good, I hope the two of you are real happy together."

"What's the dog's name?"

"Never asked Scott, never gave two shits." Davidson closed the door.

I walked behind the Samoyed. A male, I thought. It didn't take Sherlock to guess Scott Davidson would've taken his dog to the vet's office nearest to home. I opened the passenger side door for my newly adopted dog.

I knew the buyer of the GMC had to be the man in the sketch—the same man who'd driven to my office in the old Jimmy and identified himself as Deputy Scott Davidson.

It was the simplest answer. He had to be the same man, no two ways about it.

Francis Davidson lied when he said he didn't know the man in the sketch. Investigator Roberts's flip from gruff to hostile had come after I'd shown him the sketch. What the fuck was that all about?

I wondered if the man in the sketch might have shot Scott Davidson. I said aloud, "That's nothing but conjecture. You met the man who'd bought Davidson's pickup before he dropped by your office ostensibly looking for a full-time job."

I paused again, and said to myself and the dog, "So why the hell did he present himself as Scott Davidson?"

I patted the dog's head. "This case keeps falling deeper into unanswered questions, contradictions, and strange shit."

Chapter Thirty-One

You Know Goddammed Good and Well What You Heard

Clint, The Flats, Wednesday, May 16

I got home from Bakersfield around 1830 hours, carrying a twenty-five-pound bag of kibble and pet supplies, plus a bathed and groomed Samoyed named Sammy.

I'd learned the dog's name from his veterinarian. And I'd learned the name of Sammy's vet the old-fashioned way. I'd looked on the back of the rabies vaccination tag clipped onto Sammy's collar. Yup, that's why I'm the private investigator.

I set the pet supplies in the laundry room, then unlaced and pulled off my boots. My adopted dog sat on his haunches, his tongue lolling and his bushy tail thumping the floor. I bent to pet him and got my cheek licked.

I heard the whine of Ian's radio-controlled Mustang Shelby and the sound of flip-flops coming down the hall. The model car stopped dead. Ian ran in faded jeans, slid on his knees, stopping in front of Sammy. The wonderment in his big blue eyes made me smile. Dogs and children simply go together.

"Do we get to keep him, Daddy?"

"Yes, I adopted him. His name is Sammy."

"He's beautiful." Ian hugged the dog, burying his nose in Sammy's bathed, clipped, and combed fur. "He smells good too."

The challenge was dead ahead, curled up and sleeping in the hall table's ceramic bowl. The meeting of Heathcliff and Sammy started badly. Our big cat lifted his head, looked at the Samoyed, then gave me an offended glare.

Sammy had lived around feral farm cats. I imagined he'd learned to curb his attempts to herd them.

With cool, unblinking eyes, Heathcliff considered the dog with something like the look Barbara Stanwyck gave Fred MacMurray from the top of the staircase in *Double Indemnity* (JFGI). It's a shame Hollywood doesn't make film noir like that anymore, goddammit.

Heathcliff rose from the ceramic bowl and whacked the intruder on his nose. Sammy yelped and jumped back. Having affirmed his alpha male status, his highness yawned and returned to his throne.

Scooping kibble and pouring water into Sammy's new bowls, I didn't need to call him twice. I told Ian to let the dog alone while he ate. I turned and headed for the kitchen.

Raoul had his head in the refrigerator foraging.

"How did the screen test go?"

Raoul grabbed two beers and a plateful of leftover pizza. "Who the hell knows. I got the standard 'We'll be in touch.'" He snickered. "When elephants fly outta my ass."

I imagined the screen test went far better than Raoul knew. After all, I hadn't received an ear-piercing phone call from Aunt Vona for sending her an actor not up to her standards.

Raoul put the pizza in the microwave, sat on the stool beside me, and passed me a beer. "You look like you need at least one of these."

I thanked him and took a long pull of beer. "Did Ian behave after Stella went home?"

"He certainly did. When I get married, I want a dozen children like Ian." Raoul pulled the pizza out of the microwave, grabbed plates, and set one in front of me. "*Mangia, mangia.*"

I ate some pizza and drank some beer. Raoul's comment about getting married and having a dozen children struck me as either a Roman Catholic Church or an LSD flashback.

"Ian once again mentioned he gets to work for me when his, and I quote, 'penis gets big like Daddy's.' What's this fixation all about?"

I told Raoul about the phallic phase of psychosexual development and Ian's natural curiosity about male genitalia. "Not to worry, sometimes a big cigar is only a big cigar." I left it at that.

Raoul turned at the sound of Ian's flip-flops and Sammy's nails on the kitchen's hardwood floor.

"Oh, I adopted a dog," I said.

"No shit," Raoul said, petting the dog. Sammy licked Raoul's chin, then looked at his uneaten pizza crust. He lunged, grabbed, chomped, and swallowed. Raoul laughed and pulled back, dodging a second tongue swipe. "Beautiful dog, but he needs some act-right training."

"Good luck with that. He's a Samoyed." I turned to Ian. "Do you want some pizza?"

"Nuh-uh, Daddy. I had pizza for dinner."

His right hand in a fist, Ian uncurled his fingers, showing me a chunk of kibble.

"Sammy must've thought I was hungry too. He dropped this in front of my feet. Should I eat it so I don't hurt his feelings?"

I sighed inwardly. "No, son, you don't eat dog food."

"Why not?"

"It might make you sick. Throw it in the trash, then go wash your hands, please."

Ian tossed the kibble gift into the trash can under the sink and went to the main floor bathroom to wash his hands.

Raoul chuckled.

I considered having another beer.

Returning to the kitchen, Ian dropped to the floor and petted the dog. "Can Sammy sleep in my room?"

"If he wants to." No doubt about it, Sammy belonged to Ian.

"Awesome! Did you hear that, Sammy?"

The dog licked Ian's cheek.

I pulled a plastic grocery bag from under the sink. "We need to take Sammy for a walk."

The four of us took a twilight stroll. Sammy sniffed and piddled on about every bush, tree, and shrub we passed. A boy must mark his turf.

But I stopped Ian when he started to unzip his jeans. Another thread of the little boy, thinking it's socially acceptable to whip it out on a residential street and take a piss when it's not dark. A short time later, I covered my hand with the plastic bag I'd brought and cleaned up after Sammy.

Ian wrinkled his nose. "Ooh, that's disgusting!"

I tied the bag. "Uh-huh, and cleaning up after your dog will soon become your job." Yeah, right. When Pegasus soars out of my ear.

After about thirty minutes of walking, Sammy quit pulling me as if he were a sled dog mushing across the Yukon. I passed the leash to Ian a few blocks from home.

Back at the ranch, Raoul tousled Ian's hair. He wished us good night and went to his bedroom.

I pointed Ian to the shower. He slipped into bed fifteen minutes later and read about a page aloud before setting his book aside. Sammy had made himself at home at the foot of the bed. I kissed Ian on the forehead and reached for the nightlight.

"We can leave it off, Daddy. Sammy will protect me."

I said good night, petted Sammy, and headed for bed.

In the master bathroom, I brushed and flossed my teeth. And, yes, I didn't see Sierra's face in the mirror. I turned off the lights and went to bed.

It took about two minutes for my eyes to begin drooping. In about another minute, I'd fallen asleep.

Now, some noises can sound like a gunshot—for instance, a backfiring engine or a slammed metal dumpster lid. In a breeze, some types of dried weed pods can sound like the initial, slow warning of a rattlesnake. But when it's the real thing of either of the two, you know goddammed good and well what you heard.

I'd heard the muffled crack of a small caliber gunshot. The sound came from somewhere near the front of my house. I checked the child monitor. Ian slept peacefully, but I saw Sammy pacing the floor beneath the bedroom's windows.

I grabbed my Glock and a high-lumen penlight out of the safe. Yes, if I want a working flashlight, I have to keep one locked away, along with my car fob, keys, sleeping pills, and guns. I pulled on jeans, shrugged into a T-shirt, and went to Ian's bedroom. He'd rolled on his back and was breathing softly. Sammy came to me for a petting, then went back to the foot of Ian's bed. I left Ian's bedroom door ajar.

I tapped on Raoul's bedroom door—no response. I knocked harder, let myself in, and switched on the light. "Wake up, Raoul."

Raoul started awake. "Moose, what's wrong?"

"I heard a gunshot somewhere near the front of the house. I'm going outside to check."

Raoul got out of bed. His white sleep shorts glowed against his tanned skin. We headed downstairs.

I'd told Raoul I wanted tinted one-way glass installed throughout the house while he and his crew remodeled it. I like my privacy. From the bay window, I saw a familiar pickup truck parked at the curb. I said to Raoul, "Don't let anyone in. I'll text you when I'm back in the garage."

I slipped outside through the garage's pedestrian door.

Monterey pines lined one side of my driveway. Tall, perfectly symmetrical, dark green, and thickly needled, they kept me out of sight. Looking around the final tree, I saw Scott Davidson's old GMC parked at the curb. I didn't see lights on in any of the neighboring houses. Christ, had I been the only one in the hood who'd heard that gunshot, or had I imagined it?

Approaching the Jimmy from the rear, I didn't see a shadowy figure in the cab. I crept toward the driver's side door. Both windows were rolled up. Shining the powerful penlight into the cab, I saw Francis Valentine Davidson lying supine on the bench seat.

I wrapped my hand around my T-shirt and opened the driver's side door. The dome light didn't work. The mixed smells of booze, emptied bladder and bowels, blood and gunpowder struck me like a flying drop kick. I stepped back and exhaled.

Holding my breath, I took a closer look. Davidson's eyes didn't react when I pointed the pen light at them. Then I saw the trickle of blood from the bullet hole on the right side of his head. His right hand still held a thirty-eight caliber revolver. I silently closed the pickup's door.

I wondered, suicide or a handgun accident? As much as Francis Davidson drank, the crazy bastard might've pointed the revolver at one of my house's windows, fumbled the weapon, and shot himself. Not likely, but who the hell knew when it came to the mishaps of a dedicated alcoholic.

And who the hell told Francis Davidson where I lived? I kept my home address and landline number unlisted.

Hauling ass back to the garage, I unlocked and entered through the pedestrian door. Phone in hand, I started to call the Beverly Hills PD. Then I stopped. The BHPD wasn't incorporated into Los Angeles and the LAPD. No, the Hills of Beverly had its own police department.

I'd have a lotta 'splainin' to do to the Beverly Hills cops. I could either identify Francis Davidson's body or lie and tell the responding officers I'd never seen the man before and didn't know his name.

If I did tell the truth, the responding officers sure as shit wouldn't shrug off all I knew about Francis and his deceased son. I'd likely spend at least a couple of hours in an interrogation room.

A memory surfaced. About twelve hours ago, I'd seen Francis Davidson holding a gun in his left hand and a cigarette in his right.

Old man Davidson had been a southpaw. He would hold a gun in his predominant hand—his left hand.

But minutes ago, I'd seen a thirty-eight caliber revolver in Davidson's right hand and a bullet hole in the right side of his head. It didn't seem likely Francis Davidson shot himself. More likely, someone else did.

Like son, like father—a pair of identical murders.

My phone showed 0010 hours. Fuck the time. There's one man I knew who could throw some Police Administration Building high jingo (JFGI) at the Beverly Hills gendarmerie and make it stick. Oh, the glory of cop buddies in high places.

Captain Flynn answered on the fourth ring. "Steele, why the hell are you calling me at twelve minutes past fucking midnight? This better be good or I'll shove that badge I gave you so far up your ass you'll be tasting brass for a fucking fortnight."

"Wow, tasting brass for a fortnight; is that like ten days or two weeks?"

"Ahh, Jesus, Mary and Joseph. I'm hanging up."

"Don't get your cop panties in a wad. A couple of weeks ago, a man followed Diana Danning into my office." I told Flynn of my meeting with the stranger who'd lied and called himself Scott Davidson and later drove away in the pickup that was presently parked in front of my house. I told Flynn I didn't know his real name yet. I mentioned the sketch Mars had drawn of the man who'd accompanied Danning to the Laguna supermarket. "I think the face in the sketch belongs to the man who abducted Shane Danning."

"I'm not following you." Flynn's voice turned sardonic. "But since I'm half asleep, you go on without me."

"There's a dead body in that pickup. I think it's a homicide staged to look like a suicide. There's more, but I'll tell you when you get here."

"I'm on my way."

I sent Raoul a text, telling him I'd be waiting by the truck for Captain Flynn. As an afterthought, I told him to go back to bed.

Flynn arrived at the scene, shined an LAPD-officially banned eight-cell Maglite through the GMC's driver's side window, clicked off the flashlight, went to his unmarked car, and radioed the Beverly Hills PD.

I'd barely finished giving Flynn the details on Old Man Francis and Deputy Scott Davidson when a BHPD cruiser rolled to the curb. It disappointed me to see that Beverly Hills cops did not wear Gucci loafers. I let Captain Flynn do all the talking.

Flynn came across like the Police Administration Building brass he was. "Both this GMC pickup and the dead body inside, one Francis Valentine Davidson, are directly linked to an ongoing LAPD investigation of a serial felon. I'm taking this matter off your hands."

And Flynn did.

Chapter Thirty-Two

Do Not Go Gentle

Clint, Steele & Whitman Investigations, Thursday, May 17

I plopped my feet on the edge of my desk, rubbed my eyes, and leaned back in my swivel chair. I couldn't sleep after Captain Flynn convinced the BHPD's homicide commander to turn Francis Davidson's body and the GMC over to the LAPD.

Forcing myself to whip it up, I dropped my feet to the floor and returned to reading the Danning file, hoping to find something I felt certain I'd overlooked. I didn't have a frigging clue what it might be, but I'd know it when I found it. This sounded good in theory.

Two days had gone by since the kidnapper's call. The fact that he had not given Diana his instructions for Shane's release troubled me. Maybe this nameless predator, and I didn't doubt that Captain Flynn and I had such a person on our hands, liked driving home the point that Shane's release would come only on his terms and timeline. Plus he liked fucking with people.

It chilled me to consider what might have happened to Shane Danning since his kidnapping. Repetitive torture and rape seemed likely since his abductor didn't appear to be in a hurry either to let Danning go or to collect his five-million-dollar ransom.

I went back to my case notes. Goddammit, what was it? Maybe I'd heard something and hadn't written it down. I rubbed my eyes and looked up.

Sierra sat in one of the client chairs smiling at me.

I slapped the Danning file shut. "For Christ's sake, Sierra, why am I still seeing you?"

She quoted Dylan Thomas, "Do not go gentle into that good night."

"Rage, rage against the dying of the light," I said.

"I'm so pleased you love to read and got Ian hooked on books too," she said. "You're a modern Renaissance man."

I rubbed my eyes with both palms, then took another look.

No Sierra.

I crossed the room and stretched out on my office sofa. "After pulling an all-nighter, you're taking tomorrow off...unless the kidnapper calls," I said aloud.

I fell asleep in seconds.

CHAPTER THIRTY-THREE

Eye High Kicks

Raoul Martinez, The Flats, Saturday, May 19

A distant sound woke me. I'd worked eighteen hours Friday and planned to sleep in this morning, goddammit. I whacked the alarm's snooze button. The noise continued.

Then I realized the sound came from my cell's "Rock the Casbah" ringtone. That meant my agent, Del Kendal, had gotten around to returning my calls. I reached for the Levi's I'd dropped on the floor last night. I almost did a face plant into the carpet.

Grabbing the phone out of my jeans pocket, I answered with a mumbled, "Yeah, Del." I listened for a couple of minutes. "When and where?"

Thirty minutes later, showered and dressed in a polo shirt and designer jeans with stringy holes that made them especially pricy, I bounded down the stairs, jumping over Heathcliff, who lay sleeping on the bottom riser.

The big cat started awake and glared at me. He kept his distance from my dance steps and eye-high kicks. It's not a gay thing. I'd learned an ass-ton of strange and wondrous stuff at Juilliard.

In the kitchen, I opened the refrigerator and scanned the contents. At once ecstatic and scared spitless, I knew I couldn't eat anything. I sipped a glass of orange juice and checked the time on my iPhone. It was damned near noon. The house's silence reminded me Clint had taken Ian to a birthday party.

Del had warned me not to say anything to anyone until everyone signed on the dotted lines. I saw Del's directive as nothing more than industry superstitious bullshit. In particular, all actors had their own rituals and good luck belief systems; for example, on Hollywood's biggest night, some always put on the same underwear they'd worn when they'd won their first Oscar.

Del told me all about the staged drama of yesterday and this morning's negotiations: flurries of raised voices, sour faces, Khrushchevian tabletop poundings (but with a two-thousand-dollar shoe), offers, counter offers, and threats, culminating in Del declaring, "You're asking my client to give you the fucking moon—we'll talk again in a couple of hours after all of you sober up."

"You had recently tested," Del said. "I knew Vona Steele wanted you badly for her next shoot. Do you know how often you get fast-tracked in Hollyweird?"

I did, but I kept my mouth shut. Otherwise, Del would've carried on for another ten minutes regarding how often fast-tracking does not happen.

Steele Productions's representatives, all of them entertainment lawyers, returned with a proposal that looked like the original offer, but with minuscule adjustments to key percentages, Del told me. But when you considered the number of tickets sold worldwide, minuscule adjustments meant a fargon lotta cash in someone's pocket.

"It might as well land in your pocket," Del said.

"And yours too," I said to reaffirm I wasn't too fucking stupid to live.

Within a couple hours, counter offers for additional adjustments were dropped on the table by each side, with both sides rejecting most of the revisions. But in the industry, bartering and the art of compromise still flourished—until they didn't.

You've finally gotten your shot at a film career, I thought. The starring role in the Peter Remington movie belonged to me. I only needed to sign my name.

I scribbled a note to Clint, letting him know I'd been offered a contract and needed to review it with Del Kendal. Then most of the Kendal agency and I planned to celebrate. I added that I likely wouldn't get home tonight.

I again checked the time. I patted my pocket for the car fob and house key, then headed out for Century City.

CHAPTER THIRTY-FOUR

The Sky's the Limit

Clint, Beverly Hills, Saturday, May 19

Sitting on a bench under the shade of a sycamore, I scanned the Pruitts' three acres of backyard bedlam. I estimated about a hundred children, ages five to seven, accompanied by one or both parents, had come to Sage's birthday bash.

But it did not look like a little boy's birthday celebration. Oh, hell no. Spencer and Joan Pruitt had turned a child's party into a balls-out soiree, a major happening, with clowns, a wizard, pony rides, a children's Ferris wheel, a calliopied merry-go-round with pastel unicorns that probably sneezed Skittles and crapped swag bags, and a junior roller coaster. All the rides were operated by workers who looked like frat boys, not Hell's Angels. Then there was the four-piece boy band, musicians from one of L.A.'s Schools of Rock. And to maintain law and order, I must mention the ten Party Helpers, identifiable by their toothy smiles and muscular or big-boobaged chests stuffed into psychedelic-orange T-shirts. I had to wonder what the hell happened to the dancing elephants and the mime jugglers on unicycles, an obvious oversight on the part of the party planner.

I returned to watching Ian with his birthday buddy, Sage. The two boys stood side by side scrutinizing the wizard's sleights of hand. They laughed, knowing bullshit when they saw it. I thought the wizard sort of resembled W.C. Fields (JFGI) in drag.

"Do you mind if I share your shade, Clint?"

I knew that voice from somewhere. Turning, I saw a young,

blond-haired guy wearing aviators, a second-skin T-shirt, and tight, low-riding jeans.

I recognized him. We'd met almost three weeks ago at the Jugs & Mugs Saloon. I'd been working the Danning case, so I'd declined his invitation to join him for a drink. But I'd given him my business card.

"Dan, join me." I scooted over.

"You remembered my name," he said.

He sat beside me and flashed a smile. The androstanol level of his fresh summer sweat and woodsy cologne nearly threw me into a hormonal overload. And he's way too young, I reminded myself. "What brings you here?"

"Sage is my nephew. His father is my older brother." Dan raised his sunglasses. "I'll ask you the same question."

I pointed. "My son, Ian, and your nephew are best friends forever."

"They're adorable with their arms across each other's shoulders." He grinned and nudged me with his elbow. "Both of them will be breaking hearts in a few years." He paused. "You're married?"

"No, I'm a widower." Before he could offer his condolences, I said, "How old are you? I'd guess nineteen or twenty."

"Thanks for the compliment." Dan chuckled. "I'm thirty, and I recently defended my doctoral dissertation."

His age shocked the shit out of me, but I quickly regrouped. "My wife was barely thirty when she earned her PhD in economics. You're a brand-new doctor of what?"

"Medical laboratory science. I've been recruited to become part of a university consortium for basic and translational cancer immunology research," Dan said.

"Congratulations, sounds fascinating."

For whatever it is you'll be doing, I thought. People with doctorates often spoke in tongues vis-à-vis their areas of expertise. I'd learned not to ask Sierra for detailed explanations. I only became more confused.

Dan removed his sunglasses and gave me a slow once-over. Then his blue-gray eyes met mine. "I kept your business card. I won't mention how many times I came close to calling you."

I smiled. "Close only counts in horseshoes and grenades." I wanted to ask what stopped him from calling. "The birthday boy and my son are making a run for us."

Bouncing on the balls of his feet, Sage chanted, "*Un-cul-Dan, Un-cul-Dan.*"

Dan hugged his nephew and wished him a happy birthday.

"Daddy, Mrs. Pruitt asked if I'd like to spend the night with Sage."

Ian and Sage frequently had sleepovers, either here or at our house. I smiled. "Did Mrs. Pruitt invite you or did you invite yourself?"

Ian shook his head. "I did-ent invite myself."

"Let me talk with Sage's mom."

Seeing Joan Pruitt standing about fifteen feet away, I walked over to talk with her. Dan followed me, placing a hand close to the top of my ass.

Always gracious and never missing a thing, such as the location of Dan's hand, Joan Pruitt said, "I invited Ian. He's never a problem, and our boys play together so well. If you don't mind, he can stay with us through Sunday dinner."

I smiled and nodded my approval. "Thanks."

She grinned. "I'll bring Ian home Sunday evening." She winked at me. "You and Dan can let your hair down."

Dan followed me back to the shade. I liked the smile he wore. He leaned closer. "My sister-in-law believes she's a matchmaker. Got any plans for tonight, Clint Steele?"

"I've been thinking about asking this new doctor if he'd join me for dinner."

Dan grinned. "You're on."

I suggested a restaurant. Dan agreed to meet me there.

As I waited for the party's valet—yes, valet—to bring me my car, my phone vibrated. Raoul had sent a text.

Got the lead! Thnx! Won't be home 2night. 143 buddy! LD

The fact that Vona offered Raoul a contract came as no surprise. With all due modesty, I recognized great talent when I saw it. I sent Raoul a congratulatory text.

Then I went home and spent the afternoon deadheading, watering, and feeding my roses and talking to my orchids. Don't laugh. They sometimes listen.

After I finished all that, I sat poolside with a cold beer in hand. My thoughts veered to Shane Danning's abduction.

I wondered why the kidnapper continued his game of withholding his ransom payment instructions. With each passing day, the odds of Danning escaping or getting to a phone improved.

Maybe Shane's dead, I thought. But that didn't seem likely. Not with five million dollars at stake.

I kept feeling I'd missed something. I drank some beer. Maybe whatever I thought I'd missed stemmed from my overactive imagination; the same imagination that had created my Sierra echoes and hallucinations.

I took another sip of beer. Too many things surrounding the Danning case did not add up, and with no leads, I could only sit around with my thumb up my ass waiting for further instructions from the kidnapper.

But I had an ace up my sleeve: a sketch of the probable kidnapper, who would not remain unidentified for long.

My phone vibrated on the table. I checked the number. "*Que pasa,* Aunt Vona?" I already knew. I held the phone about three inches from my ear.

"You're as brilliant as your father was at spotting the industry's next superstar," Vona boomed.

I returned the phone to my ear. "Let me guess. You loved Raoul and signed him." Again, I held the phone away from my ear.

"What's not to love. Hell yes, I signed him."

When my Aunt Vona became excited or genuinely pissed off, she could out-trumpet a bull elephant. I finished my beer, reached into the cooler, and opened another.

Vona lowered her voice. "Raoul's a talented actor and a paragon of professionalism on the set. He took one look at the test script, then delivered every line flawlessly."

I grinned. "I'm not surprised." I could hear Vona signing documents and flipping pages while she continued singing Raoul's praises.

"No actor I've tested has been better than Raoul in a dramatic scene. No one's sexier, and nobody has better pacing and timing. He'll be the model for the industry's leading men to try to follow."

"That's great to hear."

I knew Raoul hadn't needed to think about what the contract said. He would have signed, even if it had been the worst deal since the Manhattan Island trade. Raoul's dream had come true and nothing else mattered.

"With all the cast members signed, we'll be leaving Los Angeles for Houston Sunday afternoon."

No surprise that; I understood production time and budget constraints. I said good-bye to Vona.

A new star would soon be born. Steele Productions's publicity department had doubtless already swung into action. Wardrobe and hair designers would create a Raoul Martinez look. Once the Peter Remington shoot began, every minute of Raoul's days would be filled. I couldn't have been happier for him.

CHAPTER THIRTY-FIVE

If I Told You, I'd Need to Kill You

Clint, Saturday Night, May 19

Dan got to the restaurant on time. Did I mention loving punctual people? He wore a dress shirt and black slacks that looked damned good on him and made him appear a bit older. But not that much older. I briefly wondered whether I should ask to see his driver's license but decided to keep my mouth shut.

After getting seated at a deck table, the cocktail waitress arrived and took our drink orders. She asked Dan for a photo ID. He sighed, pulled his driver's license, and handed it over. He frowned as he slid it back into his wallet.

"Rejoice in getting carded at thirty," I said. "As with all good things, it won't last forever."

Drinks served, the waiter took our dinner orders. Dan went for the surf and turf. I asked for grilled sea bass with parsley and lemon sauce.

Physically, Dan had a great deal going for him: blue-gray eyes, blond boy-next-door good looks, a nice smile, and a pleasant voice.

We talked in a balanced back and forth. Without giving him names, I could speak of my work as a private eye. Other than mentioning I'd been with Special Forces in the military, I could not say anything about my Delta missions. That was probably best for Dan. I didn't think he'd appreciate Delta's "Go hard or go home" maxim.

Our dinners were served. As we ate, Dan told me about the research he'd soon be conducting and explained it all in English for dummies. I thought it a sure bet his IQ went off the freaking charts.

I realized there was some chemistry between us, but our attraction was only physical. Doc Grant Stenton had recommended that I get back into the swing of life. But when it came to Dan, I knew I'd gotten on the wrong swing.

Before we'd finished eating, we'd run out of things to talk about. Dan began glancing at men seated nearby. His wandering eyes didn't surprise me. After all, he'd swooped down on me like an eagle to prey the moment I walked into the Jugs & Mugs Saloon to interview the bar's owner. It seemed a safe guess that Dan preferred quick, NSA, fuck-and-run liaisons. I did not.

"Mind if I join you?"

I'd know that voice anywhere. Mars Hauser stood beside me with a drink in one of his paws. Without waiting for an answer, he pulled out a chair and sat down beside me. As is the case with many if not most mad scientist cybertech nerds, Mars sometimes behaved a bit backward in matters of social propriety. I didn't mind.

He'd removed his contacts, opting for black-framed hipster glasses that accentuated his dark brown eyes and curly blond hair— an uncommon color combination that had captured my attention the moment we'd met in our barracks.

I made the introductions. "Mars and I were West Point roommates."

"Oh, you both attended the U.S. Military Academy."

Dan's condescending tone annoyed me. He might as well have said we had trade school written all over our chiseled faces.

"Yes, the U.S. Military Academy, also known as West Point... honor, duty, country, and all that shit." Admittedly, sarcasm is not one of my strongest suits.

"When it comes to colleges and universities, the Point is more selective than most Ivy League schools regarding standards of academic excellence and physical fitness," I told Danny Boy.

Mars chuckled and heightened the sarcasm. "Instead of 'Duty, Honor, Country,' the Point's motto should be changed to 'There's the right way, the wrong way, and the Army's way. Get used to it.'"

"Or this Army gem, 'If you're not the lead dog, you're merely sniffing the lead dog's ass.'"

"I always liked that one," Mars said laughing, "Here's another, 'Drop your cocks and grab your socks!'"

Dan didn't bother to smile.

"Will you be a high school senior or college freshman this fall?" Mars asked Dan.

Dan stiffened. "I'm afraid you're wrong on both counts. I've earned my doctorate."

"Oh wow, I get it. You're a *wunderkind* who earned his doctorate at seventeen or eighteen. That's damned impressive." He looked at Dan's empty cocktail glass. "May I get you another Shirley Temple?"

"I'm thirty," Dan snapped. "Given your build, you must be either a physical education teacher and coach, or the owner of a gym, or a personal trainer."

"Wrong on all counts," Mars said. "I do contract work for Uncle Sugar."

Dan appeared stunned. "Are you saying you're a hit man for mob boss Sucrolosi? Isn't his moniker Uncle Sugar?"

Mars's mouth quirked. One snort became a chuckle, lifting to gales of laughter.

I smiled at Dan's ignorance of common figures of speech. It happens when you spend too many years behind ivy-covered walls, separated from the facts and practicalities of the real world.

"The mob boss you're thinking of goes by the moniker Sugar Daddy and not Uncle Sugar," I said.

Mars stopped laughing, removed his metro-hip glasses, and wiped his eyes with the backs of his hands. "I'm not a mob hit man. I resolve security issues under contracts with seventeen federal agencies."

Mars had given his standard answer to questions about his occupation. Many people assumed CIA spook and either moved away from him or changed the topic. But did Dan? Oh, fuck no.

"So, what do you do for these unnamed agencies?" Dan grinned. "Oh wait, you can't tell me."

"Yes, honey, if I told you—"

"You'd need to kill me," Dan finished.

Mars looked at him sternly. "No, what I started to say was, if I were to tell you some secrets, you wouldn't have a fucking clue what I told you." He grinned. "*Then* I'd need to kill you."

We fell silent.

Finally, Dan glanced at his watch. "I need to hit some clubs. There may be a few endowed tops left." He started to pull cash out of his wallet.

"Put your money away. I'm buying dinner."

Dan forced a smile. "Thanks, Clint. Maybe I'll call you one of these nights."

Mars and I watched him walk away.

"He's goddamned cute in a jailbait sorta way," Mars said. "Oh wow, Moose, did I cock block you?"

"No, Dan and I have nothing in common." I watched his face. "Hoser, you jerk, did you follow me here?"

Mars smiled shyly and shrugged. "What, you don't believe in chance meetings?"

"Only when they are chance meetings." I looked Mars straight in the eyes. "You couldn't have tailed me. I would have spotted you."

"I know, it's what makes you the private investigator." Mars chuckled. "What difference does it make? It could be a chance meeting or not."

"True that."

I watched Mars check the time. As long as I've known him, he's worn the face of his watch under his wrist. Hell if I know why. Some people, particularly nerds, adopt strange habits.

He leaned closer to me. "Can Ian's sitter stay with him a while longer?"

"Ian's having a sleepover at his best friend's house. I've all night. Why?"

"In about an hour, my *Epiphyllous Oxypetalum* will go into full tilt, balls-out bloom. Want to drop by my house and take a look? I made a cutting of the cactus orchid for you that's ready for planting."

Mars neither wanted nor expected me to say thanks. It's a gardener's superstition that if you express your gratitude for plants, seeds, or cutting, they won't grow.

I dumped cash on the table. "I'll follow you to your house."

CHAPTER THIRTY-SIX

Lost Somehow Somewhere Sometime Along the Way

Clint, Beverly Hills, Sunday, May 20

I woke in a strange bed. Opening both eyes wide, I saw Mars's tabby, Miss Smoochies, staring at me. The set of the cat's lower jaw gave her a continuously pissed-off look. She began to purr...with her ears folded back.

I groaned. "Jesus H, only Mars would adopt a schizophrenic kitten from the shelter."

Miss Smoochies hissed at me, jumped off the bed, and shagged ass out the bedroom's open door.

I sat up and scanned the room for my clothes. My head hurt no matter which way I turned it. My day hadn't started with a hangover since the morning after Sierra's funeral.

Then I noticed the rumpled linens on the other side of the California king–sized mattress. Getting down on my hands and knees, I looked under the bed for my jeans.

"What pleasant sights to behold first thing in the morning— broad shoulders, narrow waist, and a high, muscular ass in tight black skivvies. Is it my birthday?" Mars added, "If you're looking for your clothes, I washed them. They're in the dryer."

Wearing red sleep shorts, Mars crossed the bedroom in his bare feet and set two mugs of coffee, a bottle of water, and aspirin on the nightstand.

"Thanks, buddy." Sitting on the floor, I swallowed four aspirin with water and a java chaser. I closed my eyes. "Did we sleep together last night?"

"Yeah, what about it."

"So, do I still have my honor?"

He sipped some coffee. "Well, the closest to anything sexual happening in here last night involved me getting your drunken ass undressed down to your skivvies. Then I fell asleep on the other side of the bed."

"You crawled into bed with me last night?"

Mars exhaled a laugh. "Christ, you're sounding like a scandalized Victorian queen." He said in an unmanly squeal, "Ooh, don't touch me weenie! Ooh, leave me nethers alone, you bloody brute!"

"We are not amused," I said.

He grinned. "Moose, we used to sleep closer in our barracks bunks than we did in this bed last night."

"We did," I allowed. Then I sipped some more coffee.

"I guess you don't hit the bottle much anymore. After you drank about a pint of scotch last night, I needed to fireman carry you into the house and up the stairs."

"As if I never did the same for you back in the day." Still sitting on the floor, I closed my eyes. A high-speed rerun of last night began to play.

Mars had given me a walking tour of this season's backyard ornamentals, ferns, and colorful flower beds. His *Epiphyllous Oxypetalum* cactus orchid stood almost six feet high and five feet across in a remarkable display of large white blooms with an exotic scent. I waited for the damned thing to start demanding, "Feeed me!" (*The Little Shop of Horrors*, 1960, JFGI.)

Then Mars and I sat on a bench in his backyard gardens talking in our customary ebb and flow. One after another, old memories resurfaced. We laughed, drank, and reminisced some more.

After a while, Mars looked at me with his big, dark-brown, puppy-dog eyes. "We'd planned to build a life together after we graduated and completed our military service. Moose, what the fuck happened?"

"I guess life happened." I started slurring my words. "You went milit'ry intel, I went Delta. We mustered out and open'd our own businesses. You got married first, then so did I. My wife died, and your chain of five wives each d'vorced your crazy ass." I forced a smile. "*Sic volvere Parcas.*"

"So spin the Fates," Mars translated.

I'd sipped some more scotch. The colors and lights in the nearest flower bed began to shimmer and warp. I could no longer hear the nearby fountain.

Mars had fallen silent for a while, finally asking, "Do you think we could recapture what we had back when you and I were young men?"

I yawned loud and long; then I slurred, "Recap'ure? Wha' the fuck makes you think we set anythin' free?" I forced myself to concentrate on what I was saying. "But we can't 'splore what we both feel tonigh', Hoser. Think I'm a li'l drunk." I'd sort of snapped my fingers. "Like they say, if you love somebody, fuckin' let 'im go."

"And if he doesn't come back to you, hunt him down and kill him," Mars completed the quip.

"Yeah, tha's it."

Then I'd passed out—my head landing in Mars's lap.

I'd gotten way past shitfaced last night. But this morning, I was undeniably sober.

"With both of us sporting wood that Miss Smoochies couldn't scratch, we don't need to confess our wants. But you and I need to have the talk," I said.

"Talk about what?"

The nerdy mad scientist of the cyber-tech world sometimes turned a little dense when it came to simple matters. "For shit sakes, Hoser, when did you last get tested?"

Mars winked at me. "Oh, that. I get tested every six months. I'm always negative. And I haven't had sex with anyone in over a year, except for the protected dockings you gave me and the big toys I've been practicing with."

"Negative and unlaid for a little over two years, except for our aforementioned poolside dockings. I also get tested every six months. The results are always negative." I smiled. "Throughout my life, I've had unprotected sex with only two people—you then Sierra."

The friendship, respect, admiration and love Mars and I'd shared as young men may have been set aside, but never forgotten. A decade later, we were older and a lot wiser. We now understood not to turn our backs on the few good things that come into our lives.

By 0930 hours, Mars and I had begun recapturing things we'd somehow lost somewhere sometime along the way.

All we'd shared years ago returned without a hitch. And nothing outside these four walls mattered.

Until around 1300 hours when my phone vibrated on the nightstand. I recognized the Pruitts' number.

"I'm afraid our boys got into an argument after Sage's model car collided with Ian's and knocked it into the pool. Ian's still crying and wants to come home."

"Tell Ian I'll be there in half an hour." I ended the call before she could ask how my date went with Dan, her man-whore brother-in-law.

I told Mars I needed a shower.

"I'll get your clothes out of the dryer. You'll find a new toothbrush in the vanity's right middle drawer." He nudged me. "Put it in the holder for next time."

I was showered and dressed minutes later. "I've got to go. Do you want to drop by my house for dinner this evening?"

"I'd love to, but I've an appointment with duty, honor, and country tonight." He grinned. "I'll be busy transferring several hundred million dollars American from Vlad's offshore accounts into Uncle Sugar's coffers." He shrugged. "That's only a down payment for his fucking with our democracy."

He might be joking, but probably not, I thought. Snagging my fob, phone, and wallet off the nightstand, I tapped Mars on the ass, then headed out for the Pruitt manse.

I thanked Joan Pruitt for letting Ian stay overnight, mentioned that Dan and I had a great dinner, and hustled my son to the car, his Mustang Shelby drained of pool water but still not working.

I took Ian to a toy store specializing in drones. We spent over an hour perusing the shelves, having father and son talks about the model aircraft. Ian chose a Black Hawk helicopter. Knowing he could handle a toy intended for someone two to three times his age, I didn't utter a word. I pulled my black plastic out at the register.

We got home in time to catch Raoul with his bags packed, waiting for his limo ride to the airport.

"Ian and I will miss you," I said to Raoul. "Now, get to Houston and break a leg on the shoot."

"Thanks, I owe it all to you."

"You don't owe me anything. You'd have gotten into films sooner than later."

But Raoul and I knew success in any of the industries never came to most people who'd come to L.A. to get discovered. Talent and looks weren't enough. You had to know the right people.

Raoul got a text. His ride was at the curb. He hugged Ian and me good-bye.

We watched as Raoul slid onto the back seat of a Steele Productions limo bound for LAX. In about ninety minutes, a Houston-bound jet would be wheels up.

The house felt empty without Raoul's smile, laugh, and laid-back ways. I hoped his new career would be everything he'd dreamed and more.

I held Ian as he began to cry over losing another person he loved. "Raoul will be back to L.A. before you know it."

"You promise, Daddy?"

I hugged Ian a little tighter. "I promise, son. I'll miss Raoul too."

But I had Mars. Nature's abhorrence of vacuums had finally caught up with me.

CHAPTER THIRTY-SEVEN

Nerds Love Free Food

Clint, Steele & Whitman Investigations, Monday, May 21

I got to the office after my morning session with Doc Stenton. My mild depression clouds had lifted, letting in the sunlight.

Then yesterday, Mars and I'd confirmed the sparks we'd felt as young men still crackled. I felt centered and at peace with myself. Life was great again.

I went to my desk carrying a fresh cup of coffee, sat, and opened the Danning file. Without a word from the kidnapper, the case remained at a standstill. I knew it was a waste of time worrying about things I could not change. But I wanted to find my half brother, goddammit.

Hope and I had other cases needing our attention. We did a great deal of business with law firms. Before stepping into a courtroom, an attorney needed everything his or her client claimed as an honest-to-God fact verified. Seeking light and truth had become a major source of revenue for Steele & Whitman Investigations.

I began the workday Skyping with one lawyer's client who'd been released on bail but placed under house arrest with an ankle monitor. Charged with burglarizing a Hancock Park mansion, she came across as polite, charismatic, and fascinating as only a second-story cat burglar can be—make that an *alleged* second-story cat burglar. I saw the Rodeo Drive casuals she wore and made note of the daylight diamonds in her ears and around one wrist—maybe filched out of someone's gem safe, maybe not.

Looking at her, I didn't see an accused felon. Oh, hell no, I saw a fit, petite, be-still-my-foolish-dick, dulcet-toned beautiful woman. I wondered if she offered apprenticeships.

I spent an hour asking her a series of the same questions, each worded five or six different ways like the Minnesota Multiphasic Personality Inventory exam. Her story didn't vary in the slightest. Maybe she's innocent, I thought.

Her next test would be a face-to-face, come-to-Jesus interrogation with Hope Whitman. Nobody successfully bullshitted Hope for long.

I'd emailed my Skype interview notes to Hope when my phone chimed. Mars was texting me.

Busy?

Taking a breather. Don't you have a dirty trick or two to pull on some enemy of the United States?

Recently finished fucking up a rebel leader. And it was fun too. Right now, I'm preoccupied with twitching and squirming from yesterday's horizontal mambo marathon, thank you.

But you love it!

You bet my ass. But I'm texting you because I've found nine men who resemble my sketch; probabilities of a match run from fifty to ninety-three percent. Want me to email or drop by with the photos and names of these nine hits?

Thanks, buddy. Bring what you found to my house, dinner tonight 1800 hours.

Nerds luv free food. Want me to bring anything?

Trunks.

???

Sorry, I must've slipped into writing Swahili again. Bring swimwear: manties/box trunks/Speedo for diving, swimming, getting all wet, etcetera, etcetera.

K.

BTW, it's a black tie dinner.

K. LD!

Mars missed my black tie joke. He'd probably been multitasking again, maybe giving a squad of armed insurgents instructions on how to build a pipe bomb and safely wire it to the electrical system of the dictator's Mercedes.

CHAPTER THIRTY-EIGHT

Unmasked

Clint, The Flats, Monday, May 21

Home at 1730 hours, I unlaced and pulled off my shoes. Ian's Black Hawk helicopter raced toward me, then hovered about four feet above my head. Chasing it, Sammy stopped short and barked at the drone. I petted the dog. Ian landed the Black Hawk.

"Thanks, Daddy! This Black Hawk's awesome!"

I knelt in front of him. "You're welcome, son. That was some fancy flying. And you taught yourself how to do it. I'm proud of you."

"Piece of cake, Daddy. I only needed to read the instructions."

"While ignoring this morning's American history lesson," Stella narked, carrying today's huge, blindingly colorful granny purse.

"You can't waste Stella's time, son. You only have one hour of lessons weekdays in the summertime."

"But, Daddy, history sucks!"

"Language! You *will* focus on your lessons. Don't make me ground you and your Black Hawk for a week."

"Sorry, Daddy. Sorry, Stella."

I walked Stella to the door with the Black Hawk following us like a monster dragonfly. I watched her make her customary breakneck U-turn, then slowly drive toward the street. Closing the door, I told Ian to land the Black Hawk.

"Why?"

"Your uncle is coming for dinner," I said.

"Uncle Martian!"

I went upstairs to get out of my suit and into something casual. Ian returned to playing with his Black Hawk.

Standing poolside minutes later, I fired up the grill. Mars arrived dressed in a long-sleeved tee that looked like a white-shirted, black tux with painted-on cuff links and bow tie. He'd accessorized the get-up with black shorts and black flip-flops—the funky synthetic rubber kind. He looked like a dork. I shook my head and laughed.

"You said black tie." He set his messenger bag on the glass-topped table, petted Sammy, and sat down.

The Black Hawk hovered low enough over Mars's head to ruffle his blond curls.

I sighed inwardly. "Ian, please stop doing that."

He landed the chopper poolside.

Mars raised his eyebrows. "Wow, man, I bet flying that drone is fun." He hugged Ian. "Hey, Booboo, may I see the remote?"

Ian held the remote tightly to his chest with both hands. "Do you know how to fly a Black Hawk?"

"Dude, I flew Black Hawks before you were a gleam in your parents' eyes."

"Daddy, what does that mean?"

"It means Mars flew helicopters before you were born." I left it at that.

Ian forked over the remote. "All right, Uncle Martian, show me what you can do."

I sat down to watch the children play.

"Captain Booboo, Capitol Hill miniature zombies have invaded the pool. I've got the fifty caliber bubble gun locked and loaded."

Mars flew the Black Hawk low across the pool, making staccato machine gun sounds. "Bubble encapsulated Capitol Hill mini zombies now blowing back toward DC. Mission accomplished."

"There's no such thing as zombies. Daddy said so."

Mars landed the Black Hawk. "Your daddy's right." He said under his breath, "Except for the far-right congressional automatons." He opened his messenger bag, pulled out a file, and slid it toward me. "Take a look."

I studied the first eight photos that resembled the dime-store cowboy, the likeness of him increasing slightly with every picture. The ninth was a college graduation class shot. I studied an at-least-twenty-years-younger dime-store cowboy in the top row, third from the left. With Ian standing beside me, I caught myself, and said, "Sonof a—gun. What's this man's name?"

Mars smiled. "Third man from the left, top row is one C. Judson

Tucker. He goes by Jud. He earned a BS in fire science and is a licensed paramedic. Jud worked a number of years as an LAFD fire fighter and EMT."

"And he's presently the security director at Mystic Canyon Casino," I said.

"Affirmative," Mars said.

"Do we know what the 'C' stands for?"

"I couldn't find any references to the 'C,'" Mars began. "Did you ever know what the 'F' stood for in F. Scott Fitzgerald?"

"His full name was Francis Scott Key Fitzgerald," I said. Needing to think for a few moments, I got up and put dinner on the grill.

I now had a link between Jud Tucker, Tom Andrews, and possibly Shane Danning. This gave me something to work with. At the moment, I had fuck all under the evidentiary column, but with some digging and a lot of luck in working the Danning-Andrews-Tucker angles, I might gather enough evidence that would snowball beyond circumstantial straight into compelling. It sounded good in theory.

Jud Tucker had met with me in my office. I knew getting a face-to-face meeting with him at Mystic Canyon Casino wouldn't happen unless I caught him with his guard down. As he was the casino's security director, catching him unawares didn't seem likely either.

I'd need to dig until I got enough solid evidence to get an arrest warrant. And digging for evidence I could do.

I took the steaks, burgers, and corn on the cob off the grill. As we ate, Ian didn't ask embarrassing questions and avoided making a when-my-penis-gets-big comment. Could he be growing out of his phallic phase of psychosexual development? I wouldn't hold my breath. Bottom line, we had a leisurely, relaxing, and fun dinner.

Later, Mars and I sat on the pool's coving, dangling our legs in eighty-degree water and drinking beer. I checked the child monitor I'd set on the glass-topped table. Ian remained sound asleep with Sammy curled up at the foot of the bed.

"I know you don't mind if I ask a personal question," Mars said.

"Hoser, not asking each other meddlesome questions ended about an hour after we met at the Point."

"Roger that. Did the cops think you murdered your parents?"

Home invaders had murdered my parents and their dinner guests about six months after Mars and I graduated West Point. He went to work for military intelligence, and I went into Special Forces training. Both Mars and I had worked under radio silence for years.

"You know spouses, significant others, immediate family members, and friends always top the list of suspects in homicide investigations. Plus, I inherited forty-nine percent of Steele Productions's stock. But I had an airtight alibi: I was in Afghanistan on the night of the murders. And that only motivated the investigators to dig deeper into my financial records to determine whether I might've outsourced the murders."

"And they found no suspicious cash withdrawals or transfers."

"They found nothing." I sipped some more beer. "When I flew home to bury my parents, two LAPD homicide investigators were waiting for me in the terminal. They drove me to the Laurel Canyon house where I'd lived for most of my life."

I sipped some more beer. "One of the investigators told me bloody shoeprints at the scene indicated there were four male home invaders. The other investigator said the robbery and murders came off with military precision. I told the investigators if that was the case, neither bloody shoeprints nor other forensics would've been found at the scene."

"Bet that insight was not well-received."

"Roger that. Anyway, one of the investigators said a plastic explosive blew the lock on the rear door. The invaders rushed the dining room, tied, gagged, robbed, and shot my parents' guests. The investigators surmised while one of them forced my parents upstairs, the other three invaders ransacked the lower floor. Everything had been taken from the safe, probably opened with a gun held either to my father or mother's head." I looked into the distance. "After I buried my parents, I put the Laurel Canyon house on the market. I didn't want to spend another minute in it." I let out a breath. "It sold quickly."

"Did the LAPD get assistance from the feds?"

"The FBI and the LAPD collaborated." I sipped some more beer. "As I mentioned, bloody shoeprints and other forensics found at the scene indicated there were four male home invaders; fingerprints identified three of them. Investigators think one of the invaders murdered the other three. That's likely the case, but their bodies haven't been found."

"Yes, I'd heard that much," Mars said.

"After ten years, the name of the fourth home invader remains a mystery." I nudged Mars. "Armed with a sniper rifle and scope, I'm a stainless assassin. Maybe one day I'll close the case for the LAPD."

"You didn't represent the Point at international marksman

competitions four years running because you're handsome and pack a huge rod," Mars said.

"Thanks, Hoser." I smiled. "Let's spend the night together."

"Here?"

"No, at my next-door neighbor's house." I grinned. "Yes, here. In my bed, bare-assed."

"I'm a boy who can't say no," he whispered in my ear.

CHAPTER THIRTY-NINE

O Dark Hundred

Clint, Tuesday, May 22

My bedside phone rang. Jarred awake, I checked the time. It was another unlisted O Dark Hundred call. Not wanting to awaken Mars, I lifted the handset on the first ring and stepped into the hall.

I didn't speak.

"Clinton Steele?"

The distorted male voice grabbed my attention. "This is he."

Thanks to Mars's sketch and a web search, I had a good idea the O Dark Hundred caller was C. Judson "Jud" Tucker. But I played dumb. "Who is this?"

"My name isn't relevant. All you need to do is shut the fuck up and listen carefully."

"I'm listening."

"I've been whipping Shane Danning. He's still alive, but he may not be much longer."

"You don't need to torture him. Diana and I've been waiting for your instructions," I said angrily.

"But I enjoy making him suffer. The stupid fucker's half-assed escape attempt killed Tom Andrews."

The call being digitally recorded, I now had evidence of a Danning-Andrews-Tucker connection.

Tucker's voice turned taunting. "I could get a wild hair up my ass and toss the world-famous Danning slut's only son into the hog pen." He let out a soft laugh. "Did you know once domesticated swine taste human flesh and blood, they become as unpredictable and dangerous as wild boars?"

If he hadn't handed me a line of bullshit, Jud Tucker owned a farm or ranch. "I've listened long enough. What the fuck do you want?"

"To pass along some information. Twenty minutes ago, I gave Diana Danning instructions for wiring five million dollars into an offshore account. When I know the cash has been deposited and the feds haven't gotten on the money trail, I'll turn pretty boy Shane over to you, but only to you."

"All right," I said. Then I listened for background noise. I only heard the low buzz of the electronic distortion. But with the call being recorded, Hope could use a slower playback speed that might isolate sounds I couldn't hear. More important, she could filter out the distortion that disguised Tucker's voice.

"When I've moved the five million dollars into accounts that can't be found by anyone, you and I will talk. If I get as much as a fucking feeling anyone has called the cops or feds, no one will ever find Shane Danning's body...or yours."

"Understood," I said.

"I've ordered Diana not to speak to you or anyone in law enforcement. She's going to follow my instructions to the letter, and you'd better be on the same page. I'll call you tomorrow morning and give you the rest of your orders."

Jud Tucker ended the call.

A thought had been niggling me. Sometimes the key to a crime didn't hide behind the victim, but could be found in the character of a family member or friend. I went downstairs to the den.

I did a JFGI, read, and leaned back in my desk chair. On April twenty-seventh, two days after Shane's abduction, the *L.A. Times* ran a postage stamp-sized story on the burglary of Diana Danning's Birds Neighborhood manse. The article didn't specify what had been stolen or its value. The matter remained under investigation.

Diana had given me an evasive answer when I'd asked if anything out of the ordinary had happened to her during the past few weeks.

I had questions about the burglary. Diana would follow Jud Tucker's orders and would not talk to me.

But it's always good to have friends in high places.

Next, I called Mystic Canyon Casino and asked for Jud Tucker's office. My call was transferred, and after six rings, a woman answered in a blasé tone, "Security."

"I don't suppose Mr. Tucker is at his desk," I said.

"He has the next two days off. I'm his assistant director. May I help you?"

"No, thanks. I've a personal matter to discuss with Tucker. May I have his voicemail?"

She transferred my call.

Moments later, I heard the man. Hope and I now had a digital recording of Tucker's voice to compare with the O Dark Hundred caller's. I hung up.

CHAPTER FORTY

Twenty-Four Hours

Clint, Steele & Whitman Investigations, Tuesday, May 22

As I entered the office, Hope scowled and yanked out her ear buds. I stood at parade rest beside her desk, and said, "What crawled up your rear end this morning?"

Hope pulled the pencil out of her bouffant and examined the lead. "If this dime-store cowboy Jud Tucker thinks he disguised his voice with his electronic junk, he needs to bang a Louie back to the toy store and demand a refund."

Translation bang a Louie: Make a U-turn.

I arched my brows.

Hope pushed her pencil into the electric sharpener she kept on her paperless desk. "I removed the distortion from last night's call faster than spoiled lutefisk through a short Norwegian, as Stella would put it. I also copied Jud Tucker's office voice mail recording, as you asked."

"And the voices matched."

"A perfect match at that."

"Making it easy to remove the distortion must be more of Jud Tucker's game playing," I said.

"So it seems," Hope said. "You can listen to the two voices side by each on your PC."

"I'm expecting another call from Tucker sometime this morning. Is my desk phone still wired?"

She sighed. "Your conversation will be recorded. Christ, do you think I'm about as handy as a hog winding a wristwatch?"

"I'm only checking." I took a cup of coffee to my desk and listened to the recordings. No doubt about it, both were Jud Tucker's voice.

I scanned this morning's *Times* headlines, then I grabbed another cup of coffee to handle business matters.

I reviewed Hope's math on the deposit register, then countersigned the business checks paper clipped onto the agency's invoices.

Since Hope kept the books, I made the bank deposits. She and I applied the first rule of partnership: Trust but verify. We saw our divided duties as nothing more than solid business practices.

At 1150 hours, I'd begun to worry about not getting Tucker's promised morning call.

Hope buzzed me on the intercom. "It's that dime-store cowboy asshole. And yes, I've got you on the digital recorder."

I picked up the handset. "Steele."

"Hello, Clint."

His familiarity annoyed me. "Yes, Jud."

"You identified me." His chuckle rumbled. "I knew you'd make a great player. I gotta say you're just the cat's nuts when it comes to playing the game using clever detective work."

I leaned back in my desk chair. "You made identifying you easy, starting with meeting me in my office, using shoddy equipment to disguise your voice, leaving a loud and clear message on your office voice mail, taking Shane Danning to the supermarket, and finally, returning to the same store alone—all stupid moves on your part. By the way, one of the Stop & Save's employees has an eye for men, and I got an artist's sketch of your face right down to your faded acne scars."

"I'll admit you made a masterful move bringing a sketch artist."

"Luck plays a big part in detective work, and you need to know I'm one lucky bastard."

"Well, when it comes to good fortune, I've beaten you hands down," Tucker said with a smirk in his voice. "I received five million dollars from the Danning tramp this morning. Don't bother looking for the money. It all vanished across the cybersphere." He laughed softly. "Let's see how your luck holds out on your final challenge."

"Which is?"

"Try to find where I've hidden Shane Danning."

Nothing and no one can remain hidden for long once I put Mars on your ass, I thought. "You're on."

"It's precisely noon. You have twenty-four hours to find Shane. Miss the deadline and I'll kill your half brother."

He caught me off guard. How the fuck did he know Shane was my half brother? Who'd known besides my late father, Diana, and me?

I didn't speak.

"Should you find where I've hidden Shane Danning, you'd best come alone. I'm no stranger to murder. I killed Deputy Scott Davidson, then put a hole in his alcoholic father's head right in front of your house. But I'm guessing you figured that out."

"I did." He mentioned murdering two people as nonchalantly as if we were talking baseball.

"Here's something else you need to know. The firebombing of your buddy's house didn't happen out of the fucking blue. My only regret being he wasn't home that night. It would be a shame if your white colonial went up in smoke too."

Jud Tucker ended the call.

I called home and told Stella to get herself, Ian, Heathcliff, and Sammy into her car and come straight to the office.

I asked bomb expert Hope to check the office for explosive and incendiary devices.

Then I called Mars.

CHAPTER FORTY-ONE

The Usual Suspects

Clint, Tuesday, May 22

I heard Hope and Stella talking in the reception area while I watched Ian playing with his Black Hawk outside my office. Heathcliff had made himself at home on my lap, and Sammy lay asleep in my desk's leg well. White dog hair covered the lower half of my jeans; red cat fur clung to my thighs.

"Isn't all this lovely," I said to Heathcliff, meaning it. The big cat opened one eye, blinked, and went back to sleep. For the first time since Tucker's none-too-subtle threat to destroy my house, I could relax.

I'd come to work today intending to call Captain Flynn about the burglary of Diana Danning's house before Jud Tucker's five alarm shit show. I considered how much to tell Flynn about Jud Tucker's O Dark Hundred and today's 1150 phone calls. With cops' loose lips, don't tell him much until you know where Tucker has hidden Shane, I thought, then decided, the fuck! I'm deputized and need to tell Flynn everything.

I punched in Flynn's number and caught him at his desk. I spoke without preamble. "On the twenty-seventh of April, someone burglarized Diana Danning's manse. What can you tell me about it?"

"Oh, to be sure, I fuckin' live to serve you," Flynn said.

He kept me on hold. When it came to keyboarding, Flynn was a hunt 'n' pecker. The one time I tossed that archaic idiom at Flynn, his response had been: "In a pig's ass I'm huntin' anybody's pecker."

I think he was joking.

Flynn finally came back on the line. "The investigating officers found no signs of forced entry, and the place hadn't been ransacked."

"What was stolen?"

"Diamond jewelry, but whoever did it knew the real stones from the fakes."

I tapped a pencil on my desk. "Sounds like an inside job."

"Or the burglar wanted us to think it was an inside job," Flynn countered.

"When did Diana last see her diamonds?"

"Ahh, Jesus, Mary and Joseph, she's not absolutely certain. She thinks she last saw her diamonds on or around March tenth. She didn't discover the safe had been emptied until April twenty-seventh."

"Could that alleged cat burglar who's under house arrest account for her whereabouts from March through April?"

"No, but if this wasn't an inside job, it's the work of a professional. Our local cat burglar is at the top of our suspects list," Flynn said.

I couldn't tell Flynn Hope and I had been retained by the alleged Hancock Park cat burglar's lawyer to investigate his client's alibi. Hired by her legal counsel, attorney-client privileges applied on the matter. "What about Diana and Shane's alibis?"

"Both of them keep day planners. Since we don't know the exact date of the robbery, we're up shit creek as to any suspect's guilt or innocence."

I told Flynn about the calls I'd received from Jud Tucker, his claim that Diana had paid the five-million-dollar ransom, his confession to committing multiple homicides, and his none-too-subtle threat to destroy my house. "When we learn where Tucker lives, let me go there alone, assess the situation, and find probable cause for you to get a search warrant in advance."

Flynn spoke firmly: "If you find where this asswipe lives, don't even consider heading out until I can arrange backup."

"No, I'll go alone. Must I remind you that I used to gather intelligence and assassinate terrorists from a thousand yards away?"

I patiently waited for Hal to stop yelling. "Don't get your balls in a pinch," I said. "You know if Tucker spots one unmarked car behind me, Danning's a dead man."

Flynn reluctantly agreed.

"I suspect Tucker owns a farm or ranch, and I've put together a plan to find it," I said, ending the call.

I hugged Ian, spoke with Hope and Stella, then headed for Mars's office.

CHAPTER FORTY-TWO

Algorithm

Clint, Hauser Security, Tuesday, May 22

I parked in front of the bland beige building and stepped onto the pavement. Turning, I saw Mars's brick-shithouse security guard, Alesandro, standing beside the Viper's passenger's side door. Worried and edgy over Tucker's barely veiled threat, I said irritably, "Why don't I ever see and hear you coming or going?"

Alesandro grinned. "I'm like a whirlwind—here, there, all around you, and *poof*, gone."

"Uh-huh. Before you poof your ass out of here, you need to know my family and I have been threatened by a suspected kidnapper and killer named Jud Tucker." I pulled a copy of Mars's sketch from my messenger bag and passed it to Alesandro. "I made several quick turns on my way here, but I can't say with certainty whether I had a tail."

"I've a copy of the boss's sketch." He studied the drawing, then slid the page into a pocket of his suit jacket. He pulled his SIG, checked the mag, racked a round, and holstered the semiautomatic. He smiled. "I'll be watching for him."

"For the record, I'm also armed," I said.

He sighed. "Oh, that's a gun in your pants pocket. I thought you got excited seeing me."

"Don't flatter yourself." I laughed. "And no, Mae West (JFGI), that's not my gun you're seeing in my pocket."

Alesandro walked me to Hauser Security's main entrance. He held up his proximity card and entered a PIN. I heard the deadbolts unlock. "The boss man's waiting. You know the way."

I stepped inside. Keyboards clicked, phones warbled, and soft voices rose from the first floor's maze of cubicles. I turned back to the doors. Alesandro had vanished.

I caught Mars on the phone. He smiled and waved me in.

Wearing a vintage second-skin Ramones T-shirt and distressed cutoff jeans, Mars completed his extreme office casual dress code with a two-day stubble and unruly mop of blond curls. As I sat down, he plopped his bare feet on top of his desk and crossed them at the ankles. With his tight T-shirt and all that skin on display, I felt as if I was on the set of a soft porn shoot.

When Mars and I first met in our plebes barracks, we instantly clicked and soon recognized our shared bisexuality. Once we'd confirmed our mutual love of both genders, we instantly became best friends. Over the past fifteen years, I'd never seen him acting like an uber manly man. He didn't need to. With his muscular body and surfer looks, Mars turned heads without macho affectations.

"Consider it done." He held up his left index finger at me and pressed a switch on his desk phone, taking him off the secure line. He pressed a series of numbers, waited, and said, "Go."

I knew better than to ask Mars what brave new hell would soon be unloosed on some despotic enemy of the U.S. of A.

He turned his full attention to me. "We've a lot of work to do. Get your ass over here and sit beside me."

I pulled my chair behind his paperless L-shaped desk. Before he dropped his big feet to the floor, I noticed the metro hip nerd sported a recent pedicure. We private dicks miss nothing.

"I take it Ian's in a safe place," Mars said.

"He'll be staying with Hope and Stella in Simi Valley."

"With all those LAPD cops and LAPD retirees living in Simi, there's no place safer," he said. He checked his legal pad. "When you called, you said you wanted to find C. Judson Tucker's address."

"Yes."

"I ran the preliminary searches. I found no property deeds or vehicle titles issued to a C. Judson Tucker or C. J. Tucker, or Judson Tucker, or Jud Tucker; no utility, landline or cell bills; no driver's or other licenses; no birth certificate, no real property deeds, no federal or state tax returns, and nothing for anyone of that name in a nationwide criminal background check."

"Holy shit, it doesn't look promising," I said.

Mars cracked his knuckles. "We need a search algorithm."

"Excuse me, you're speaking nerd."

"Sorry, Moose. An algorithm uses data stipulations for solving a problem or group of problems. Algorithms are effective methodologies expressed in a finite amount of space and time."

I hesitated then said, "Okay."

"Simply put, a search algorithm with a computer is a step-by-step procedure for finding someone. We'll begin by making notations on everything we know about C. Judson Tucker."

"Which isn't much," I said. "Christ, we don't even know whether C. Judson Tucker is his real name or an alias."

"Bear in mind that computers cannot deal with ambiguities. We'll begin by assuming we have his birth name or a known alias."

"He might be found under several aliases," I said.

"That's my guess," Mars said. "Chances are the name C. Judson Tucker will point us to an alias or aliases. Another possibility is at some point, Tucker fucked up and left us an incongruity."

He saw my confusion.

"By that, I mean he used a part or parts of his real name on some official document we haven't yet considered."

We began listing what we knew with some degree of certainty about C. Judson Tucker. Mars entered algorithm notations into his computer.

He continued keyboarding. "We'll be working with a finite number of steps which will likely involve repetitions of the search. As data are processed, the algorithm will perform automatic reasoning tasks that, when executed, proceed through a predetermined number of well-defined successive states, eventually producing output. You'll want to note that the transition from one successive state to the next won't necessarily be deterministic."

"Mars…"

"Yeah, buddy."

"Your nerd speak is making my brain smolder." And to think when he was a plebe cadet, the cybertech genius once dressed hurriedly, forgot to pull on his boots, and reported to formation in his socked feet. He's hated wearing shoes all the years I've known him.

"Since we know when he graduated college, we'll begin our search by limiting the time period to the past twenty years and restrict the quest area to run from Sacramento to the Oregon border." Mars made a few additional key strokes, then hit enter.

"Now we wait," Mars said.

CHAPTER FORTY-THREE

Algorithm Redux

Clint, Hauser Security, Tuesday, May 22

About twenty minutes later, the first search ended. Neither an address, nor phone number, nor current employer had been located in the northern half of the state for either C. Judson or C.J. Tucker or Jud Tucker over the past twenty years.

"Well, it's a safe bet he hasn't lived or worked in the northern half of the state under the name Tucker," Mars said.

We refined the notations and revised the quest area to search from south of Sacramento to the Mexican border. Mars hit enter again.

We played poker while waiting for the new algorithm to complete its search. About forty minutes later, we had neither Tucker's current address, nor his phone numbers, nor any other relevant information. After he'd graduated from college, completed his paramedical training, gone to work for the Los Angeles Fire department, and quit his job five years later, it seemed as if he'd beamed himself off to Jupiter.

Mars let out a breath and leaned back in his desk chair. "Ain't this the screamin' shits." He glanced at his watch and dropped his pen on his desk. "We're spinning our wheels." He slid his feet into his flip-flops and stood. "Maybe a food break will help us see whatever it is we're missing in our search notations."

My stomach growled. We went to Hollywood's In-N-Out Burger on Sunset.

As we chowed down on burgers and fries from one of L.A.'s best-known fast-food franchises, I had a couple of new notation ideas for our next search.

And the clock kept ticking toward Tucker's twenty-four hour deadline. But if needed, I had a delay tactic for Tucker's game.

Back in Mars's office, I said, "Since Tucker works at Mystic Canyon Casino, and I'm presuming his residence is a farm or ranch, it seems likely we'll find his address somewhere within forty miles northwest or southwest of the greater Los Angeles metro."

"Okay," Mars said, entering in the new notation. "You got anything else we can work with?"

"Maybe we'll find everything Tucker owns, all his utility bills, his licenses, vehicle registrations, and his farm or ranch under a corporate name."

"And how the hell do we separate the oats from the horseshit in the greater Los Angeles corporate cluster fuck?"

"Let's assume his farm or ranch isn't a nonprofit organization, which narrows the corporate search algorithm to either limited liability companies, or C or S corporations," I said.

"All right, but why not a nonprofit organization?" Mars asked.

"Although it sounds logical a farm or ranch might be seen as a nonprofit corporation, attempting to file taxes thusly would not be well-received by either the state's Department of Revenue or the IRS."

"Got it. I'm entering limited liability companies, or C or S corporations in the notations." He stopped for a moment. "Supposing we don't find licenses, tax returns, property deeds and/or auto registrations under something like the Tucker Corporation, or the Tucker Company, or Tuck LLC. What's the purpose of taking the corporate route in the first place?"

"Because most corporations must conduct at least one meeting of the governing board annually and elect officers. The names of a corporation's board execs and the CEO must be registered with the secretary of state," I said.

"Shit, that's a good idea. I knew there's at least one reason why I liked you beyond your looks," Mars said while working the keyboard.

We played more poker while waiting for the new algorithm to do its thing. In the time it took me to call Hope to check that all was well, then win twenty bucks from Mars, the computer completed its search.

And again, nothing, *nada*, zero, zip, bupkis.

Mars pulled a bottle of single malt out of a desk drawer and poured each of us two fingers, neat. We discussed a couple of new notation ideas, then we debated and dismissed them. I would've tossed something across the office had Mars anything on his desk to pitch. I briefly considered the scotch tumbler I held in my hand, but it felt and looked a bit too expensive to willfully shatter against a wall. I settled for a string of curse words.

I leaned back in my chair, sipped my scotch, then helped myself to more. A thought struck me. What if Tucker operated a farm or ranch vocational training program for troubled teens or an agricultural training halfway house for newly paroled inmates? Either of the two could be established as a nonprofit organization.

I told Mars what I thought. He made a new notation for a Tucker serving on the board of directors of a nonprofit organization.

In minutes, Mars yelled, *"Well, fuck me raw, we've found the sonofabitch!"*

I read the monitor. A Cletus J. Tucker served as president and CEO of a nonprofit vocational training program for troubled teens and young adults. The tax-exempt corporation did business as "the Ranch." And I now had the property's legal description and location. I felt certain it was at this rural address that I'd find Shane Danning.

"I see why he goes by Jud. I mean, Cletus? His parents should've been locked up for child abuse," Mars said.

Although it was a holdover from our years at the Point, we bumped fists.

"Anything else I can do for you?" Mars asked.

"I've several things I'd like you to do tomorrow at precisely 1145 hours." I told Mars what I needed from him.

"That's a big 10-4." He winked and smiled. "We still make a helluva team."

"We do," I said.

And once again, he and I teamed up for the night.

CHAPTER FORTY-FOUR

You Win

Clint, Wednesday, May 23

Arriving at the office about a minute behind Hope, I watched her unholster her S&W thirty-eight special and return the gun to her desk's middle drawer, leaving it open about six inches.

"Everyone's safe?" I asked.

Hope frowned. "Would I be here otherwise?"

"Update me, please."

"Ian, Stella, and your pets are fine. Two retired cops are guarding them while I'm here. A bomb squad buddy of mine checked your Flats property and double-checked our office building. He neither found explosive nor incendiary devices here, nor on your house, nor in your lawn, nor in any of your gardens."

"Thank you."

"You are most certainly welcome." Hope aimed her hazel eyes at me. "I don't like this plan of yours. We don't know enough about Jud Tucker even to guess his next move."

"At 1145 hours, Tucker will be too busy stomping out brush fires to be coming after anyone." I checked my watch. "Is the digital recorder ready?"

"Locked and loaded," Hope said.

I went to my office and called Jud Tucker.

"Good morning, Clint," Tucker said. "How's the search going?"

"I've been searching nonstop since you called yesterday. It's as if you vanished after you quit the L.A. Fire Department. Nothing about you or any of Mystic Canyon Casino's employees is listed anywhere on the web. I can't find your address." I turned up the despondency. "I guess you've won."

Jud Tucker chuckled. "Looks like I did."

"You have your five-million-dollar ransom." I paused. "What can I do to save Shane Danning's life?"

Tucker said, "Meet me in my casino office at 1200 hours. If you're late, your half brother is dead. If I even suspect you contacted the cops or feds, both you and Danning are dead. You got it?"

"I'll come alone."

Tucker ended the call.

I called Captain Flynn. He answered on the first ring.

"I'm heading out," I said.

"Steele, I don't like this plan of yours one fucking bit."

"I'm still your deputy," I said.

"And I can undeputize your ass fucking fast."

"I emailed you my recordings of Tucker's and my conversations. You have his admissions of the homicides and kidnappings he committed. If you find the right judge, you should have enough to get both a search and an arrest warrant. I want to find Danning before you come charging in with your posse."

"I'll have warrants, all right." Flynn paused before saying, "I know you're former Delta and can take care of yourself. I still don't like this."

"Make certain your FBI buddies are at Mystic Canyon Casino at 1145 hours. You bring the state and local cops to Tucker's ranch at 1300 hours. Shane Danning and I will be waiting for you."

Always on top of everything, Hope handed me my backpack. "Be safe, Clint." She hugged me.

I ran to my car.

CHAPTER FORTY-FIVE

Inexorable Force

Clint, The Ranch, Wednesday, May 23

I love Los Angeles—L.A. traffic, not so much. There are occasional exceptions, but in general, driving here is a frigging nightmare. And I had no time to spare.

I inched along Sunset, made a right on Sepulveda Way, and finally merged onto the 405. Fifteen miles later, I got onto the 5N. Eventually, traffic thinned slightly. Everyone began behaving like Angeleno motorists, speeding and driving like assholes. In about thirty minutes, I passed Valencia. About twenty miles north of Magic Mountain, the landscape changed to farmhouses and fields.

I followed a two-lane highway until the GPS lady told me to turn at the next right. Minutes later, I stopped outside a high gate posted with "The Ranch—No Trespassing."

The bolt cutters I kept hidden in my car got me past the chained and padlocked gate, which I stopped to close. Even when breaking and entering, private investigators can be courteous.

I drove past truck gardens of lettuce, sweet corn, tomatoes, green beans, and squash. Fields of stubble told me the winter wheat had been harvested. A beef herd grazed in a meadow. I rounded a sharp curve, and a white Western Reserve–style house came into view.

Parked and concealed in a stand of pines, I got out of my car, pulled binoculars from my pack, and did a thorough reconnaissance of the area. I neither saw nor heard anyone in or around the house, barn, or outbuildings. I did not spot ranch hands working anywhere.

I pulled my Glock, chambered a round, then checked my pack.

I smiled to myself. As if seventy-year-old Hope Whitman could ever forget anything I needed for a job.

I followed a line of conifers to the garage and kept myself concealed as I worked my way to the east side of the two-story house. Glancing around a corner, I saw no one. I crept along the back side of the building.

I stopped beside a window and peeked into a sparsely furnished barracks. The two rows of bunk beds, all tightly made, could've each bounced a dime. I saw no one.

Squatting beneath the windows, I listened. No birds chirping and no dogs barking. A stench in the air confirmed that Tucker raised a few pigs.

The breeze shifted. From the direction of the barn came an unforgettable, unmistakable battlefield odor—a distinct, repulsive stench that would remain in my nose, mouth, and throat for hours. I considered checking it out but thought better of it. Without a doubt, the barn was a crime scene, which Captain Flynn and his posse would handle. I had only one job: find Shane Danning.

Continuing along the house's rear wall, I peeked in the window of an unoccupied kitchen. Staying low, I ran to the jalousied all-season porch, opened the screen door, and stepped inside.

Shoes and boots in differing sizes, all scuffed, many with holes or split seams had been placed in matching pairs along the porch's baseboards. Tucker's trophies, I inferred.

A six-panel solid oak door led into the kitchen. I pressed an ear against the wood. I heard nothing. Turning the doorknob, I softly growled, "Fucking locked." I reached into my pack for my burglar tools.

I shot graphite into the keyhole. Armed with a torsion wrench and pick gun, I unlocked the door on the first try. If anyone had been standing near the kitchen, I'd lost the element of surprise.

A hallway led to the kitchen. Staying low and moving fast, I swept my Glock from left to right.

Behind me, a pantry door opened on oiled hinges.

"Dude, your ass belongs to me," a vaguely familiar voice said, laughing.

I turned and saw Blaine Vogel, one of the two university students who'd witnessed Danning's abduction.

Vogel pointed a revolver at my chest. His eyes narrowed. "Is that a semiautomatic?"

"Yes, it is." I knew I'd soon get the opportunity to take that gun away from Vogel.

"I'll be taking that off your hands. Put down the gun and kick it out of reach. Fuck with me, and you'll get a round in your guts." He smiled. "A wound like that gives you plenty of time to feel some serious hurt before you die."

"You watch way too many crime shows."

"Don't piss me off. Do what I said."

I bent at the waist, set my Glock on the floor, stood, abruptly turned, and kicked Vogel's weapon out of his hand. I spun Vogel face first into the wall.

"You should always cock a revolver before pointing it at some-one," I said while twisting his right arm behind his back, lifting it to about an inch from dislocating his shoulder. He started bawling like a little boy, but I kept him pinned to the wall. "Don't fucking move." I cuffed his wrists behind his back and grabbed my Glock off the floor. I slid Vogel's revolver into an evidence bag and dropped it into my pack.

"Sonofabitch, I think you broke my wrist. It fuckin' hurts."

"Shut the hell up."

Vogel tried not to cry, but tears kept lining his tanned cheeks. "Dude…I was only fucking around. I never would've shot you."

I considered knocking out Vogel's front teeth for lying, but held back. "Where's your playmate?"

"At home."

I exhaled a laugh, grabbed a fistful of hair, and pounded Vogel's head against the plastered wall a couple, three times. Or maybe four. "I don't think I heard you right."

"Blake's asleep on the living room sofa," Vogel whimpered.

I frog-marched Vogel to a six-panel envelope door, slid it open about a foot, and saw Vogel's fuck buddy asleep on the couch.

I wrapped my left arm around Vogel's throat and held my Glock to the side of his chest. "Tell your sleeping princess to come to the kitchen."

"Blake, come here and see what I got," Vogel called in a phlegmy voice.

Blake Walsh entered the kitchen in less than a minute, rubbing sleep from his eyes with both hands. He had a gun in the left front pocket of his baggy shorts. "Woo-hoo! Detective Mouthwatering! No fuckin' way we're giving this one to Tucker."

Blake Walsh froze, seeing my gun pointed at his chest.

"With your thumb and forefinger, set your gun on the floor." I watched Walsh's eyes and hands. "I'll put a hollow point in your eye before you can lift that revolver out of your pocket and above your balls. With your thumb and forefinger on the stock, pull the gun out of your pocket and drop it."

Blake Walsh dropped the revolver. I kicked it out of reach and holstered my gun. I spun Walsh around and cuffed his hands behind his back.

I pushed Vogel and Walsh to the floor and propped their backs against the kitchen cabinets. I shook my head in disgust. "Tucker shouldn't let you little boys play with matches, let alone firearms." I retrieved and bagged Walsh's revolver, pulled out one of the kitchen table's chairs, and straddled it backward. The wall phone rang. Their eyes wet, Vogel and Walsh turned their heads toward the sound.

Apparently, voice mail answered the call after four rings. I glowered at Walsh and Vogel. "Quit crying and start talking."

"We're not telling you jack shit," Vogel said, his face and voice jagged with defiance.

I let out a tired sigh, pulled my gun, and fired a single round into the strip of kitchen cabinetry between their heads. Walsh screamed. Vogel pissed his pants.

"I'll begin shooting off ears until someone's lips start moving." I waited a beat before pointing my gun at Blake Walsh.

"*No!*" Blake screamed as if I'd slammed a kitchen drawer shut on his dick. "What do you want to know?"

"Everything." With my phone on video, I pointed my gun at Blaine Vogel's forehead.

"Tuck likes them fifteen to twenty-nine, male or female, athletic and fit." He shrugged one shoulder. "Blaine and I cruised the streets, bars, bus, and train depots…you know, any place we can find runaway teens or down-and-out young men and women who haven't gotten the look and stink of the streets on them yet."

"Any of these people happen to be friends or classmates of yours?"

Vogel snorted. "Fuck, dude, do we look like retards?"

I looked into Vogel's face and saw the cold, black eyes of something reptilian. Human life meant nothing to him.

Walsh spoke up. "We especially like cruising bus depots. Blaine and I can spot hungry runaways who don't have a dollar to their names and no one to meet them in the City of Angels…except us."

Vogel sneered. "Besides all those runaway teens, there's an ass-ton of twentysomething vets from Bumfuck-ganistan all messed up with PTSD. Then there are all the young people from East Shitztown Indiana and other Deep Hole America spots who think Hollywood's never seen a face as handsome, or an actor as talented, or a musician as gifted, or a porn star with a cock as big."

Walsh smirked, shaking his head. "We might tell a young male or female runaway that we work for a talent agency, and we like his or her looks."

"We buy them something to eat," Vogel said. "Shit, they're all starving, and we listen to their sob stories. We get them drunk and bring them here." He shrugged. "It's that easy."

"Tucker gives them three meals a day, a place to sleep, and in return, they work the fields. Those needing medical care get that from Tucker. Blaine and I get to fuck and torture those who slack off in the fields or somehow turn difficult. Then we process them, as Tucker calls it." He smiled. "Eventually, they all get processed off the Ranch."

I stared into Walsh's eyes. "When you say processed, you're telling me that Tucker and you Bobbsey Twins from hell kill them, harvest their organs, and sell them on the transplant black market."

"Yeeeesss," Vogel said, stretching the word. "Hearts, kidneys, lungs, livers, corneas, tendons, intestines, large blood vessels, skin— they're all big sellers. Parts that don't have much of a market value get fed to Tucker's pigs."

"We wait until we have the chest freezer full of bones, then use Tuck's backhoe to bury those remains in a mass grave."

My blood ran cold. Among other mental issues, Vogel, Walsh, and Tucker sounded like pathological sadists. "Where's Shane Danning?"

Vogel smirked. "Danning's in lockup."

"Here in the house?"

"Shit no," Walsh said. "He's locked up in what we call Tuck's private prison for wayward boys and girls."

"Where is this prison?"

Walsh shrugged. "It's a short walk away."

"How many people are in there?"

"Three," Walsh said.

"The dorm's empty right now. Blake and I will begin recruiting the throwaway children and veterans who aren't too fucked up to work in time to harvest the soybeans and plant next summer's wheat."

"Is Shane Danning all right?"

"Dude, he's a hurting motherfucker, that's for sure," Walsh said, "but he was still alive when I checked on him last night."

"Danning won't be going shirtless to the beach anymore," Vogel said.

I lifted Vogel and Walsh by the fronts of their shirts. "Who has the keys to the prison?"

"In my left front pocket," Walsh said.

"What else do you have in that pocket?"

"Nothing," Walsh said.

I held my Glock against his head. "I know where to put a bullet in your brain that will make you a living, breathing vegetable." I slid my left hand into the pocket of Blake's baggy shorts and pulled out a ring of keys. I flipped through them, one larger, five slightly smaller. "One to the prison's main door, the other five to cells," I said.

Walsh nodded.

Vogel grinned. "If you liked the feel of my partner's junk, maybe you'd like to get your hands on the deluxe package."

I gave Vogel my crooked grin. "And maybe you'd like to swallow some of your teeth."

The kitchen's wall phone rang again. Walsh and Vogel glanced at each other.

Again, I let the call go to voice mail, then cuffed their left and right arms together. I pushed them to the door. "Take me to Danning."

CHAPTER FORTY-SIX

Going Home

Clint, The Ranch, Wednesday, May 23

I followed Vogel and Walsh along a path edged with wild fennel, coarse grasses, and eucalyptus bushes. The two young men had not shut their goddammed mouths since leaving the farmhouse, dropping dime after dime on Jud Tucker. I still had my phone on video.

According to Vogel and Walsh, they assisted Tucker in most areas of the Ranch's operations. But their primary duty involved recruiting and kidnapping the slave laborers. Calling and reporting to the cops that they may have witnessed an abduction had been their role in snatching Danning.

Disgusted, I shook my head. "What about Tom Andrews?"

"Tuck did that abduction on his own." Vogel shrugged. "Andrews, the dumb fuck, electrocuted himself while trying to escape with Danning." He grinned. "You've no idea how dangerous the Ranch can be."

Vogel and Walsh admitted to participating in the murders of the kidnapped victims. But, according to them, they had no choice. Tucker had kept them fearing for their own lives over the past five years.

"Sure, any court will buy that argument," I said. "It went over well during the Nuremberg Trials."

According to Vogel and Walsh, they'd also followed Tucker's orders for five years because he'd guided them through the commission of perfect crimes.

Vogel looked over his shoulder and smirked. "Did you know Jud promised to pay Blake and me each two hundred and fifty thousand dollars for reporting the Danning kidnapping and lying to you and the cops?"

"If Tucker ever pays you, that amount won't even cover your legal fees. And I'd suspected someone paid you to lie."

"Very good, Sherlock," Vogel said. "The rest of the five-million-dollar-ransom went to Tucker for planning and committing Danning's abduction." Vogel turned and grinned. "Tucker's following Diana Danning into your office...that was ballsy and brilliant, don't you think?"

"No, I call it balls-out brainless. Tucker made an ass-ton of mistakes, but the worst had to be his coming into my office using his buddy's name."

Vogel scowled. "How did you know about Tucker and Scott Davidson?"

"I'm a detective. People tell me shit, I put everything together and reach conclusions." I shoved Vogel's ass with the sole of my boot. "Shut the fuck up and keep moving."

"Blake and I want to turn state's evidence," Vogel began. "Our testimony will put Jud Tucker on death row. For that, we want full immunity."

"Full immunity, or worst case scenario, a few months in county lockup, and a couple years of probation," Walsh said.

"Your lawyers will need to negotiate a plea deal with the prosecutor," I said.

And good luck with all that. Miniature elephants would fly out of these psycho boys' asses before any prosecutor would even consider a plea involving county jail time and probation. At best, Vogel and Walsh might get life imprisonment without the possibility of parole in lieu of them joining Tucker on death row.

Life without the possibility of parole or death row, whichever or what-the-fuck-ever, I hoped the Bobbsey Twins from hell and Tucker would never again step outside prison walls. Manipulative, organized, and able to fly under society's radar, they struck me as textbook psychopaths. They saw nothing wrong with abduction, rape, torture, and cold-blooded murder for profit. I could not venture a guess as to how many nameless victims' bones would be found buried on the Ranch. I doubted Tucker himself knew the exact number.

I briefly considered putting bullets in Vogel and Walsh's heads, saving taxpayers the cost of finding them guilty of multiple felonies.

Their prints were all over the guns they'd pulled on me. Staged properly, I could claim self-defense.

Then I considered Nietzsche's warning about gazing long into the abyss. *Beware, that when fighting monsters, you yourself do not become a monster.* I would trust law enforcement and the criminal justice system to do what needed to be done with Blake Walsh, Blaine Vogel, and Jud Tucker.

I followed Vogel and Walsh through a narrow opening in a long row of tall spruce trees. A windowless cinderblock building stood ahead, backed by a second windbreak of towering pines.

I pulled out the keys I'd taken from Walsh. "Try running, and I'll put your little dicks in the dirt without thinking twice about it. Do I make myself clear?"

Vogel and Walsh nodded. I shoulder-holstered my Glock.

Fisting their shirt collars, I lifted them and dropped them on their asses. With their hands Plasticuffed behind their backs and their arms tied together, standing without my assistance would take teamwork and effort.

The key slid into the lock and twisted easily. I pulled open the thick steel door.

Hot air and the pong of emptied bowels, urine, and the coppery tang of blood rushed out the opened door like explosive vomit. I stepped aside, gulped semifresh air, and exhaled a string of expletives. Regaining my equilibrium, I slid a hand along the right side of the jamb and found a light switch. Twin rows of fluorescent tubes flickered, then glowed steadily.

Again grabbing their shirt collars, I lifted Vogel and Walsh to their feet and shoved them into Jud Tucker's private prison. We entered an open room with a small kitchen, threadbare sofa, and an antique console TV. The hallway to my right had a row of five solid steel cell doors. Two of them stood open.

I again frisked Walsh and Vogel, shoved each into an empty cell, then closed and locked the doors.

I checked the next cell. A man who could've been twentysomething or sixtysomething lay supine and nude on his bunk. He appeared to be breathing, but didn't respond to my voice. The stench of shit and the ammonia burn of the piss-soaked bunk forced me to hold my breath. But another odor lay beneath this unknown man—the reek of decaying flesh. I did not need to roll him over to check; I recognized the smell of decubitus ulcers. Attempting to move him would do more harm than good.

Another nude man, awake and breathing evenly, sat still as death in the next cell. Dried drool caked his chest. He'd also emptied his bowels and urinated on the thin mattress. He gave no sign of either seeing me or hearing my voice.

I found Shane Danning in the next cell. He lay on his stomach in the nude, his face pointed toward the door. His eyes remained closed at the sound of my footsteps. His back wounds had remained open from repeated whippings. The deeper slashes appeared to be infected. I touched Shane's forehead. He felt feverish. His hands and feet were roped to the bunk. I pulled my KA-BAR knife and cut him loose.

"Shane, can you hear me?"

His eyes opened to slits. He spoke in a hoarse whisper. "No more...please."

"I came to get you out of here."

Danning's eyes opened wider.

"You need water. Can you sit up?"

He closed his eyes. "No."

I checked my phone. I did not have a signal. I told Shane I'd be back with water. Stepping outside the cinderblock prison, I checked again for a signal, frowned, and ran for the farmhouse.

In Jud Tucker's kitchen, I lifted the wall phone's receiver and punched in Captain Flynn's cell number. I waited for it to ring.

The Ranch lay far beyond the captain's jurisdiction, but the Danning case belonged to Flynn. I didn't doubt there would be cooperation between law enforcement agencies and jurisdictions. Flynn answered my call on the first ring.

"I found Danning and two other men alive. All of them need immediate medical attention and hospitalization."

"Roger that. I'm on my way with an interdepartmental posse and EMTs."

"It's bad, but once the staties and feds bring in the cadaver dogs, sensor probes, and a helicopter with an infrared camera, it's going to get far fucking worse."

"Ten-two," Flynn said, letting me know he'd received my message and its core meaning.

"I also have two suspects cuffed and subdued. Since Jud Tucker isn't one of them, I'm assuming he's at the casino."

"Not to worry. He's presently in his office under surveillance by the feds and local police."

"What's your ETA?"

"About ten minutes," Flynn said.

I hung up the kitchen wall phone. Seconds later, it rang. Expecting Flynn, I answered, "Did you forget something?"

After a few seconds of silence, I started to hang up. Jud Tucker's voice sounded way beyond pissed. "You fucking lied to me."

"It doesn't matter. You're out of time," I said.

Tucker fell silent, but I heard him breathing and sensed his rage. I gave the knife another twist. "You know, there is some honor among thieves. Child killers are at the bottom of the prison pecking order. While you're in county lockup awaiting trial, you'll likely get gang-raped repeatedly until someone shivs you."

"Fuck you," Tucker said.

"But hey, should you make it out of county lockup alive, enjoy your short stay as a guest at one of California's beautiful maximum security prisons. You won't stay alive for long, as Jeffrey Dahmer didn't." Letting the handset fall to the kitchen floor, I heard Tucker's tinny condemnations. Grabbing three bottles of water from the refrigerator and sliding them into my pack, I ran back to Tucker's private prison.

I returned to Shane's cell. "Let me help you to sit up." Kneeling, I wrapped his arms across my shoulders and told him to lock his fingers. Emaciated, Shane wasn't heavy. I gingerly lifted his legs, sat him up, and began giving him sips of water.

Distant sirens drew nearer. "Do you hear that? You're going home."

Shane tried to smile. Tears streaked his dirty cheeks.

I gave him another sip of water. I'd found Danning injured and scarred for life in more ways than one. But soon, I'd let him know he had an unknown brother, nephew, and aunt.

Flynn and I had closed the Danning case.

It sounded good in theory.

CHAPTER FORTY-SEVEN

Lied To and Locked In

Jud Tucker, Mystic Canyon Casino, Wednesday, May 23

I'd ordered Steele to meet me in my office. But the motherfucker
outsmarted me. How the hell he discovered my ranch's address went
way beyond my realm of understanding. My certainty Steele couldn't
find Danning had been the ace up my sleeve.

Taking a CCTV look at all the casino's parking lots, ramps, and
the valet underground garage, I spotted three beige four-door sedans
and a pair of black SUVs with tinted windows. The fucking cops had
invaded my workplace. I'd gotten lied to and locked in.

Steele evidently overpowered Vogel and Walsh. Adding insult to
defeat, the two college boys doubtless spilled their fucking guts. They
would turn state's evidence, no fucking doubt about that.

I looked up as the lights in my office flickered.

I'd underestimated Steele again. When I heard his voice on my
kitchen's wall phone, I knew I'd gotten fucked seven ways to Sunday. I
pounded my fist on the desk.

But I had one more move to make.

I'd found all of Steele's email addresses and phone numbers. I
turned to my office keyboard and sent a message to Steele's home PC.

Then I deleted all the files and the operating system in my office
computer. I checked my watch. It was 1140 hours. I knew I didn't have
much time left.

I pushed away from my desk, crossed my office, and stood before
the floor-to-ceiling one-way glass to watch the players seated at the
high stakes poker tables. Cameras gave me a view of every square inch
of the casino's gaming floors, all the common areas, and every gambler.

But I enjoyed looking through the mirrored glass, watching the hope in players' eyes turn to dismay as they lost this month's rent or mortgage and car payments, not to mention the money to feed themselves and their families. Most of these fucking fools would lose every dollar they had until their next payday. Then they'd return.

Some people considered casinos a fool's paradise; some called them dens of iniquity. But all players knew the first rule of gambling: The house always wins. Still, they came.

The lights in my office flickered again. I wondered what the fuck was causing that. I checked the time. It was 1145 hours. My desk phone rang. I answered the call.

"Mr. Tucker, there's something hinky going on with the power. Every slot machine that's in use has locked up and is playing jackpot music. You need to get down here."

"Get everyone out of the casino now," I said.

A minute later, a recorded announcement told casino guests to go immediately to the nearest exit and follow security guards' instructions.

I turned to the line of CCTVs and watched the casino's guests being shepherded to the doors. All the lights went out, and three thousand slot machines went dark. The emergency lighting came on.

I watched four federal agents and six uniformed cops push their way through the casino's main doors. I no longer gave two shits about either the cops storming my casino, or anything about my job, or the Ranch's black-market organ business, or my latest killing game miscalculations.

But I would not spend the rest of my life in prison.

It wouldn't be long before the feds and the local cops took a battering ram to my office door. I pulled my Beretta from my middle desk drawer. They'd catch me all right—with the back of my head missing.

Hearing the cops outside my office door, I slid the gun into my mouth.

The door crashed open.

CHAPTER FORTY-EIGHT

Hocus Pocus

Jane Day Child, The Houston Shoot, Friday, June 15

As my surname suggests, I'm an indigenous American; what it does not say is I'm a six-foot-two, male-to-female transgender.

Topping off my bio, I'm the first person a Steele Productions actor calls when she or he gets busted for lewd conduct, domestic violence, public intoxication, making an indecent proposal to an undercover cop, shoplifting, assaulting a photographer, ass-ending a police cruiser, and so on. I'll mention that with little or no provocation, an actor can turn crazier than a rat trapped in a tin shithouse. It's my job to post bail and hustle the artiste's sorry ass out the police station's back door before the media swoops in.

Presently, I'm working the Houston shoot of *Peter Remington*. It's often hella boring on the set, but I figure it beats working in a reservation's salmon cannery.

Someone above my pay grade changed Raoul Martinez's name to Raul Martin. His hair color went from a sun-streaked brown to blond, emphasizing his green eyes and golden complexion. Raul Martin is a hot devil all right.

As to the Peter Remington movie, Steele Productions's marketing and promotions department continued to wage a media blitzkrieg. It's hard to miss seeing Raul Martin and his costar, Vanessa Holmes, on the covers of tabloids, Sunday newspaper inserts, movie magazines, and in skimpy swimwear on fourteen-feet-high and forty-eight-feet-wide billboards. Together, they've been making the rounds of the TV talk-show circuit. Stills and videos of Raul and Vanessa from the Peter Remington shoot can be seen all across the worldwide web simply by entering "Raul Van" in your browser. Steele Productions's dreamweaver machine created two hot new stars before the release of their first film. It's all Hollywood hocus-pocus.

For the filming of tonight's scene, the location manager rented a Houston area roadhouse. The set decorator, prop master, and art director gave the old joint a warmer, less dumpish look, and the set was ready to go.

The gaffer, grips, camera operators, and their assistants patiently waited for further instructions and/or changes. The scene's extras included folks dressed as a ranch hand, a cable technician, a pair of auto mechanics, an oil rigger, a gaggle of buxom bottle blondes, run-of-the-mill rednecks, and a smattering of store managers with their white collars loosened and their Sunday pants on, all in their places with sunshiny faces. And all this for a scene that would run under five minutes.

I stopped Rick Jackson, a reporter-photographer with the tabloid *Worldwide Tattler*, at the roadhouse's doors. Looking straight into Jackson's beady eyes in his shit weasel face, I demanded his phone. He gave it to me. Then I held out my hand for his other phone. "Don't make me frisk you." He handed me his backup phone.

"Mr. Jackson, you know how it works: No photos or videos of anything or anyone before the end of the shoot. If you break the rule, I'll smash your camera, then I'll bust your sorry ass while I'm kicking it out the door and down the street." What can I say—I'm not at all pleasant when I'm forced to deal with tabloid tools.

Following a final adjustment of the lights, Vona Steele, the film's director-producer, ordered, "Roll sound, roll cameras."

A four-piece band played an old Hank Williams tune. Raul and Vanessa two-stepped around the dance floor. They began speaking their lines.

I could literally see and feel the chemistry between the two actors. If I, jaded broad that I am, recognized it, theater audiences and critics couldn't miss the magic between Raul and Vanessa. I've been on enough shoots to know this movie would be fucking *huge*.

I kept my eyes peeled for potential problems. An extra wearing brand new rigger boots stood at the edge of the dance floor, smirking at Raul and Vanessa.

I ambled over and wedged myself between the rigger and a rhinestone cowboy.

"They sure can dance," I whispered in the rigger's ear.

The cute bastard put his hand on my ass. If the cameras hadn't been rolling… I'll leave it at that.

Still watching Raul, the rigger leaned closer and whispered in my ear, "He's too good-looking not to be a fag." He added, "Course, all fudge packers can dance like darkies." His lips curled into a malicious smile. "Think I'll follow his pansy ass out the door, shove him into an alley, and give him a taste of real Texas beef."

I didn't reply, but thought, Fucking great, we got a homophobic racist, queer-in-denial rough trader, rapist, and overall shit rag on the set. I'd report this asshole to Vona. Maybe she could see that he lost his SAG card.

The song ended. Vona Steele yelled, "Cut, print it."

The rigger extra moseyed behind Raul and Vanessa as they headed for the bar. I followed one step behind him. I squawked my rover twice, alerting security guards of a potential problem.

I saw the tabloid's Rick Jackson taking candid shots of Raul and Vanessa as they talked at the bar. I focused my attention on the pretend rigger.

The rigger extra shoved Raul against the bar and kissed him on the lips. I caught the flash of that shitshow Rick Jackson's camera.

Raul connected his fist with the extra's nose, dropping him screaming and bleeding to the floor. A real lightweight, the extra doubled over and puked. Two company security men manhandled him off the set.

Sure as I'm standing here, Rick Jackson and the pretend rigger staged this little incident. I could see the tabloid's cover photo and headline: "Raul Martin Gay As Springtime!" Or something similar.

I told Raul and Vanessa to stay where they were. Then I chased after Rick Jackson.

I followed the tabloid tool down the sidewalk. In about fifteen seconds, give or take, Jackson's photo card would be gone; that, and his ass kicked.

My security coworkers don't call me Jane Wayne for nothing. Yeah, this job seriously beats the hell out of working in a salmon cannery.

CHAPTER FORTY-NINE

Hold My Beer and Watch This

Clint, Friday, June 15

I'd boarded a flight to San Francisco this morning to meet with Anna Acerbi. If memory served, Acerbi meant "heartless" in Italian. She's the principal of Acerbi, Kline, and Emerson, one of San Fran's most prestigious law firms.

Anna Acerbi read about Steele & Whitman's work on the Danning case. In her letter, she said she needed a competent, reliable, and thorough detective agency to monitor and direct her firm's in-house private eyes. Ms. Acerbi offered Steele & Whitman Investigations a two-year contract with serious money.

Hope and I discussed the firm's offer and decided I should meet with Acerbi in person to see how I felt about the principal and the firm. When I got back to the office Monday morning, we'd decide to accept, decline, or make a counter offer to the proposal.

I knew going into my meeting with Ms. Acerbi that the firm sometimes handled high-profile criminal defense cases.

I knew this criminal defense work would be about as well-received by Hope as a turd in her chowder bowl. And after falling prey to one of California's most prolific serial killers, I didn't know whether I wanted the contract either, no matter how lucrative it was.

My insomnia had returned after I'd found my half brother nearly whipped to death at the Ranch. Had I been a day or two later in finding him, what remained of Shane's body would've been dropped into a mass grave.

Since Shane's rescue, I'd been stopping by his private hospital room daily, bringing him real food, books, and candy after Diana told me her son had a weakness for chocolate. Initially, I did most of the talking. On my second visit, I held his hand and told him about our family connection. He lifted his brows and gave me a slight smile. Then we began talking.

On my third visit, I brought Ian to meet his uncle. My son asked with an earnest look, "Did you ever see that movie where the little boy yells, 'Shane! Come back!' I totally liked it. Daddy watched it with me. I asked why Shane wouldn't come back. He said cowboys had to keep riding the range. I think he wouldn't come back cause it's another one of those things I'm not supposed to know about until I'm older."

Shane laughed warmly and tousled Ian's hair. "When I get back to work, would you like to sit in the cockpit with me on a short flight?"

"Awesome," Ian said.

Shane smiled and winked at me. At that moment, we knew we'd bonded. It took the innocence of a child to bring the three of us together as a family.

I yawned deeply in my first class seat. Tired as I felt, I'd been unable to sleep last night; ditto on this return flight.

I loosened my tie. Then I sent Mars a text, asking if he wanted to get together this evening. He replied that he had an assignment but would drop by around 2100 hours, possibly earlier. I let him know I'd be waiting for him.

I stared out the window as the jetliner neared the greater Los Angeles area. The voice brought me out of my stupor.

"Before we begin our descent into Los Angeles, may I bring you another drink?" The cabin attendant added, "Or anything else, anything at all."

"I'll pass on another drink, thanks." But I flirted back. "How far down the path of anything at all were you thinking of going?" Having no interest in him, I wondered why the hell I'd said that.

The cabin attendant grinned, reached across the empty seat beside me, cleared away my scotch bottle and glass, then returned the tray to its fully upright and locked position.

Something lightly brushed my crotch. My cock started to stiffen—the shameless prick.

The cabin attendant noticed. "I believe that answers any doubts I had." He pushed the drink cart back to the galley.

I found the business card between my thighs. I chuckled as I read, "Landon Cox, Licensed Masseur & Personal Trainer," followed by a Los Angeles phone number.

Anyone of the LGBTQA+ tribes knew the connotations of "masseur" or "masseuse" combined with "personal trainer." And if Landon Cox wasn't a website alias, I'm the lost heir of Warren Buffett.

I folded the card and slipped it into the magazine pouch beneath the tray. I didn't need a massage from a stranger. I had Mars dropping by tonight.

The feds and the Mystic Canyon cops had gotten to Jud Tucker before he could kill himself. Tucker, along with his assistants, Blake Walsh and Blaine Vogel, were in county lockup, awaiting trial. I pinched the top of my nose between my thumb and index finger. Something about Jud Tucker's crimes did not compute. Specifically, how the fuck had he known that Shane Danning was my half brother? I'd thought Shane's paternity had been one of the film industry's better-kept secrets. Maybe I needed to have a long talk with Diana. Then it hit me like a kick in the head: Diana might've had a one-time get in, get off, get out liaison with Jud Tucker as she'd had with other men, including myself. It hadn't escaped my attention she liked to pillow talk.

I tightened my seat belt as the jetliner began its long glide toward LAX. I closed my eyes.

I jolted awake as the plane touched down, then slowed and taxied toward a Jetway. Pulling my laptop bag out of the overhead bin, I waved buh-bye at Landon Cox as I disembarked. He smiled and winked at me. I winked back in recognition of his entrepreneurial spirit.

I got out of LAX, saw it was past 1630 hours, and decided to stop for a drink. Ian and his buddy Sage had a weekend sleepover at the Pruitt manse. Tonight through Sunday belonged to me and Mars.

Being a Friday rush hour, it only took me seventy minutes to drive the nine miles from LAX to Santa Monica. Yup, that's bitterness you're hearing. I pulled into the first bar I saw without a car bearing a faded "MAGA" sticker on a bumper held in place with duct tape and coat hanger wire.

I stepped into a lounge filled with men in suits and ties, and women in business attire all ready for a drink and dinner at the end of another work week. I found an empty stool on the shadowy side of the bar.

An attractive bartender smiled at me. "What can I bring you?"

I smiled back. "Do you have a bottle of Utopia?"

She raised her brows, spoke to the bar back, who hustled off and returned cradling a bottle of beer that cost two Franklins. A boy must treat himself now and then.

Pulling my money clip from my pocket, I laid two hundred bucks plus a forty dollar tip in front of the bartender. She thanked me, slid the bills off the bar, and went to the till. It hadn't escaped my attention she wore a wedding ring. Private investigators miss nothing. I slowly poured beer into the chilled mug she'd set in front of me and sipped.

The thirtysomething guy to my right tried to interrupt my quiet enjoyment of a luxury beer. I ignored the stranger beside me. But I saw the bartender shoot a dirty look at him.

I drank some more beer.

"You like expensive beer," the thirtysomething man sitting to my right stated.

"Sometimes," I said.

"I know I haven't seen you in here before. I'd have remembered you." He burped. "Excuse me. I've had a few."

I gave him a quick once-over. His sandy hair had begun to recede, which didn't look bad on him. Add pale blue eyes behind thin glasses and a nice smile. The trite pickup line and belch aside, I thought him an all right looking guy.

I drank some more beer.

Looking closer, I saw the indentation of a long-worn wedding band on the man's left ring finger. Ahh, fuck, I thought, but said, "Are you recently divorced or looking for something you can't get at home?" Watching for a reaction, I noticed the stranger's eyes appeared a bit dilated. He had a nervous energy barely beneath his skin that had one knee jiggling and his right hand tapping the bar. I knew goddammed good and well he was an addict, probably crack. I turned back to my beer.

"Don't turn away from me. I'm talking to you."

Great, he had a crack addict's irrational temper.

"Listen," he began in a low voice, "for a hundred bucks, I'll give you a blow job to remember. For two hundred, you can fuck me, and that'll be something you'll never forget."

"Uh-huh, and for nothing, I can go home and jerk off." I finished my beer, stood, and made it to the door without being followed. On the sidewalk, I pulled the car's fob from my pocket. Christ, even in a pleasant lounge with expensive drinks and a mellow crowd, I had to sit next to a crack whore. I went to a steak house for dinner.

At home, I pulled off my dress shoes and kneeled for Sammy's sloppy kiss, playful growls, and tail wags. Heathcliff peeked at us from the laundry room door. "What's up, pretty boy?"

The fat cat swaggered over and let me pick him up.

"So, your highness, did you make certain the whelp didn't pee on any of my rosebushes while I was gone?"

Heathcliff purred and squirmed. I set him on the floor. At least the family pets were always here to welcome me home. Seeing they had plenty of food and water, I grabbed my shoes and headed upstairs.

I was standing in my bedroom in my underwear when my phone vibrated on the nightstand. It was a call from Mars.

"I finished early."

"So you're on your way," I said.

"Incoming, baby, and close enough to see the light from your bedroom windows."

I looked toward the street and affected a Brooklyn inflection. "I see you. I got your incoming right here."

He adopted the same inflection. "Moose, buddy, hold my beer and watch this."

I laughed, hearing squealing tires as Mars raced up my driveway.

Marston Hauser could always make me laugh. And I suspected he could keep me happy for a long, long while.

And for the first time today, I genuinely smiled.

CHAPTER FIFTY

Where's the Rest of the Story

Clint, Beverly Hills, Saturday, June 16

The waiter served our drinks: a Jack Daniel's single barrel on the rocks for Flynn, and I'd ordered the same, but neat.

Our waiter, sufficiently handsome and well-built to be a CK underwear model, asked if we'd decided what we'd like for dinner.

I asked for the tenderloin cooked medium, stuffed baked potato, and stir-fried vegetables.

The waiter looked at Flynn. "And for you, sir?"

"What are your specials?"

The waiter rattled them off.

"Who in the hell eats swordfish?" He moved ahead. "Then do you have lamb belly sweetbread?"

"Sorry, no sir."

"Ahh, Jesus, Mary, and Joseph, then can you bring me either a tongue or a head cheese sandwich?"

I lightly kicked Flynn under the table. "You're about to trip my gag reflex." The restaurant specialized in steaks and seafood, and being Saturday night, the place was packed. "In the interest of time, double my order, please."

"But I want my steak cooked well, and I'll take mashed, not baked, with chicken gravy." Flynn glanced at the menu one more time. "Do you have corn or peas in the kitchen instead of that stir-fried shit?"

"I'm certain we have fresh pea pods, baby carrots, mushrooms, green beans, and zucchini," the waiter said.

"We used to feed pea pods to the hogs," Flynn grumped. "Well then, can you shuck the peas and boil them?"

"Sir, each pea is slightly larger than the head of a pin, but I'll ask the chef what he can substitute for your stir-fried vegetables." The waiter hung in there. "Since you want it cooked well, may the chef butterfly your tenderloin?"

"What the hell does that mean?"

I answered for Flynn as if he were in an early stage of dementia. "He won't mind." I held a fist to my mouth and yawned. I would've preferred having dinner with Mars, but one of the intelligence agencies had an emergency contract for tonight. Not interested in eating alone, I'd called Flynn.

"My name is Brennon," our waiter said. "Let me know if you need anything before I serve your dinners." He snapped up the tall menus, turned, and fled.

Flynn squinted, watching Brennon's departure as if the young man were a park restroom perv. He took a sip of his whiskey, took another sip, and set the tumbler on the white linen tablecloth. "I imagine Steele & Whitman got a shitload of new clients after the Danning case made the newspapers."

I nodded and mentioned the Acerbi, Kline, and Emerson contract proposal. I did not say how lucrative the San Fran law firm's offer was. I also kept quiet about their luxurious offices.

Hope and I had discussed the offer this morning before I went to my desk. I'd known Hope felt as I did: Who the hell needed the headaches.

I told Flynn that Steele & Whitman Investigations had all the business we needed.

"Business is booming," Flynn said. "Ain't you a lucky so-and-so."

"You know every investigation hinges on a degree of good fortune. Working together, you and I had all the necessary skills and ten times the luck."

Our waiter brought our salads. "I'll bring your dinners shortly."

Flynn scowled at his salad. "You want this?"

"No thanks, go ahead and try it. You might like it," I said.

Flynn stared with disgust at his salad for several seconds as if it were a fresh, colorful cow pie. He shoved the plate aside. "I'm told the two men Tucker kept drugged and locked away will make a full recovery in time. As to Shane Danning, he's been released from hospital."

"I know," I said. "Shane decided to try some talk therapy before the flight surgeon examines him and makes a determination on his fitness to fly." I shrugged. "He's going to postpone plastic surgery on his back."

I ate some salad. "You know, Captain, we still need to learn the rest of the story behind the Danning case."

"Well now, your gut instincts are telling you this?"

"No, Flynn, it's my Delta Force preternatural powers, my private eye's spidey senses, and my Captain America decoder ring." I dropped the matter.

Flynn ignored my sarcasm. "I hear Jud Tucker, Blaine Vogel, and Blake Walsh's attorneys will argue their clients have been legally insane for years."

I knew California used the two-pronged McNaughton Rule in determining a defendant's sanity at the time of a crime: First, the defendant understood the nature and quality of the act, and second, the defendant could distinguish the difference between right and wrong. I also knew in California, a defendant could not be found insane solely on the basis of personality, adjustment or seizure disorders, or the addiction/abuse of intoxicating substances.

I figured Tucker, Vogel, and Walsh had the slightest chance of acquittals by reason of insanity. If so, all three of them would spend the rest of their lives locked away in a state mental hospital. It's merely another type of penitentiary.

Our salad plates were whisked away and our dinners served.

"To Vogel and Walsh's credit," Flynn said, "they told detectives they watched Jud Tucker shoot Deputy Sheriff Scott Davidson in cold blood, and made the murder look like a suicide."

"Why did Tucker kill the deputy?"

"Seems Scott Davidson wanted a sexual relationship with Mr. Tucker."

"Deputy Davidson didn't deserve to die for that. What a fucking brainless approach to saying 'No thanks.'" I chewed a piece of fabulously seasoned steak and swallowed. "What about the five-million-dollar ransom Diana paid Tucker?"

"The feds found a couple thousand Tucker deposited in his checking account, but they're not saying much about the rest of the ransom."

I nodded. Then Flynn and I focused on eating.

In a while, a busboy removed our plates and cutlery. Moments later, waiter Brennon arrived. "May I tempt you gentlemen with dessert, coffee, or an after-dinner drink?"

Flynn and I declined. Brennon set the leather check holder on the table. I picked it up.

Flynn grunted his thanks.

On top of the bill, I found a note written in a masculine cursive: *Off at eleven. Call me about dessert, if you're so inclined.* Brennon included his phone number.

I tucked Brennon's note into the breast pocket of my sport coat. I paid for our meals with black plastic. This was, after all, a deductible business dinner. I pulled cash from my money clip for the gratuity and closed the check holder.

When the waiter returned, he ran my card at the table and shot me a smile that went all the way to his eyes. "Thank you, gentlemen."

"I suppose you left that handsome and probably queer"—he pronounced it "quare"—"waiter too much of a tip. A couple of dollars would've been sufficient."

"Only in a Bangladesh restaurant. In Beverly Hills, two bucks wouldn't cover the tip for the glacier ice in your drink. But you did get one thing right."

"And what would that be?"

"Our waiter is one handsome devil. He gave me his phone number. Do you want it?"

"Now, why would I want that? All I need to do is wait for him at the bar until the end of his shift."

"He's off at 2300 hours." I stood then pushed my chair under the table. "Good night, Captain Parsimonious Tramp." I held a fist to my mouth and yawned. "Do you need an escort? I'd hate to learn your 1965 Vauxhall wouldn't start again."

Flynn stood. "Get outta my face. I've gotten tired of your smart-assed remarks left and right."

"Flynn, it's always a pleasure." We shook hands. "Love you like the big brother I never had."

He actually smiled. "Same here."

Chapter Fifty-One

You Got Mail

Clint, The Flats, Saturday, June 16

I walked into my house around 2200 hours and felt the rumble of its silence.

Ian and Sage's sleepovers always included both Friday and Saturday nights. Heathcliff lay curled up in the entry hall's big ceramic bowl. Beneath the table, Sammy slept with his muzzle under his tail. (It's something Samoyeds do, along with digging holes in the yard to lie in.) Both pets stirred, opened their eyes, and granted me talking and petting time before going back to sleep.

I went upstairs to my bedroom, emptied my pockets, and set everything on the nightstand except Brennon's handwritten invitation for dessert. I crumpled it and tossed it into the wastepaper basket. I'd let Flynn have him, as if. Then I went to the walk-in closet and stripped down to my skivvies, leaving my clothing on the floor.

The ambient glow of the street lamps cast my bedroom in twilight. Thanks to Jud Tucker's atrocities, I hadn't slept well for over three weeks. And tonight, I felt it.

But tonight, I fell asleep without the crutch of pharmaceuticals.

And I dreamt of Sierra.

"You are the most bullheaded, my way or the highway pain in the ass I ever knew," dream Sierra said.

"Tell me how you truly feel." I shot a crooked grin at Sierra who, after weeks of no-shows, made her appearance wearing the black bikini and the Prada flip-flops I'd boxed up and donated to Goodwill.

Pulling off one of her pricey flip-flops, she whacked me on top of my head with it.

"That stung, dammit!" I rubbed my head. "Why the hell did you do that?"

She frowned and folded her arms across her chest. It was body language she reserved for hate groups, anything championed by far-right wingnuts, and one student who'd forcefully argued in his first semester macroeconomics class that trickle-down would work only when all the goddammed screaming liberals and whining poor got a one-way ticket to Mexico.

And yes, I used to find myself on the receiving end of that same body language whenever she thought I'd done something painfully stupid...as if.

"I whacked you for two reasons. First, you made me leave the top deck of a ghost cruise ship where I was sitting poolside, chatting with two nicely muscled Aussies, each having a large basket tucked in minimal swimwear."

"As if you've never seen and experienced a big crank and large balls before," I said. "Without hitting me, what's reason number two?"

Sierra whacked me again. "My second reason for hitting you on the head is to capture your attention. Before I'm assigned to the next string of my life's continuum, I must resolve the greatest concern of my former life."

"Which is?" I asked with interest.

"Your happiness. I'd hoped to be granted the time to recruit, fully research, interview, analyze, and train my replacement." She paused, then said, "How about you and Mars?"

"Mars and I are doing fine—better than we did during our West Point years," I said. "Didn't you think I could find your replacement on my own? I mean, I'm the one who found you."

Sierra snorted. "No, I could've dropped dead waiting for you to talk to me at that second-rate coffee shop."

I chuckled. "If that's how you recall it, you go right on believing. Why do you think I kept returning to a place where the baristas learned the craft of coffee brewing at a frigging truck stop?" I exhaled a laugh. "When you finally looked at me and smiled, I came straight to your table and started talking fast before you changed your mind."

"Oh," she said.

I grinned. "Oh?"

Dream Sierra sat on the edge of the bed. "Oh, Clint, we're no longer on the same playing field, but you still bring back such wonderful memories."

She stood and ran her hand over her hair, an unconscious habit she had whenever she'd become uncertain about something. But this time, blue and silver sparks crackled above her dark auburn locks. "One day soon, you need to marry again because you're a commitment kind of man."

"You know I will." Looking into her eyes, I asked, "Do you know what's next in your life's continuum?"

"I hear rumors."

"Such as?"

She sighed. "One of the sprites gave me a wild-assed story about the next string of my life's continuum."

"I'm listening."

"This sprite said I'd return as a baby boy who becomes a con man."

"Pardon me?"

"I'll return as a Southern televangelist whoremonger with a depressed, alcoholic wife and ten children, all of whom have become utterly fucked up over Old Testament fairy tales." She affected the marginally prissy tone she often used during faculty meetings. "The good news being one can't believe anything a sprite says. As you and I used to remark, never let it be said that all the gods and goddesses don't share the same sick sense of humor."

My phone rose off the nightstand and dropped onto the head of my cock. "Ouch, dammit."

Sierra winked. "I know Mars is a great match for you. I'm fine with your partner replacement choice."

She whacked me on the head again. "The next thing you must do is stop being so damned bullheaded, and check your home email for May twenty-third."

I rubbed the sore spot on my head. "You know I never check my home inbox. It's nothing but spam. All my friends and clients know to contact me at my office email address."

I felt a cool fingertip touch my lips.

"Check your home email now, sweetheart. You won't see me again."

Her visage became fainter as she walked away.

"Good-bye, Sierra, a piece of my heart will always belong to you."

CHAPTER FIFTY-TWO

The Fourth and a Fifth

Clint, The Flats, Saturday Night, June 16

Sitting on the edge of the bed with my phone in hand, I pulled up my May twenty-third home email.

I scrolled past spam for Russian hooker mail-order brides, a plea for assistance from exiled Queen Latisha of Kwabena in retrieving her family's stolen fortune; Girls, Girls, Girls waiting for your call; and *Trump University's Big Pop-up Book of Jelking Exercises* (JFGI).

I wondered who came up with this shit. Were there people dumb enough to buy it? I recalled the words of H. L. Mencken: "Nobody ever went broke underestimating the tastes of the American public."

I stopped on an email from Jtuck, MCC Security Director. It had a cryptic subject line: *The Fourth and a Fifth.* I opened and read Jud Tucker's message.

You won the game, but not the war—not yet anyway.

The cops got it right when they concluded four people invaded your parents' house. I was that fourth man. The other three men, all Special Services soldiers dishonorably discharged for snorting too much Colombian marching powder, were dead a few hours after the murders of your parents and their guests—mind you, those military boys are long dead, but not wasted. Their hearts, lungs, livers, and kidneys saved the lives of many, their corneas returned sight to the blind, and their skin soothed patients in hospital burn units.

I know Shane is your half brother because the Danning tramp likes to pillow talk. She told the fifth man the name of Shane's father. And it was that fifth man who told me of your father's bastard son; he also told me about the gold bars, cash, bearer bonds, and jewelry your father kept in his home safe. It seems Liam Steele liked to talk about his holdings with Vona in her office.

You know this fifth man well. He's behind it all. Find him if you can and ask him why he hired me to kill your parents and their guests.

Still sitting on the edge of the bed, I read the message again and sent it to Captain Flynn.

Then I called Flynn.

CHAPTER FIFTY-THREE

Thus Always to Tyrants

Clint, Hollywood, June 16

I saw him sitting alone in his boxers, gently rocking the swing and staring into the night. I sat on the top cap of the porch's white picket railing and waited for him to speak.

He said, "I've been expecting you to drop by unannounced one of these days." He scooted over on the porch swing. "The railing's paint is chalky. Before you ruin the seat of your jeans, come sit beside me like you used to do."

I sat beside him and waited for him to speak.

He went back to staring into the night, softly chortled, then said, "I don't need to be a private investigator to guess Jud Tucker somehow contacted you."

"Before Tucker got arrested, he sent a message to my home email. I didn't find and open it until this evening," I said.

"You didn't read it for weeks," he said. "What the hell motivated you to open it tonight?"

I didn't tell him my late wife prodded me. "My friends know to email me at work. I finally got around to cleaning out my home inbox tonight."

He shook his head and sighed. "If it weren't for bad luck, I'd have no fucking luck at all."

"If a jury finds you guilty of conspiracy, you'll win a long, all-expenses-paid vacation to one of California's one-star crowbar hotels."

He exhaled a laugh. "Nah, a prosecutor couldn't even hang an indictment on me, and you know it." He nudged me with his elbow. "It doesn't matter whether you're talking about one felony or a dozen.

The cops have nothing on me because I've never done anything illegal in my fucking life." He faced me. "Thing is, your daddy liked to talk to Vona in her office, telling her about everything he kept in his home safe."

"Where you could hear everything they said by keeping your headset on and Vona's intercom open," I said.

He shrugged. "Guess your lotharious daddy never heard the one about loose lips sinking ships."

"How do you know Jud Tucker?" I asked.

"Jud and I met in high school. That poor sonofabitch looked and dressed like a war orphan. Everyone shunned him, but I didn't. Jud was malnourished and slowly starving to death." He shook his head. "We'd sit together in the cafeteria, and I'd give him my lunch, then go buy another tray for myself. He'd eat some of that too." He added, "Thing is, Jud is fucking smart. He won several scholarships. Then he and I spent four years at the same university."

"So, Jud Tucker was your best friend in high school and college," I said.

"You could say that."

I suspected he'd given me only part of the story, the part I'd told Captain Flynn we were missing. Flynn thought I was full of shit.

"What aren't you telling me?"

He let out a low chuckle. "It's one of the oldest tales known to mankind." He stared into the night. "I wanted Diana Danning. Christ, I loved her, and she worshipped my crank. I would've married her in a New York minute." He looked straight into my eyes. "Diana slept with lots of men and women, but she truly loved one man and one man only: your fucking father." He angrily shook his head. "Did you know all six of Diana's husbands were gayer than the robins in springtime?"

"No," I said.

"To hide her long-term affair with your father, Diana tied the knot now and again. But she only married very butch, deeply closeted actors."

"Who wouldn't ask her for sex," I said.

"Yes." He said offhandedly, "I'd lay odds you personally know Diana never saw a handsome man with a low-hanging basket that she could resist."

I didn't take the bait. But I'd bet Devin had been the man who'd kept calling Diana and hanging up without saying a word, prompting me to go to her house to check things out.

He said, "Not one of her marriages was consummated. But none of her husbands needed to stay with her for long. They each signed a contract promising to be seen around town exclusively with Diana. After six or eight months, Diana divorced them, paid them, and cut them loose."

"I see."

He shook his head in disgust. "From the day Diana met your father, she went head over heels, deep into all-fucked-uppery over him. But she had me as her backup dick when your daddy couldn't get away from a shoot or your mother."

"I recently learned about Dad's extramarital relationship with Diana," I said.

He said heatedly, "Diana was barely sixteen with all that youthful beauty and big-eyed innocence when your father first fucked her and knocked her up. Did you know that?"

"No." But I'd done the math. Diana mentioned Shane had recently turned thirty. She still would've been sixteen when she gave birth to Shane. Disgusted by my famous fucking father's pedophilia, I changed the subject. "I've seen Diana's first movie. She was a knockout."

"You bet your ass she was beautiful then and still is. But Christ, she believed your dad would someday leave your mother; then he'd marry her, they'd raise their son together, and live happily in love and laughter ever after."

"I guess no one told Diana family men don't always divorce their wives to marry their mistresses," I said.

"I tried to tell her, but everything I said blew in one ear and out her lovely ass."

"So you knew Jud Tucker who needed cash, and hired him to rob and kill my father," I said.

"Hold it right there, goddammit. I never hired Jud to kill anyone."

He returned to looking into the night. "Jud would've known without anyone telling him that emptying the safe, ransacking the place, and killing everyone in the house would look like another home invasion."

He turned back to me. "After your daddy died, Diana wouldn't let me near her. She didn't return my calls or reply to my email messages." He let out a long breath. "Diana finally told me she wanted nothing to do with me, and to let her the fuck alone."

"*Sic semper tyrannis,*" I said.

"What?" he said.

"Thus always to tyrants," I translated the Latin phrase. "It's what John Wilkes Boothe shouted after he shot President Abraham Lincoln. It's also Virginia's state motto."

He chuckled. "Using all them fancy wordages, are you calling your father or me or both of us tyrants?"

Captain Flynn and two Hollywood Station officers stepped onto the porch. Flynn flashed his gold shield, introduced himself, and said, "Devin McLean, I'd like to talk to you about an unsolved home invasion and six homicides. Would you mind coming to the Hollywood station with me?"

Devin McLean, Aunt Vona's executive assistant, said, "Sure, but I know nothing about any crime." He stood. "Do you mind if I get dressed first?"

"Is anyone in the house?" Flynn asked.

Devin told Flynn there wasn't. Flynn got Devin's okay to check the two-bedroom bungalow.

The two cops returned to the porch in less than three minutes. "Clear," one of the officers said.

"Go ahead and get dressed," Flynn told Devin.

With their gun holsters unsnapped, the Hollywood officers shepherded Devin into his dimly lighted living room and up the stairs.

"Are you all right?" Flynn asked.

Looking at the smoggy night, I turned to Flynn and said, "I'll work through it."

I'd known since I was seven that my parents had neither the time nor the inclination to nurture their only child. I loved Devin for all the hours he spent listening and talking to me. He, not my parents, attended my high school baseball, football, and basketball games. He had been here for me right up to the day I boarded a jetliner for New York and the U.S. Military Academy.

Our lives had been woven together. Now he needed my help.

Regardless of Devin's innocence or guilt, he had a constitutional right to a competent defense and a fair trial, if it came to that.

I would retain one of the best criminal defense attorneys in California—Anna Acerbi—the San Francisco lawyer. It was the least I could do for Devin.

Male voices began shouting inside Devin's house. The sounds of three gunshots followed.

Flynn ran for the door. I followed him. We rushed up the stairs.

In his bedroom, Devin lay supine on the floor, bleeding and gasping from the three bullet holes in his chest. A gun lay on the floor.

The gun looked real. But I instantly recognized it as a goddammed stage prop.

I'd spent enough time in war zones to know Devin was mortally wounded and didn't have much time left. Something visceral pulsed upward, making me feel as if my chest would split in half. I knelt beside Devin and held his hand.

Devin looked at me, and only for a heartbeat, I'd swear I saw that mischievous gleam return to his eyes. He tried to speak, but the words wouldn't come. His lungs drowning, blood began to trickle out of the corners of his mouth.

I said, "Don't try to speak. Help is on the way."

He weakly squeezed my hand, shuddered, and let out a rattling breath.

As I heard the medical techs pounding up the stairs, Devin McLean's eyes went blank.

The techs tried to revive him. But he was gone.

CHAPTER FIFTY-FOUR

Cast-Iron Certainties

Clint, One Month Later, Sunday, July 15

Jud Tucker claimed he knew nothing about a home invasion, robbery, and mass murder. He did not point a finger at his old friend, Devin. He asked the guard to take him back to his cell. He's still remaining silent.

Officially, the robbery-homicide case of my parents and their guests remains closed-unsolved.

Captain Flynn, Vona, and I thought Devin McLean may have passed information to Tucker about the contents of my father's home safe. But with his fake gun and "suicide by cops" kiss-off, Devin was innocent in the eyes of the law, and would forever remain innocent. After all, you can't arrest, try, and convict a dead person…not even in Los Angeles.

Maybe I knew the truth. Maybe I only thought I did and was full of shit.

Even a bottom-of-the-barrel defense lawyer could've pulled all kinds of reasons out of his or her ass why Devin was innocent. The email I got pointing at Devin McLean could've come from anyone. With Tucker's silence, the state of California had nothing on either Jud or Devin's involvement in the robbery and murder of my parents and their guests.

Early this beautiful Sunday morning, I cut a perfect white rosebud from my backyard garden and headed to Devin McLean's final resting place. This being the City of Angels where nothing is ever too strange, of course there's a story here.

The crypt of a handsome actor who'd died in the early 1960s

was located right above the final resting place of the movie industry's beautiful blond bombshell of the same era.

The handsome actor's elderly widow, strapped for cash, disinterred her husband's ashes and gave him a burial at sea. She then offered the valuable prime-location vault to the highest bidder.

Devin loved beautiful women. I thought the vault right above the blond bombshell's final resting place the perfect spot for Devin's ashes. I went in exceedingly high, and won the bid.

After Devin's remains were interred with military honors, I was handed the folded flag that had covered his urn. As Vona and I walked away, she told me that for seventeen years, my father had paid Devin to serve as my stand-in dad.

Devin McLean had been a lifelong bachelor with neither family ties nor children of his own. He'd been my mentor, hero, role model, confidant, and friend until I went to the Point.

Over the weeks since Devin's death, I'd come to appreciate one of life's cast-iron certainties: We're all the products of the children we used to be. For the first seventeen years of my life, Devin never failed me and had always given me his best.

I walked in leaf-dappled sunlight to the memorial park's stone wall of crypts. I slipped the white rose into the bud holder, then wiped a few specks of dust off the bronze plaque reading "Devin Patrick McLean." Beneath his name were the years of his birth and death. At center bottom: *Semper fi.*

Brothers in arms, I snapped a salute then whispered, "Oorah, Devin." I owed him so much more.

I'd return each month to pay my respects. It was the only thing I could give him for all he'd done for me. I would never forget him.

I started for home to spend the rest of Sunday with Ian. We'd talk, swim, and sit in the shade at the poolside table, playing his new love, cards. I'm not talking Go Fish or Crazy Eights. Oh, hell no, Ian loved to play blackjack. (His buddy Sage taught him the game.) I'm all but certain Ian counted cards and knew when the odds favored him to take another hit on sixteen or seventeen. Maybe my little boy was simply lucky; that, or a card shark in the making.

Fatherhood had provided me with another of life's cast-iron certainties: I loved my son unconditionally. I'd learned all about absolute love and trust from Devin.

And like a gold watch, I would hand down Devin's teachings to Ian.

EPILOGUE

Wefts And Warps

Clint, Hollywood and Highland Center, Seven Months Later

Aunt Vona despised ostentatious displays of wealth. She drove a slightly dented, six-year-old Impala to work, where she wore off-the-rack business suits and office casuals. She lived in a ranch-style house in the West Los Angeles neighborhood of Beverly Glen.

But on Hollywood's biggest night, she went balls out, so to speak. Riding in the back of a limousine service's chauffeured stretch, she looked elegant in her Dior haute couture with enough diamond bling to give off a sparkle or two under the lights.

Our hired white land yacht inched along the queue of limousines and hybrids, heading south on Highland to the Hollywood Boulevard drop-off point. From there, we had a short walk to the red carpet.

Nominated for best actor and best supporting actress in *Peter Remington: A Deadly Match*, newlyweds Raoul Martinez/Raul Martin and Vanessa Holmes held hands in the back seat of the stretch. Mars, Vona and I sat in the seat facing them.

"We're about four minutes to the drop-off," the chauffeur announced.

Vona, Raul, and Vanessa each pulled down a lighted mirror.

Vanessa touched up her lip gloss.

Raul added a spritz to an unruly strand of hair.

Vona gave her understated makeup and hairdo a final check.

The three of them snapped the lighted mirrors shut.

I tapped Raoul/Raul on the knee. "In this light, you remind me of Brad Pitt in his younger days." I quickly added, "But you're better looking."

Vanessa looked closely at her husband. "You know, in the shadows, you do look like a young, blond, and way more gorgeous Pitt."

Raoul/Raul chuckled, shaking his head. "Thanks, but I think you're both hallucinating from my finishing spray's fumes."

It hadn't been easy, but I'd convinced Mars to get his wild blond curls trimmed, shave off the two-day stubble, and play "Mr. Dress-up" in a black tux, white shirt, cuff links, and a bow tie. I'd insisted he would wear neither designer flip-flops, nor cowboy boot sandals, nor go barefoot to the Oscars. I'd handed him a new pair of black Salvatore Ferragamo formal loafers.

I leaned forward to look at Mars's big feet. He hadn't removed his shoes.

Mars and Doc Grant Stenton had helped me come to terms with the greatest tragedy of my life, losing Sierra. During my final talk therapy session, I'd told Doc Grant that Mars had asked me to move in with him.

Grant said, "And you're hesitating because?"

"My life and everything in it is perfect. I don't want to change a thing."

Grant smiled and shook his head. "Here you are worrying about upsetting the apple cart, and you know goddammed well the apple cart always gets upset."

I loved Doc Grant's therapy directives.

So Ian, Heathcliff, Sammy, and I moved into Mars's steel, stone, and glass circular multilevel, an architectural design Ian said looked like a house from *The Jetsons*.

I'd put my white colonial on the market. Diana Danning bought it for Shane. After closing on the property, I showed Shane how everything in the place worked—from the water softener, to the programmable thermostats, to the self-cleaning oven, to setting the timer on the underground sprinkler system, to arming and disarming the burglar alarm. I taught him the basics of tending what were now *his* shrubs, flower beds, lawn, and roses. But you don't acquire a green thumb overnight. I'd continue working with him.

But I took my potted orchids to my new home, knowing they'd die on Shane for the sole purpose of spiting him. Orchids can turn seriously pissy that way.

Shane and I regularly talked, laughed, and sat together over coffee or a drink. After he'd been reissued his FAA fit-for-flight medical certificate, he kept his alcohol intake to a single beer.

Shane and I had grown as close as two brothers could get. Ian hero-worshipped his uncle Shane, as he adored his "Uncle Martian."

During one of our brotherly talks, I'd asked Shane if he had ever been a compulsive gambler.

He'd chuckled. "I'll make a wild-assed guess on that one. My ex, Kristina Morgotti, told you I had a gambling addiction."

I'd nodded.

"Hell, bro, I've never made enough money flying the wild blue yonder to piss a dime of it away in a casino." He smiled. "And starring in porn isn't as easy as it looks. I don't waste my ill-gotten booty either." He'd sighed. "You know Krissy is a frigging drama queen. And I'll guess she gave you a sob story about my faithless love. Then she asked you to fuck him."

"Uh-huh, but I declined the offer," I said.

Shane shook his head. "She earns an ass-ton of money by making shit up and delivering it with flair. She doesn't know how to turn it off. Kristina and Kristopher are about as bat shit as one person can get."

I guess I'd known it.

The same way I'd known Mars had called it right: The white colonial I loved held too many memories of my life with Sierra.

Mars studied my face in the limo's semidarkness. "You're thinking again. Stop it. This is your night to celebrate."

He was right. I knew this year's Oscars belonged to Steele Productions. *Peter Remington: A Deadly Match* had received rave reviews during its November platform release. The movie opened nationwide on Thanksgiving, and continued to break box office records. I smiled inwardly. Steele Productions had gambled on the making of a multimillion-dollar movie that seemed all wrong demographically in the minds of most industry moguls.

But the "all wrong" movie became not only a holidays hit, but was on the way to becoming the blockbuster of the year.

In addition to best actor, supporting actress, and the grand prize, film of the year, Vona's and my roll of the dice had netted numerous other nominations, including screenplay, editing, music, sound, cinematography, and best director. All too familiar with Hollyweird's politics, I knew a clean sweep for Steele Productions wouldn't likely happen.

But then again, it might.

I squeezed and released Mars's hand as the limo rolled to a stop at the drop-off point. "Sparkle time," I told him. Then I checked that he was still wearing his shoes.

Raul Martin stepped out of the stretch's door and smiled at the cameras as he gave Vanessa a hand to the sidewalk. The two walked onto the red carpet leading to the Dolby Theater.

The fans seated in the bleachers went wild, screaming and snapping photos of Raul Martin and Vanessa Holmes, putting the LAPD officers handling crowd control on edge. One never knew when a crowd of adoring fans might turn into a mob.

Vona, Mars, and I stepped out of the white limo. He and I walked on either side of Vona, whom I suspected would be named director of the year.

We could not guess what we'd encounter in the wefts and warps of our lives. We couldn't predict the outcomes of our decisions in relation to life's vagaries.

But with Mars's cyber nerd mad scientist genius, his spirit of a child, and the smiles that went all the way to our eyes when we were together, I knew we could keep each other happy and young at heart for the rest of our lives.

And for the first time since I'd lost my wife, I looked forward to finding out what awaited around the next corner, and the next, and the next.

So spin the Fates.

About the Author

Louis Barr (http://www.louisbarrauthor.com) directed a federal civil rights program for forty years. He and his spouse reside in suburbia, where they are owned by their two cats.

Barr enjoys hearing from his readers but believes cell phones, text messaging, and social media are indicators of civilization's decline. You can send Barr a letter by old-fashioned email at: louisbarrauthor@gmail.com.

Books Available From Bold Strokes Books

Everyday People by Louis Barr. When film star Diana Danning hires private eye Clint Steele to find her son, Clint turns to his former West Point barracks mate, and ex-buddy with benefits, Mars Hauser to lend his cyber espionage and digital black ops skills to the case.(978-1-63555-698-8)

Cirque des Freaks and Other Tales of Horror by Julian Lopez. Explore the pleasure of horror in this compilation that delivers like the horror classics…good ole tales of terror. (978-1-63555-689-6)

Royal Street Reveillon by Greg Herren. In this Scotty Bradley mystery, someone is killing the stars of a reality show, and it's up to Scotty Bradley and the boys to find out who. (978-1-63555-545-5)

Death Takes a Bow by David S. Pederson. Alan Keys takes part in a local stage production, but when the leading man is murdered, his partner Detective Heath Barrington is thrust into the limelight to find the killer. (978-1-63555-472-4)

Accidental Prophet by Bud Gundy. Days after his grandmother dies, Drew Morten learns his true identity and finds himself racing against time to save civilization from the apocalypse. (978-1-63555-452-6)

In Case You Forgot by Fredrick Smith and Chaz Lamar. Zaire and Kenny, two newly single, Black, queer, and socially aware men, start again—in love, career, and life—in the West Hollywood neighborhood of LA. (978-1-63555-493-9)

Counting for Thunder by Phillip Irwin Cooper. A struggling actor returns to the Deep South to manage a family crisis but finds love and ultimately his own voice as his mother is regaining hers for possibly the last time. (978-1-63555-450-2)

Survivor's Guilt and Other Stories by Greg Herren. Award-winning author Greg Herren's short stories are finally pulled together into a single collection, including the Macavity Award–nominated title story and the first-ever Chanse MacLeod short story. (978-1-63555-413-7)

Saints + Sinners Anthology 2019, edited by Tracy Cunningham and Paul Willis. An anthology of short fiction featuring the finalist selections from the 2019 Saints + Sinners Literary Festival. (978-1-63555-447-2)

The Shape of the Earth by Gary Garth McCann. After appearing in *Best Gay Love Stories*, *HarringtonGMFQ*, *Q Review*, and *Off the Rocks*, Lenny and his partner Dave return in a hotbed of manhood and jealousy. (978-1-63555-391-8)

Exit Plans for Teenage Freaks by 'Nathan Burgoine. Cole always has a plan—especially for escaping his small-town reputation as "that kid who was kidnapped when he was four"—but when he teleports to a museum, it's time to face facts: it's possible he's a total freak after all. (978-1-163555-098-6)

Death Checks In by David S. Pederson. Despite Heath's promises to Alan to not get involved, Heath can't resist investigating a shopkeeper's murder in Chicago, which dashes their plans for a romantic weekend getaway. (978-1-163555-329-1)

Of Echoes Born by 'Nathan Burgoine. A collection of queer fantasy short stories set in Canada from Lambda Literary Award finalist 'Nathan Burgoine. (978-1-63555-096-2)

The Lurid Sea by Tom Cardamone. Cursed to spend eternity on his knees, Nerites is having the time of his life. (978-1-62639-911-2)

Sinister Justice by Steve Pickens. When a vigilante targets citizens of Jake Finnigan's hometown, Jake and his partner Sam fall under suspicion themselves as they investigate the murders. (978-1-63555-094-8)

Club Arcana: Operation Janus by Jon Wilson. Wizards, demons, Elder Gods: Who knew the universe was so crowded, and that they'd all be out to get Angus McAslan? (978-1-62639-969-3)

Triad Soul by 'Nathan Burgoine. Luc, Anders, and Curtis—vampire, demon, and wizard—must use their powers of blood, soul, and magic to defeat a murderer determined to turn their city into a battlefield. (978-1-62639-863-4)

CPSIA information can be obtained
at www.ICGtesting.com
Printed in the USA
FSHW011656290320
68562FS

9 781635 556988